Never Mess with Mistletoe

by Edie Claire

Book Ten of the
Leigh Koslow Mystery Series

Dedication

In loving memory of Thomas W. Moore, DVM (1937–2016), longtime owner of the Avalon Veterinary Hospital and my first boss. Dr. Moore and his wonderful wife Nancy were always unfailingly supportive of me, first as a newly graduated clinician and then as a budding novelist — and trust me, the first part wasn't easy! For decades, Dr. Moore provided skilled, compassionate, and affordable care to any creature brought to him, whether it be feathered, furred, or scaled. More rare still, he provided that care to all of his patients, with a smile of kindly good humor, whether their owners be rich or poor, famous or homeless. Thank you, Dr. Moore. You are greatly missed.

Cast of Characters

The Family

Leigh Koslow Harmon	Our hapless heroine
Warren Harmon	Leigh's husband
Allison & Ethan Harmon	Leigh & Warren's children
Frances & Randall Koslow	Leigh's parents
Lydie Dublin	Leigh's aunt, Frances's twin sister
Cara Dublin March	Leigh's cousin, Lydie & Mason's daughter
Lenna & Mathias March	Cara's children
Mason Dublin	Lydie's ex-husband, Cara's father
Bess Cogley	Leigh's aunt, Frances & Lydie's older sister

The Floribundas

Olympia	Chapter president, married to **Melvin**
Lucille	Has assistant **Bridget** and son **Bobby**
Virginia	Married to **Harry**
Anna Marie	Married to **Eugene**
Delores & Jennie Ruth	Housemates
Sue	Stayed at home sick

Chapter 1

Leigh Koslow Harmon did not believe that her future could be determined by a fortune cookie.

She hesitated anyway. Two cookies were left on the break room table, a red one and a green one. She'd never seen brightly colored fortune cookies before this Christmas, but some marketing team somewhere must be having a toast, because the plastic-wrapped treats were currently being thrown in every bag of Chinese takeout in Pittsburgh. The employees of Hook, Inc., the advertising firm of which Leigh was a principal, had to admire the brilliance of the scheme. The leftover cookies might all be thrown out in January, but as far as the manufacturer was concerned, that was a plus. In the meantime, countless people like Leigh were wasting inordinate amounts of time staring at the product while contemplating an otherwise unnecessary decision.

Red or green?

Her time was up. She'd been leaning toward the green, but in the last second, the red cookie called to her. She made a grab for it.

"Are you sure?" her co-worker Alice said mockingly as she speared a bite of moo goo gai pan. "You could be making a terrible mistake, you know."

Leigh smirked. She and Alice had been good-naturedly sparring with each other for a very long time now, ever since they'd shared a cubicle together as twenty-somethings at another communications firm that had dumped them both. Now in their mid-forties and making a comfortable living at Hook, both women spent much of their time working from home. But the dynamic between them remained unchanged.

"You can't have the red one," Leigh argued. "I don't care what you say, you're not getting it."

Alice sighed dramatically as she reached for the green cookie. *"Fine."*

Both women tore apart the plastic wrappings. "I really wanted the green one the whole time, you know," Alice insisted.

"You wish." Leigh broke her cookie in two, popped half of it into her mouth with a flourish, and unrolled the slip of paper inside.

> The blaxe you brew for your adversary often burns you more than him.

Leigh rolled her eyes and tossed it.

Alice cracked up laughing. "What? You know you have to share!"

Leigh groaned, retrieved the paper, and read the message out loud.

"No way!" Alice chuckled. "Let me see." She took the paper from Leigh and read it herself. "What the hell is blaxe?"

"How should I know?"

"Maybe it's an ancient Chinese herb that tastes great unless you cook it a certain way — and then it turns into a deadly poison!"

Leigh scowled. "Read yours."

Alice returned Leigh's fortune and unrolled the paper inside her own cookie. She smiled. "Unexpected romantic and financial gifts surprise and delight you."

"You are such a liar!" Leigh protested. She snatched the paper from Alice's fingers.

The words were printed exactly as read.

"Merry Christmas to me!" Alice said in a sing-song, grinning from ear to ear as she snatched the fortune back.

"Better watch out for me and my blaxe," Leigh warned.

Alice stuffed the whole cookie in her mouth and responded with an enthusiastic double thumbs-up.

Leigh ate the second half of her cookie and reread her own "fortune." It still made no sense. Whatever the original meaning, it had obviously been butchered in translation. There was no reason for something so silly to leave such a bad taste in her mouth, over and above the bitter tang of the cheap red dye. Yet the words bothered her. They left her feeling... unsettled.

The blaxe you brew for your adversary often burns you more than him.

She fought back a shiver. She should forget it. Why all this talk of brewing and burning at Christmas, anyway? There was no need to be unpleasant. Besides which, the language was sexist. With so many tidbits of ancient proverbial wisdom floating around the internet, putting *that* quote in such an otherwise innocent-looking holiday treat was practically criminal.

She knew she should have taken the green one.

The cell phone in her pocket began to play soothing, melodic notes of harp music, and Leigh tensed. She had set up the ringtone as an antidote to that reaction, but the attempt failed. Her nervous system could not be fooled. She knew who was calling. *Again.* Worse still, the caller knew that Leigh was working at her office today. And interruptions at work by said caller never boded well.

She put the phone to her ear and forced a cheerful greeting. "Hi, Mom. What's up?"

"The regionals are coming!!!"

Leigh held the phone away from her head and took a deep breath. Her mother was hysterical, yes, but at least she wasn't hysterical-horrified. She was hysterical-excited, which was better. Although both states generally resulted in Leigh's having to drive somewhere, clean something, rescue some family member, or atone for some sin, the happy lilt in Frances's voice did seem to preclude a mad dash to the local hospital, police station, or jail.

"Mom," Leigh soothed. "Take it easy. You know I have no idea what you're talking about."

"Of course you do!" Frances shrieked. "I explained all this yesterday! Olympia made the submission but she didn't think anything would come of it because it was so last minute and everything has already been printed and she was sure they'd just cancel but after all the two were so close together and all that needs to be done is a simple map guiding people from one to the other and they must have agreed with her because they told her they wanted to see the house and she just called me and told me and I should have asked for more time but I was so surprised I couldn't think quickly enough and now it's too late, and oh — Leigh, *whatever will we do?"*

While Frances paused long enough to breathe, Leigh's brain struggled to filter key words from the gibberish. Submission? Map? Nope. No sense there. Last night her mother had rambled on for half an hour over speakerphone while Leigh folded laundry, but Leigh hadn't paid much attention. Doing so for every conversation simply wasn't possible anymore. Ever since her Aunt Lydie, Frances's twin sister, had become engaged, the sisters' normal volume of chatter had been curtailed. Leigh had been elected to pick up the slack, and the closer Lydie's wedding approached, the more frequent and long-winded Frances's calls became.

The calls were never about Lydie or her wedding, however. They were about random nonsense. Like whether Leigh's father was due for a new coat this winter. Or what line item from what committee threatened to ruin the church budget. Or who was causing the latest drama at the garden club.

The garden club!

"Wait!" Leigh cried triumphantly, remembering. "Are you talking about the Holiday House Tour?"

"The regionals are coming!" Frances repeated an octave higher.

Leigh pulled the phone away from her ear again. *Ouch.* "You mean the regional garden club people? The ones who make the final decisions about which houses go on the Christmas tour?" She paused in disbelief. "They're coming to see *your* house?"

Surely not. She must be misunderstanding. The Holiday House Tour was a big deal. It was sponsored by a cluster of garden clubs in both Pittsburgh proper and the surrounding suburbs, and every December five showplace homes were chosen to be decorated to the hilt and toured by throngs of gawking admirers. Leigh had attended once or twice and toured mansions in Shady Side, renovated Victorians on Mount Washington, and unique architectural wonders à la Frank Lloyd Wright. The houses weren't always huge, but they were always interesting.

The Koslow homestead, in contrast, was one of thousands of modest Foursquare houses that filled the working-class neighborhoods of Pittsburgh. It sat in the middle of the northern suburb of West View, a sturdy brick two-story with three small bedrooms and a bathroom upstairs and a kitchen, living room, dining room, and retrofitted half-bath downstairs. Leigh's dad kept a workshop in the somewhat dingy basement. It had a wide concrete porch in front and a small yard in the back. There was absolutely nothing unusual or special about it. Her parents had owned it since the late sixties and had always kept it in immaculate condition. But still.

Why?

"Oh, for heaven's sake, don't give me an inquisition!" Frances chastised. "I'll explain when you get here! But you've got to hurry!

They're coming in *fifty-two* minutes!"

Leigh rubbed her free hand over her face. Across the table, she could hear Alice chuckling. Frances's distinctive shrill tone carried well, even if her words did not, and Leigh's facial expressions told the rest. This was hardly Alice's first brush with a Koslow family "emergency."

"Shall I fetch your coat?" Alice offered in a whisper.

Leigh ignored her. "Mom, I'm at work, remember? Why do you need me there when they come?"

"I don't need you *then!*" Frances protested. "I need you *now!*"

At long last, Leigh's charge became clear. It was the cleaning one. *Crap.* "Can't Aunt—"

"Your Aunt Lydie is out for the day, and I already called your Aunt Bess and she had the nerve to hang up on me! I even thought about calling your cousin Cara, but I know she's working on a project this week," Frances explained with no trace of irony. "There's nobody else I can call right now — only family knows everything that has to be done to ensure the proper level of cleanliness! And it's never been more important that this house be spotless! Never!"

Leigh could take issue with that point. But reliving the various incidents that had spurred her clean-freak mother to strive for new heights in "spotlessness" was not her idea of a good time. She let out a breath slowly. There really was no hope for it. Frances knew that Leigh's work hours were flexible. And although Bess could thumb her nose at her little sister with impunity, Leigh could never get away with hanging up on her mother.

"Fine, Mom," she said, defeated. "I'll come over."

"Oh, wonderful!" Frances trilled. "I'll be waiting!"

"But I—" Leigh stopped herself in mid sentence. Her mother had just hung up on her.

Twenty-two minutes later, Leigh pulled up in front of her parents' house and made haste towards the front door. Any normal person wouldn't expect her to arrive from her office on the North Side any faster than that, but she couldn't be seen as shirking. Fifty-two minus twenty-two was thirty, and no matter what Frances thought needed to be done to the house, Leigh doubted it could be achieved in half an hour. Not that the state of the house truly mattered, of course. Leigh was here only to prevent a spontaneous combustion of Frances herself.

Leigh knocked on the door, but then walked in without waiting for an answer. "I'm here!"

"Oh!" Frances's muffled voice drifted in from the kitchen. "Wait! Wait!"

Leigh hung her purse and coat on the rack. A second later, Frances Koslow emerged from the kitchen doorway and pulled a respirator mask off her face. Dressed from head to toe in bright yellow hazmat-style garb, she looked more like a CDC investigator than a self-described "dedicated homemaker."

"Tell me you can't smell the oven cleaner," Frances demanded. "This grade can release toxic fumes, but it leaves less residue and there's no lingering odor."

"I can't smell anything," Leigh said honestly. It was unacceptable, according to Frances, for a house to smell like cleaning products at any time. If a guest were to pick up the scent of lemons, for example, it would be obvious that you had *just* cleaned, which somehow indicated that your house was *not* clean before that. Never mind that Frances always cleaned immediately before guests arrived, and expected that everyone else ought to as well, just to be on the safe side. It was all in the perception.

The face behind the elastic bands of the respirator crinkled into a smile. "Excellent."

Leigh surveyed her mother critically, then relaxed a little. The hysteria phase was over. Frances was well into the steamroller phase now, which was safer, at least for her blood pressure. To say that Frances was mellowing with age would be an overstatement, but in terms of her response to crises, the hysteria phase did seem to be shortening. In Leigh's memory, the soundtrack for the sticky-hands and mud-pies part of her childhood consisted of one protracted scream. Now, Frances shifted from reaction into action much quicker. Of course, the steamroller phase had its own drawbacks.

"Help me tidy up the supplies," Frances ordered, losing the smile. "Then we'll move to the second floor."

Leigh followed her mother to the kitchen, caught the "cleaning apron" that was tossed at her, and tied it around her neck and waist with a grimace. Protesting the garment was not worth the effort. Although she despised the decades-old burlap apron with the embroidered mushrooms and orange bric-a-brac trim with every fiber of her being, she was even more tired of throwing away good clothes with bleach spots. And there was no way anyone as clumsy as she was could clean anything with her mother's powerful arsenal without splashing something on herself.

"You have to tell me what's going on, Mom," Leigh insisted as she helped Frances gather up the various kitchen-cleaning supplies as if striking a surgical theater. "Is this house seriously being considered for the Holiday House Tour?"

Frances's cheeks flamed bright red, and her dark eyes shone with a feverish glint. "It's conceivable," she answered in a hushed tone, as if afraid that speaking too loudly would jinx her. "They had all the houses selected months ago, but as I mentioned last night when you clearly weren't listening, the Marsh house up the street had to be dropped as of yesterday. They started drilling holes to put up the decorations and a section of wallboard disintegrated before their eyes! Apparently, the roof has been leaking for some time and there was black mold all through one side of the house. The organization couldn't expose the public to any part of that... just think of the liability!"

Leigh nodded. She honestly couldn't remember her mother telling her any of this. Maybe Frances's memory was going. Then again, her own wasn't the greatest these days. Ever since she turned forty, she'd noticed an alarming uptick in the number of times she walked into a room and had no idea why.

"Well," Frances continued as she carefully placed the bottles, brushes, and sponges Leigh handed her in their assigned spots in the cupboard. "That's when Olympia got the idea. You know she's been fuming ever since the Flying Maples got their house on the tour in the first place. The nerve of them!"

Leigh searched her brain. She knew that Olympia was the newest president of Frances's local garden club, which covered the suburb of West View as well as some of the neighboring communities. The Floribundas had been in existence since Noah beached the ark, Frances had been a member as long as Leigh had been alive, and most of the remaining members were older than Frances. "Who are the Flying Maples?"

Frances rolled her eyes and gave her head a shake of irritation. She shut the cupboard door and made haste out of the doorway, gesturing for Leigh to follow her. "The Flying Maples are a bunch of upstart women who wouldn't know a hydrangea from a rhododendron. As far as we can tell, they don't do a blessed thing at their meetings but drink cheap wine from a box and plan their next fundraiser!"

Frances began a determined march up the stairs, her feet slamming down with unnecessary force on each step.

Leigh regretted asking the question. Clearly, her mother was sensitive on the topic. The Floribundas, she knew, had always considered themselves to be *the* garden club for the area. In their heyday, they'd had a thriving membership of close to a hundred, but in recent decades, like many women's clubs of their ilk, they had struggled to attract the younger generations.

"Our club has submitted a house to the regional committee every year since 1978," Frances went on. "And we know, because our historian, Sue, looked it up. And *not once* has one of our own been chosen! But these *Flying Maples,*" she said derisively, "turn in their very first submission, and it is accepted! Have you ever heard of anything so ridiculous? Until fourteen months ago, they weren't even *affiliated!*"

Frances reached the second floor landing and jerked open the door to the linen closet. "We had a spy go to one of their meetings once, just to see if they were doing anything untoward, you know. We had to know… it's important for the sanctity of the brand! And we couldn't believe some of the things she reported. When those women conduct their meetings—" Frances whirled around and made a point of holding Leigh's gaze. Her voice dropped to a guilty whisper again. "Why, they don't even follow Robert's Rules of Order!"

The puce cast to Frances's face looked so unhealthy, Leigh managed to stifle her first response. "You don't say?" she choked out instead.

"It's true," Frances continued, handing Leigh several dust cloths and a spray bottle. "We believe the only reason they submitted an entry to the Holiday Tour in the first place was to irritate us! It's an obsession they have, you know. Preoccupied with what *we're* doing." She made a scooting gesture urging Leigh towards the master bedroom.

"Mom," Leigh attempted again. "I still don't understand why—"

"You dust. I'll talk," Frances ordered. She picked up a tray of cleansers and disappeared into the bathroom.

Leigh moved into her parents' bedroom with a sigh. There was, naturally, not a speck of dust in sight. She squatted down to the nearest section of baseboard and ran a fingertip along the perfectly smooth, shiny surface. Nothing.

"By the time the black mold was discovered, you see," Frances called out, "the Flying Maples' house had already been included in all the advertisements and the printed program maps. So Olympia had the most wonderful idea: why not give the committee an alternative right down the road? That way, we could do a last-minute switch just by handing out fliers at the door! But there was a catch."

Leigh looked around for some other surface she could claim to have wiped down. "What catch?" she asked.

"The theme of the tour this year is 'A Century of Christmas.' They have a house that was built a hundred years ago and an enormous brand new mansion out in Franklin Park. Then there's a lovely house in the city from the late thirties that they're fixing up like it's Christmas of 1945, and some other place I can't remember that was built at the turn of the millennium. That cheap little mold incubator of Judy Marsh's — she's the president of the Flying Maples, you know — was supposed to represent the seventies."

Leigh paused in confusion. No way was the house in which they were standing built in the seventies. Leigh had grown up in the seventies and the neighborhood had seemed old then. "When was this house built?"

"1930," Frances called back. "I don't understand it, either. But as soon as we got the news, Olympia insisted the chapter nominate this house. She said it was 'absolutely perfect.' When I asked her why she thought that, she stared back at me as if she didn't understand the question! I thought the woman had lost her mind — she is a bit odd, you know — but then she called me back and said the regionals were coming!"

Leigh's brow wrinkled in thought as she pulled back the bedspread and leaned down to run her dust rag in the groove between the mattress and the support rail. She'd gotten in trouble for missing that spot before. She pulled the cloth back up and examined it.

Nothing.

Leigh gave up. She looked around the room again with a sigh. Her parents' full-sized bed had been covered with the same flowered spread and crocheted throw blanket for as long as Leigh could remember. On the wall by the door hung a metal clock shaped like the sun. At the foot of the bed was a bench with a cushion upholstered in burnt orange. The walls were papered with stripes of giant gold fleurs-de-lis.

Wait a minute.

"Be right back!" Leigh called as she ducked out of the bedroom and made her way down the stairs again. She reached the living room and did her best to set aside a lifetime of habituation and look at the house through unbiased eyes.

Woah.

The long, low squarish sofa that dominated the Koslow living room was the exact same shade of burnt orange as the bedroom bench. The wingchair by the window was olive green. Her dad's reading chair was beige with a brown pattern of windmills and covered bridges. Every stick of furniture was the same furniture Leigh had been looking at her entire life. How could it be?

Leigh knew how. Her parents had slowly and gradually collected a whole houseful of furniture during their first decade of marriage, and although they had never bought extravagantly, Frances did know quality craftsmanship from junk. And while most families eventually wore out their living room sets, most families did not include Frances Koslow.

The whole time Leigh was growing up, every upholstered piece of furniture in the house had been encased in plastic. Leigh remembered well, because visiting any house where she didn't sit down and stick had made her feel like royalty. Frances had abandoned the covers only after they had turned yellow with age and replacements were no longer manufactured. Frances being Frances, however, she had managed to keep her furniture in pristine condition even without the plastic. The burnt orange sofa looked as "cheerful" today as it ever had, and the olive-green seat cushions on the dining room chairs denied ever having been touched by carbohydrate. Throw pillows in various shades of harvest gold, many of them embroidered with birds, bees, and sequins, lay in the same assigned locations as always, and the walls were still papered with a raised pattern that was fuzzy to the touch.

Deep in Leigh's imagination, strains of Carpenters' music began to play.

"What on earth are you doing?" Frances called down. "Is something wrong?"

"Um, no," Leigh answered, turning around and starting back up the steps. She got it, now. She understood all too well. The question was, did Frances? "So, what you're saying is that this house will be decorated by the garden club like it's Christmas in the nineteen seventies, and —"

"Oh, don't say it!" Frances interrupted. "Nothing's been decided. We mustn't get ahead of ourselves. Do you have any idea how *important* this is?"

Frances's expression was half panic, half euphoria. Leigh decided to hold her tongue. For her mother, showing off the fruit of forty-some-odd years' worth of hard labor to every garden club in Pittsburgh as well as any interested member of the public would indeed be a dream come true. Despite the accidental nature of the situation, Frances's retro tastes would truly — and finally — be appreciated. Leigh should be happy for her.

And yet…

A sense of doom percolated deep in her gut. Somehow, she couldn't shake the feeling that inviting huge numbers of people to eat, drink, and be merry in the epicenter of team Koslow was akin to flipping one's middle finger at fate.

Did she have any grounds to back that up? Or was she still freaking out over the stupid fortune cookie?

She decided it must be the latter. There was nothing wrong here. Everything would be fine. Her mother was certainly happy enough, and lately, that was saying something.

"You're not done already, are you?" Frances asked skeptically. "Have you popped open the windows and cleaned the ridges of the sills?"

"I was getting to that." Leigh tried to shrug off her concern as she headed back into the bedroom. Surely she was being ridiculous. She herself might have bad karma — okay, when it came to her personal proximity to other people's "end-of-life transitions," she had really, *really* bad karma — but that curse had no bearing on her mother. Frances Koslow's participation in the Holiday House Tour was not

Leigh's affair. Never mind that Leigh would rather be boiled in oil than have hundreds of people tromping through the Harmon family home — this was what Frances wanted. What right did Leigh have to naysay, based on nothing but a nebulous feeling of impending disaster brought on by a poorly translated fortune cookie?

She popped open the window and began to clean the sill.

"Do take this seriously, dear!" Frances called from inside the bathroom again. Her words were barely audible over a vigorous scrubbing sound. "You have no idea how important this is to the Floribundas. We simply *must* make a success of it!"

Leigh breathed deeply of the cold air that poured into the room. She still felt anxious.

"It's a matter of life and death!" Frances finished.

Leigh dropped the cloth out the window. The still-spotless dust rag drifted down and away, then snagged on a naked limb. Leigh reached out to try and grab it, but the cloth was just out of reach. Its corners fluttered in the breeze, mocking her.

Frances really should know better than to use that word.

Chapter 2

"We have six minutes!" Frances reported as she finished peeling off her protective gear. "You'd best be leaving now, dear. Unless you want to meet the officials?"

Leigh's already elevated pulse rate increased. No, she did not want to meet the officials. She was quite sure that there were many garden clubs in many places filled with lovely, wonderful, friendly women who enjoyed horticultural pursuits, worked well together for the common good, and were perfectly sane. The Floribundas were not among them.

The Floribundas were a flock of loons.

To be fair, Leigh had never met Olympia. The club's newest president had only joined within the past few months after moving into the area from New York State. But every other member had been a part of the group since avocado-colored toilets were in style. Over the course of the club's history many other women had come and gone, women of all ages and stripes, women who were nice, women who were normal. But in the last decade or so all of Frances's less eccentric fellow Floribundas had slowly but surely fallen away from the fold.

The eight that remained did nothing for Darwin's theory.

Perhaps Leigh was being uncharitable. As far as she knew, all of the women in question did manage to lead semi-normal lives. As her always-diplomatic Aunt Lydie once put it, "There's nothing pathological about any of them. They simply have personality traits that stretch the boundaries of social acceptability."

That said, Lydie herself had quit in the nineties.

"I'll leave," Leigh announced, pulling off her apron and handing it back to her mother. "Who exactly is coming? How many people?"

"Two, besides Olympia. The chair of the Holiday House Tour committee and the Regional Coordinator," Frances said with reverence. She put the apron away, then darted into the powder room to fluff her hair.

"No other Floribundas? No Flying Maples?" Leigh asked with

relief. Her mother had never been prone to violence, but Leigh did not trust the rest of the Floribundas as far as she could throw them, never mind that a third of them were over eighty. The additional backstory Leigh had learned over the last half hour wasn't pretty. The "upstart" Flying Maples could be a bunch of nutcases every bit as diabolical as the Floribundas believed them to be, or they could be normal women whose only crime was wanting a garden club that was whack-job free. Either way, Leigh didn't want the warring chapters to wind up facing each other in the Koslows' living room. Certainly not unless all the glassware was removed first.

Frances sniffed. "It's not a *local* decision."

"Well, good luck," Leigh offered, slipping on her coat. "I'll head out the back."

"Oh!" Frances jumped out again. "You came in the front door, didn't you? Heavens! You'll have left prints on the knob!" She scurried back into the kitchen and returned with a wipe. "Would you mind polishing that up on your way out?"

Leigh took the wipe without comment. She reached out to open the door.

Frances tut-tutted.

Leigh bit back a sigh as she polished the inside knob, then twisted it open with the wipe still beneath her fingers. *Leave no trace,* Frances had lectured her as a child. Leigh had always thought her mother would make an excellent burglar.

She swung open the door to repeat the process on the outside knob. Three women in winter coats smiled back at her.

Uh-oh.

"Well, hello!" the tallest of the three said loudly. "You must be Frances's daughter, Leigh! My goodness, don't you look just like her!"

Leigh stared back at the stranger, mute, as Frances popped up at her side. Leigh and her mother were both average height and pear-shaped, but the resemblance ended there. Frances's now snow-white hair had been cut short and molded into its proper matronly form since her twenty-third birthday, and her posture and bearing were straight out of illustrations from the *Ladies Home Journal.* Leigh's shoulder-length brown hair had always been allowed to roam free, and she had a bad habit of crossing her arms over her chest and slouching. She didn't think she looked like either of her parents in the face, but when pressed, most people said she looked more like her dad.

"Thanks," Leigh and her mother said together, glumly.

The tall woman tittered with laughter, and her companions on either side tittered too.

Leigh plastered on a fake smile. How soon could she get out of this?

Frances swept the front door open, and Leigh stepped back into the house. Other than running the trio over, she had no choice.

"Welcome! Welcome!" Frances began, shifting into full hostess mode. The women commenced with introductions all around, and Leigh kept up the fake smiling.

The tall woman was Olympia Pepper, the president of the Floribundas. She stooped a little, as if attempting to shave off a few inches of her six feet of height, but otherwise her bearing was self-assured. Her arms and legs were bony and angular, without an ounce of fat. She showed a little too much gum when she smiled, and her orthodontia had been sorely neglected. But her blondish-gray hair was cut neatly into a short bob, and her beige suit was crisp and professional. According to Frances, Olympia was in her early sixties, newly retired from her career as a tax attorney, and flush with both time and energy.

As yet, Leigh didn't know what was wrong with her. But the fact that she had assumed the presidency of the club within a month of joining did not lobby in favor of normalcy.

"Frances is one of our most decorated members," Olympia bragged. "She's been a past president of the chapter, and she's even won awards at the state level! *And,*" She turned to Leigh. "I understand that her daughter here is a master rose gardener!"

Say what? Leigh shot a questioning glance at her mother. The only roses Leigh had ever planted either turned black with mold or were nibbled into oblivion by aphids. Why would Frances tell Olympia such a thing?

Frances's wide eyes were blinking nervously. Her face had gone pale.

Leigh pulled herself together and faced Olympia's companions. "My talents are grossly overstated," she said smoothly. "My mother is the gardener in the family."

The other women smiled back, and some of Frances's color

returned.

"Oh, that's true, too!" Olympia gushed, animating her words with grand hand gestures. "If only you were here in spring! Frances's azaleas are simply to die for!"

Leigh watched as her mother's face went pale again. The burning question had been answered even sooner than Leigh expected, seeing as how the only shrubs around the Koslow home were boxwoods and holly.

Evidently, Olympia Pepper was a congenital liar.

Fabulous.

"Can I take your coats?" Leigh asked after a moment, concerned that her mother had yet to make the offer. Frances seemed nearly frozen with anxiety. Leigh gathered the other women's things and hung them.

"We have to be honest with you both," Leigh heard the Regional Coordinator say grimly, "we're not at all sure that making a substitution at this late hour is a good idea. Particularly when it would mean having two houses from the nineteen thirties."

Leigh looked over her shoulder to see her mother's face go from stricken to crestfallen. Did Frances really want her home on the tour that badly?

Yep.

Leigh shrugged off her own coat and replaced it on the rack. She wasn't in the advertising business for nothing. "Ah, but the construction of a house is about architecture," she said pleasantly. "A configuration of bricks and mortar representing a single point in time. Creating a mood with one's decor, on the other hand, is a living art. An art that everyday American families have practiced in every era, making use of whatever space they're given. And this space…" She swept her arms out over the room. "This space lives and breathes with the seventies. Can't you feel it?"

She would give anything to have a Barry Manilow ballad cued up.

"Oooh, Yes!" Olympia agreed happily. "Can't you, though? Frances has done an amazing job. Her expertise in retro fashion is simply exceptional. She has people all across the country begging for her advice!"

"Oh, but it is marvelous, isn't it?" cooed the petite, mousy woman who had been introduced as the chair of the tour committee. "Just look at that vintage windmill pattern on the upholstery! And the colors! And... and this!" She moved around the furniture and stopped in front of a metal lamp whose painted base and paper shade were the same ghastly orange as the sofa. "My father used to have one just like this in his study!"

Leigh watched as the Regional Coordinator, an impeccably dressed woman in three-inch heels who looked like she should be a lawyer, surveyed the room. "You do have a point," she said thoughtfully. She turned to Frances. "Wherever did you find so many original pieces?"

Frances looked confused, and Leigh tensed. Her mother had never quite grasped the concept that her furniture was out of style. The idea that it was now so out that it was technically back in was beyond her comprehension. To Frances, good-quality furniture was good-quality furniture. Being a slave to ever-changing fashions was wasteful and imprudent.

The disconnect was not lost on Olympia, who jumped into the awkward silence with enthusiasm. "Oh, Frances has always loved the era! Most of the pieces are her own. She's simply taken excellent care of them over the years, so she's been able to recreate the original effect with only a few adjustments. Others may pluck their decor from here or there, changing everything willy-nilly" — Olympia's gestures here were especially emphatic — "but when it comes to color and consistency of style, Frances has always been a purist. Haven't you, Frances?"

Frances's lips made the slightest of movements.

"Of course she has!" Olympia answered for her. "Now, you may see some pieces sitting out today that don't quite fit our needs for the tour, but of course this isn't the finished product. The Floribundas are prepared to make this home a quintessential *museum* of middle-American family life at a nineteen seventies' Christmas!"

The Regional Coordinator's eyes suddenly widened. "Oh, my," she said in a whisper, moving toward the entrance to the dining room. Everyone followed as she stepped to the table, her eyes fixed on the display of fake fruit at its center. "Glass grapes!" she exclaimed, crossing her hands over her heart. "I'd nearly forgotten these existed! My grandmother used to make them. She had a kit!"

"And wax fruit!" the committee chair exclaimed, rushing up

with a clap of her hands. "In a cranberry-glass bowl! Oh, doesn't that take you back!"

Leigh stole a glance at her mother and saw a healthy rose color returning to her cheeks. "Why, thank you," Frances said meekly, even as her chest puffed up with pride. "I do love my fruit. Like I always say, 'Quality will last, as long as one takes proper care.'"

Olympia laughed loudly. "Oh, Frances, dear, you are such a hoot!" She shot an arm around Frances's shoulders, which remained stiff. "One of the funniest women I know! Would you like to see the kitchen, ladies? It's practically famous. It's been in a magazine!"

The muscles in Frances's jaw tightened briefly. "Yes, please," she managed with grace. "Come see the kitchen. We had it completely remodeled after we bought the house. We had to, actually, because there had been a small fire previously. A malfunctioning toaster, we were told. Of course, the timing was perfect for us, because we were able to purchase the house at a very reasonable price..."

The group shuffled into the next room, and Leigh fought an internal debate. Her mother was going to be fine; Leigh could slip out now. But she gave in to her own curiosity. She was dying to know what fictional magazine had done a spread on the Koslow kitchen.

"You've probably never heard of it," Olympia trilled on, hands flying. "It was called *Living Retro*. Or was it *Retro Living*? Something like that. Anyway, they ran some sort of contest and Frances sent in a picture, and she won! They sent a photographer out, and he did a lovely article. Of course, that was before she redid the floor. This tile is beautiful, of course, but such a shame to have to cover that gorgeous vinyl! For two bits, I'd pull all this up just for the tour!"

Leigh blinked with amazement. Olympia's series of off-the-cuff fabrications had included one accidental truth. There was indeed a vintage vinyl floor underneath the ceramic tile on which they stood. The old floor had been covered only a few years ago, when Leigh's Aunt Bess had been redoing her own kitchen and had mistakenly ordered enough tile for Frances's kitchen also. It was an "accident" that Leigh was certain had more to do with Bess's hatred of the old vinyl than any error of math. The flooring Leigh grew up with had a daisy-yellow background and repeating globules of green, brown, and orange that were big enough to play hopscotch on.

Leigh winced slightly at the memory. Seventies nostalgia was all well and good. But some things were better off covered by a quarter inch of earth tones.

"Oh, but the rest of the room is just darling!" the chair of the tour committee exclaimed. "If these appliances were only green instead of white, it would look just like the kitchen on *The Brady Bunch!*"

Leigh grinned. She and Cara had been saying the same thing ever since they watched the reruns themselves as kids. The Koslows' countertops were a vivid orange. The cabinets were all smooth-faced, covered with a fake-wood veneer and lacking any hardware pulls. The sink was — and always had been — stainless steel. The curtains, dishtowels, and toaster cozy were all dull green. Every potholder was emblazoned with a mushroom.

"I can definitely see potential," the Regional Coordinator announced.

"Well, you will have absolutely no worries whatsoever about the physical condition of this house," Olympia bloviated. "As you can see yourself, it's been kept immaculately, both inside and out. Frances's husband is a registered electrician and plumber, and we can assure you there will be no problems *whatsoever* with public safety!"

Leigh fought to keep from laughing aloud. The image of her workaholic veterinarian father being certified in two other professions was too amusing. She wondered if Olympia even knew what Randall did for a living.

"Well, let's see the upstairs, shall we?" Olympia continued. "You're just going to *love* what she's done with the master bedroom! Frances, dear, shall you tell them how you acquired that absolutely gorgeous metal fish sculpture on the wall in the bathroom, or shall I? Ooh, never mind! I will. I simply must! Well, ladies, Frances and her husband happened to be tooling around the Three Rivers Arts Festival one summer back in the day, and they came across one particular artist who simply amazed them..."

Leigh hung back, listening from below, as Olympia led the other women up the staircase. Frances trailed behind, rubbing her hands nervously, no doubt hoping that none of the women would look too closely at the fish sculpture, which — although it had indeed hung in its current location since the seventies — had probably been purchased from JC Penny and made in Taiwan.

Within a few minutes the women trooped back down again, the

impeccably preserved rooms and outrageous commentary having
left broad smiles on every face except Frances's. Frances was still on
tenterhooks.

"Well, I think we've seen all we need to see," the Regional
Coordinator said, exchanging a nod with the committee chair. "We
shall make the substitution! Ladies, can your chapter have this
house decorated for Christmas in — she looked at her watch with a
grim set to her lips — twenty-three and a half hours?"

"Absolutely!" Frances and Olympia said simultaneously,
Frances's face now beaming.

"Well, we'd best be on our way, then. We'll have to see about
making some fliers to redirect people. We'll have to make
adjustments with the parking zone and look into the insurance
situation..."

"Oh, of course, of course!" Olympia agreed, handing the women
their coats. "Let me walk you out. Frances, we simply must inform
the rest of the Floribundas right—"

"We'll convene an emergency meeting immediately," Frances
interrupted. "There are a million things to be done!"

The women exchanged their final pleasantries in brisk fashion,
then Frances shut the door behind the three of them and whirled
around, her dark eyes twinkling. "Oh, Leigh! Do you believe it?"

Leigh couldn't remember the last time she'd seen her mother so
happy. Certainly not in the last few, tension-filled months that she'd
been feuding with her twin. "Congratulations, Mom," she praised.
She grabbed her own coat again.

"A substitution the day before the event is unthinkable!" Frances
said breathlessly. "I never believed that Olympia could talk them
into it. I still can't believe it!"

Leigh smirked. "I can't believe that Dad is a registered plumber."

Frances waved a hand dismissively. "Oh, poo. That woman lies
like a rug."

"So I noticed," Leigh agreed. "And yet you elected her
president?"

Frances's eyes rolled. She headed off toward the kitchen in a
flurry. "Well, for heaven's sake, who else is going to do it? There
isn't a member among us who hasn't taken on that miserable job at
least twice now. Complaints, always complaints, always a better
way to do something, nobody's ever happy! Women calling you up

at all hours telling you who said what and what went wrong and how somebody else used to do it better and how they would do it differently if they were in charge but of course they don't want to be in charge because they have more important things to do with their own time!" She picked up her ancient landline phone. "I've served four terms already and I'll be dee-diddly-darned if they're ever talking me into it again!"

Leigh's mouth dropped open. If serving as president of the Floribundas was considered more of a burden than a privilege, this was the first she'd heard of it. Frances had always given the impression that such work was, at the very least, a sacred duty.

"Hello, Anna Marie?" Frances barked into the phone. "Frances, here. Activate the phone chain! Olympia did it! We're on the tour!"

Leigh took a step back as a noise erupted from the handset that sounded like the squawking of a very large parrot. *I'll be going now,* she mouthed with a wave. She moved quickly to the back door, not wanting to bump into a returning Olympia.

Frances returned her wave absently. "I know! Isn't it marvelous!" she gushed into the phone.

Leigh opened the back door and stepped out. Getting the house completely decorated and ready for hundreds of people to tour in less than twenty-four hours would be a huge undertaking for eight women of the Floribundas' age. It would be a pain in the butt for eight people of any age. Leigh had no doubt that she would get roped into the process, the only question was how long she could avoid the summons. The Harmon family would all be busy with her son Ethan's party tonight; whatever else Leigh had to get done before Sunday she realized she had better do now.

"You most certainly are responsible for the phone chain, Anna Marie!" Frances insisted, her voice rising with frustration. "No, that was last year! I will not ask her! It's your—"

Leigh quietly clicked the door shut behind her.

Chapter 3

The street outside buzzed with activity as the two garden club officials drove away, Olympia started back toward the house, and Lydie's car pulled up next door. Leigh waited for her aunt and soon-to-be-uncle to park, then walked over.

"Hello there!" she said cheerfully, noting how happy the couple looked. They were carrying multiple red and green shopping bags and their cheeks were flushed with cold... or something.

"Hello, Leigh," Lydie replied warmly, but with a twinge of concern. "What brings you here at this hour? Is everything all right?" She stole a glance toward Frances's house. "What's all the commotion?"

Leigh began to answer, then was struck by the odd impression that Lydie looked an awful lot like Frances. Leigh blinked and did a double take. The thought was a strange one. Granted, the sisters were identical twins. But in Leigh's lifetime they had always looked far too different to be confused. Not only had Frances always been plump, but she dressed formally and carried herself with the utmost in self-confidence. Lydie was nobody's doormat, for sure, but she always seemed too busy to be proud of herself. She was in constant motion, dressed for practicality, and had always been thin — sometimes painfully so, especially in the face and shoulders.

Leigh cocked an eyebrow. Her aunt had most definitely put on weight. Her natural pear shape was more pronounced and her cheeks were full and rosy. She wore a colorful new outfit that Leigh had never seen before and there was something different about her hair, as well. "Believe it or not," Leigh explained, "the Koslow home is going to be an official stop on the Holiday House Tour. *Tomorrow.*"

Lydie used a word Leigh had never heard her speak before. Leigh laughed out loud as Mason Dublin walked around the car and took the packages from his fiance's hands.

"I don't know what a Holiday House Tour is," he said jovially. "But if it's got you swearing in the middle of a Friday afternoon, I'm guessing you'd better go on over there."

Lydie swallowed. She looked from Mason to Leigh to Frances's house, and then back to Mason again. "I don't have to."

Leigh watched as a silent exchange ensued between the couple. Their history with each other and with Frances was a long and complicated one. Lydie and Mason had met when they were young, and after a whirlwind courtship they had gotten married and Leigh's cousin Cara had been born. But Mason had been a bit of a scamp, to say the least, and Frances had never approved of him. The marriage ended quickly and disastrously, just as Frances had predicted, and the couple went on to lead separate lives. But recently, their more mature counterparts had reconnected, and slowly but surely they'd discovered what turned out to be an amazingly long-burning flame.

Lydie and Mason were very happy together, and everyone in the family was happy for them. Everyone except Frances.

"Go on, love," Mason insisted, giving Lydie a quick peck on the cheek. "You know you want to."

Lydie's face tightened with concern. "Her blood pressure has been on the high side lately."

"Go," Mason repeated.

Lydie kissed him back. On the lips. Then she said goodbye to Leigh and went.

"Can I help you carry something in?" Leigh asked, looking at the bags Mason was juggling.

The blue-green eyes which looked so much like Cara's twinkled at her mischievously. "You may not," he replied. "It's Christmas. There are things in these bags no one may see until Santa comes."

Leigh smiled back at him. She had always liked Mason, despite his earlier challenges in law abidance. "Can I at least open the door for you?"

He squirmed around and produced his keys. "You may."

Leigh took the keys and let them both into her aunt's house, which was nearly identical to the Koslow home except for lacking a half bath downstairs. Much like the twin sisters themselves, the resemblance was in structure only. Lydie's house was brightly colored and cozy, filled with low-budget and second-hand furniture that was clearly selected for comfort over style. The house was always reasonably clean, but just cluttered and messy enough to feel like home. When Leigh was a child, coming over to Cara's house had felt like taking off your church dress and slipping into a cotton romper.

"So tell me," Mason asked as he set the packages down and waved Leigh toward a chair. "What's all this about a house tour?"

Leigh offered a brief summary. Mason sank back in his own chair and whistled. "Francie will be in high clover, for sure. And her diastolic will be getting up there too, I'll bet."

Leigh nodded in agreement. Her mother's diagnosis of high blood pressure the month before had been troubling to all concerned. The family had long since learned how to take even the most full-blown Frances freak-out in stride, but now, with the risk of stroke added into the equation, they'd all been walking on eggshells.

"Maybe I should take off for the weekend," he said thoughtfully, scratching a jaw covered with several days' worth of stubble. Whether he knew the look was sexy or whether he'd simply been too lazy to shave, Leigh didn't know. They had all been pretending not to notice, for the children's sake, how much time Mason spent at her aunt's house these days, as opposed to his own apartment in Bellevue. The man might be nearing seventy, but with his full head of hair and devil-may-care smile, Mason Dublin could still catch women's eyes. It was easy to see how Lydie had fallen so completely for his younger incarnation, reckless troublemaker though he may have been.

"Why would you need to leave?" Leigh asked.

Mason threw her a look, then sighed. "You know why, kid," he said ruefully. "Things haven't been the same between the sisters for months, and it's all because of me."

Leigh felt a heavy weight in her middle. She couldn't deny the truth of that. "But it's not your fault, Mason."

He shook his head. "Well, that's neither here nor there. Facts are facts. And I hate what it's doing to Lydie."

"I know," Leigh agreed. "But I do think my mother is trying. She's... not openly hostile, at least. Right?"

Mason chuckled. "She smiles and looks right through me. I can deal with that. The problem is that she won't set foot in this house if she knows I'm here. She won't even call. She'll only talk to her sister — *really* talk — when they're alone. Which means the more time I spend with the woman I love, the less time the two of them spend together. And they're so used to being close… it's getting to both of them, I think."

"My mother doesn't want to be difficult," Leigh tried to explain. "The problem is that she genuinely believes Lydie is making a mistake. She *can't* make peace with the situation as long as she believes that, even if she does manage to control what comes out of her mouth. We all know she's wrong… maybe we need to try harder to convince her."

Mason smiled sardonically. "It's been forty-three years, kid. How much more time are we talking about? Lydie and I are pretty well preserved, but we're not immortal."

Leigh had no response to that. Mason rose again. "I think I'll head out to Jennerstown for the weekend. I have a few more things to tie up before the sales are final on the farm and the store."

"You can't be gone all weekend!" Leigh protested, rising with him. "Ethan and Allison's birthday is Sunday."

"Oh, right!" he exclaimed with a start. "Can't miss that! Don't worry. I'll be back by Sunday afternoon. But if this house tour thing is as big a deal as you say, it's best I make myself scarce. Lydie's been firm about not giving in to her sister's tantrums — she insists if she wants to spend time with me, that's what she's going to do. But if I'm not around, she won't feel conflicted."

Leigh frowned with frustration. "*This* is the Mason my mother never sees," she mumbled. She gave him a quick hug and headed for the door.

"You keep your mother out of trouble, now," he called after her. "This will be quite a milestone for Francie. I didn't think she'd ever get over the trauma of that sweet sixteen party. She used to say she'd rather march straight to hell than throw another big to-do in her own backyard ever again! But I guess time heals all wounds."

Leigh stopped moving. She turned around. "Sweet sixteen party?"

Mason stared at her a moment, his eyes slowly widening. "Your mother never told you about that?"

Leigh frowned. She really did hate those particular words. "Evidently not."

"Oh," Mason said with embarrassment. "Never mind, then. Have a good weekend, kid. I'll see you on —"

"Don't even," Leigh said heavily, taking a step closer. "You brought it up, now you're spilling it! What happened at their sweet sixteen party?" She wasn't sure why it mattered. But she was getting that bad feeling in her gut again.

"Nothing!" Mason lied. "I don't even know why I thought of it. This event is just people walking through the house, right?"

"As opposed to what?"

"I just mean," he asked, "there's not a bunch of food being served at every stop, is there?"

The bad feeling grew worse. Leigh had enough of her own misgivings; she didn't need to add Mason's to the mix. "The hosting garden club usually does serve some light refreshments at each station, yes," she answered. "Why?"

Mason relaxed a little. "Oh, well if it's just Christmas cookies and such…"

"What happened on Mom and Aunt Lydie's sixteenth birthday?" Leigh repeated.

Mason exhaled and rubbed his chin again. "Look, I didn't mean to step into it. I just didn't think, after all this time… Maybe Lydie had better give me a cheat sheet of what I'm allowed to talk about and what I'm not."

"You mean there's more?" Leigh practically exploded. She was still smarting over the lies the family had told Cara and her both about Mason, all under the guise of "protecting" the girls. "How many things is my mother still censoring from my impressionable middle-aged ears?"

"Now, calm down, kid," Mason said evenly. "Your mother's entitled to a little privacy. Surely there's a thing or two in your own history you wouldn't want me tattling to Ethan and Allison?"

Leigh went quiet.

Mason cracked a small grin of triumph. "I thought so. Look, don't let anyone know I said anything, will you? The last thing I need right now is to give your mother another reason to hate me."

Leigh bit her tongue. Literally. Mason was right. Besides, what possible bearing could such ancient history have on the current situation? Surely none. Still, she couldn't quell her curiosity. Now that she thought about it, she couldn't remember Frances ever having hosted an actual full-blown, non-family adult party at the Koslow house. Of course, not everybody enjoyed doing that sort of thing, but it seemed like Frances should. She did love showing off her clean house. She was always inviting family and small groups of friends over for dinner, and she was constantly making casseroles for donation to the church freezer. But although she did have meetings at her house for all sorts of groups, she never hosted receptions or showers or large events with food, ostensibly because "that many people eating make too much of a mess."

If Frances really had vowed once upon a time that she would never again "throw a big to-do," then it appeared she had kept that promise for fifty some-odd years. And tomorrow, she was going to break it.

Leigh blew out a frustrated breath. "Fine," she conceded to Mason. "I won't ask my mother anything about her mysterious sweet sixteen."

Mason thanked her, they exchanged another round of goodbyes, and Leigh headed for her car.

But I'm going to find out anyway, she added silently.

Chapter 4

Leigh steadied her gun and aimed carefully in the dim light. She squeezed the trigger, and an explosion sounded in her ears. She smirked with satisfaction.

She had shot her husband. Again.

Warren threw his hands up in the air with good-natured frustration, then whirled around and dashed off toward the recharging station.

"Good one, Mom!" Allison called out from the darkness below.

"Thanks!" Leigh shouted happily. She hadn't realized her daughter was hiding there, crouching behind a low barrier in the foggy chaos of the laser tag arena. Allison would turn twelve the day after tomorrow, but she was small for her age, she was dressed in solid black, and she crept around so low to the ground and so stealthily that she was able to make herself virtually invisible. Which was excellent for the red team.

"Have you died yet?" Leigh shouted out over the din. Weird techno music blared over the speakers, punctuated by the occasional wail of a siren when someone hit a base target.

"Of course not!" Allison returned indignantly.

An explosion sounded in Leigh's ears again. But this time, it came with an unpleasant deflating sound. *Dammit.*

"Recharge!" an obnoxious voice taunted in her headset. She looked over to see her son laughing at her from behind an enemy barrier not eight feet away. Gone were the days when Leigh had to pretend to let Ethan beat her at anything. The boy had begun a massive growth spurt over the fall and now looked her straight in the eye, which was beyond disconcerting.

"Allison," she cried in frustration. "Kill your brother!"

"Okay," her daughter called back cheerfully.

Leigh scurried back through the maze of walls and barricades that defined the red team's territory until she reached her designated recharging station. Her heart was pumping wildly, which she knew was ironic. She'd never played with toy guns as a child, had never even handled a real gun as an adult, and had never had the slightest desire to do either. But there was definitely something cathartic about running around in a dark room with blinking strobes and shooting laser beams at little lights that glowed over your enemies' ears, particularly when those enemies were friends and family.

Go figure.

She had to recharge her gun quickly. It was pure random chance that she and Warren had been on opposite teams both games they'd played so far, but his team had pounded hers the first time, and she was *not* going down again. His personal player stats were better than hers, too, and that could not be tolerated. Warren was a wonderful husband and father, he was brilliant with finance, he was one of those rare men who only got better looking as they aged, and she loved him dearly. But no way in hell was he beating her at laser tag.

Self-possessed as Warren J. Harmon III might look now, Leigh knew that underneath that mantle of sophisticated maturity lay a too-tall gawky misfit who had been the only other freshman at Pitt who could make her sorry butt look good in Tennis 101. Although he loved laser tag with a passion — the flashing lights and geeky techno environment were like a drug to his sci-fi obsessed soul — the sad fact was that Warren was no more athletic than she was, which put him roughly two levels above a tomato. How the two of them had combined their genes to produce a strapping son like Ethan, who had natural talent at any sport he played but was too easy-going to be seriously competitive at any of them, was an enduring mystery.

Leigh *should* be the better player. Warren lacked the dexterity to aim a gun or weave amongst the barriers, and his tall form and broad shoulders were impossible to hide. The green lights on his headset were always sticking up somewhere, making him a pathetically easy target. Leigh was much more difficult to strike, partly because she was smaller and partly because she knew a thing or two about covert operations, for reasons she didn't care to think about in the middle of a kids' birthday party.

Leigh stuck her gun under the light on the recharging post. One of Ethan's friends arrived just after her, carrying with him the distinctive aroma of twelve-year-old boys everywhere: the pungent combination of foot and body odor. He was sweating so much his glasses kept slipping down his nose, but he was smiling from ear to ear. "I got the base!" he bragged.

"Good job!" Leigh praised, forgetting the boy's name. She'd known most of Ethan's friends for years, but this fall in middle school he'd picked up several new ones. She felt a pang of sadness whenever she remembered that this was the first party of Ethan's that his cousin Mathias hadn't attended, but she tried not to dwell on it. Matt was two and a half years older, after all. He was a high school freshman while these boys were all in the sixth grade. Socially, that made a huge difference.

She supposed she should be glad that Ethan tolerated his sister and parents playing along. Most boys wouldn't, but it worked out well enough, since Warren was in his glory and all the boys enjoyed making mincemeat of the parental units. They paid little attention to Ethan's quiet, bookish sister, much to their regret when they got back their scorecards. *Hey! Who is number 13? They shot me 8 times!*

Allison never said a word.

Leigh heard the happy zipping sound that meant her gun was reloaded, and she headed back out to the battlefield. Only a few minutes remained, and the red team was behind again. She slunk around the barriers until she reached her favored spot, a mound-shaped shield from behind which she could shoot at Warren when he perched at his favorite spot.

An explosion sounded in her ears again.

Dammit!

Leigh moved farther behind the shield. She had no idea who had fired at her. But she was down to two lives again already. Where was Warren?

"Don't kick me, Mom," Allison grumbled.

"Oh, sorry!" Leigh apologized to the darkness.

"You need to shoot at Ethan," Allison instructed. "He can hit the base. Dad can't."

"Roger that," Leigh agreed. She moved carefully out from behind her hiding place, only to immediately hear another explosion.

She remembered not to swear this time.

"Don't go that way, Mom!" Allison said with frustration. "Jonathan's just going to keep shooting you! Go the other way, and duck down! I'm going to try for the green base again."

Leigh had no idea where Jonathan was hiding. If only she were canine, she mused to herself. Then she could sniff out every one of them! She slunk away in the direction Allison instructed and tried harder to keep her own headset hidden behind the barriers. She could see Ethan moving around in the fog ahead of her. He was going to attack the red base again, and they really couldn't afford that. She slipped after him, moving quickly from hiding place to hiding place, twisting her neck around whenever she was out in the open to make the lights on her headset a more difficult target. She was *going* to win this thing.

She heard a siren in the distance and looked up at the scoreboard. Yes! Allison had scored against the green base. The reds were ahead again! She watched as Ethan approached the red base and prepared to shoot. Their time was almost up. Less than ten seconds left in the game now. Leigh raised her gun and waited for Ethan to step out, but just as her son made his move, Warren stepped boldly right out in the open.

The nerve! Leigh swung her gun over and aimed a fierce volley of shots at the man she loved. Ripples of explosions blasted through her headset, and she smirked with triumph to watch as the lights over his ears blinked repeatedly, indicating she had finished him off. Unfortunately, she heard something else at the same time. She heard the siren sound, which along with the giant flashing red light on the nearby ceiling meant that the red base had been hit.

The buzzer sounded to end the game, and the room lightened. Ethan shouted out a "woot" and gave his dad a high five, and Leigh looked up at the scoreboard with apprehension. Ethan had hit the base. The red team had lost. Again.

Oh, well. At least the birthday boy was having a good time. "Good shot, Ethan!" she praised. Then she turned tail and trudged back around the maze to the exit, where she was forced to face her daughter's glower. "You shot at Dad again, didn't you?" Allison accused with a pout.

"No comment," Leigh answered.

The teams exited to the equipment room and took off their gear, then the boys all piled back into the lobby to await their scorecards. A sweaty and exhilarated Warren met Leigh by the giant claw machine and threw an arm around her. "You just can't resist me, can you?" he smirked.

Leigh's eyes narrowed. "You did that on purpose."

He laughed out loud. "Call it taking one for the team."

Allison stood before them, her arms crossed over her chest. "It's my birthday too, you know," she reminded.

Warren straightened a bit and smiled at his daughter. "You raise a good point. My condolences on the loss. But I'm sure you were the red team MVP as usual, Allie."

The girl seemed mollified. She smiled with satisfaction. "I hope so."

Leigh felt a twinge of unease watching her daughter hanging with the parents as the boys tumbled around the arcade shouting like maniacs. In the past the twins' parties had involved their cousins and friends of both genders. But this year Ethan had only wanted boys from his grade, and Allison hadn't wanted a party at all. She claimed that the girls she would invite were in different "friend groups," that they didn't all get along with each other, and that it "wasn't worth the drama." Leigh knew that such changes were inevitable as the kids grew up, but that didn't mean she was ready for them. It had been entirely too convenient, for all these years, for her children and Cara's to be a self-sufficient social unit.

Warren started a bit, then pulled his phone from his breast pocket and looked at the screen. His eyebrows tented. "It's your mother," he said to Leigh. "Any ideas?"

"Help with the house tour, I'm sure," she answered, her happy mood deflating further.

Warren looked back at her with a puzzled expression, then turned to move to a less noisy location. "Hello, Frances!" he answered with enthusiasm, as if he'd been waiting for his mother-in-law's call all day. The man was a born schmoozer.

Leigh watched through the glass as he spoke on the phone in the entryway for a few minutes. Then he came back in, found Ethan, and motioned for the boy to join him. After Ethan spoke on the phone, he returned to the party and gestured for Allison to go out.

Leigh joined Warren in the entryway as he handed the phone to their daughter.

"What's up?" Leigh asked. "What does she want, exactly?"

"Height," he answered.

"Excuse me?"

Warren laughed. "Apparently, the Floribundas' enthusiasm for decorating does not extend to climbing up ladders. They need some taller and preferably younger people to help out tomorrow morning."

"Oh," Leigh replied dully. She had expected to be summoned herself, but she hadn't thought about Warren and the children becoming involved. The idea unnerved her.

"Here, Mom," Allison said. "Grandma wants to talk to you."

Leigh took the phone from her daughter's hand, and Allison rushed back into the lobby where the boys were receiving their scorecards.

"Leigh, dear," Frances began, sounding as if she were checking items off a list. "Thanks so much for helping out. What time can you be here tomorrow? Warren says he'll bring the children between eight and eight-thirty, but it would be positively marvelous if you could make it here by seven."

Leigh's shoulders sagged. "Seven *AM?*"

Frances made no response to that.

"Fine," Leigh capitulated. She would like to think she could sneak out once the tour started at two, but she knew that wouldn't happen. Whatever time she arrived at her mother's house tomorrow, she would not be returning until it was all said and done.

All said and done. Why was her gut starting to ache again? "Are you sure you need the kids there?" she asked.

"For heaven's sake," Frances said irritably, "we need all the help we can get! We've only got four husbands among us, and your father is *working,* as always. Anna Marie's husband can't help; he has too much trouble getting around. Virginia's husband Harry is right as rain, but he's always been a horse's rear; he makes more trouble than he's worth. Olympia's husband Melvin is a lovely man — he's a proctologist, you know — but the poor dear is only five foot two, and we've got lights to string!"

Leigh raised no further objection. Frances rang off, clearly in a hurry to reach the next person on her list, and Leigh handed the phone back to Warren.

"What's that look for?" he asked.

"What look?"

He shook his head at her. "Don't give me that. Something's

bothering you about this house tour. What is it? Sounds to me like it's your mother's dream come true."

Leigh sighed. "It is. Maybe that's what worries me."

They returned to the lobby, and Allison ran over and handed them their scorecards. "Two-time MVP!" she said proudly.

They congratulated her in unison. Although Allison was smart as a whip and good at many things, competitive sports were not among them. Her peculiar abilities at laser tag made the game a rare treat for her, or else she would more than likely have spent another Friday night at home in front of her computer.

Leigh and Warren bent their heads and studied their own statistics. Then they looked over to study each other's.

"*Yes!*" Leigh cried triumphantly, pumping a fist.

Warren rolled his eyes. "So competitive!"

"You gloated after the first game!" Leigh shot back.

"I did not," Warren protested.

They turned to Allison as if to settle to the dispute. "I'm out of here," the girl announced, moving off.

"Well, what do you say?" Warren suggested cheerfully, gesturing to the boys, who had begun to scatter across the arcade. "Shall we go for a third round or just let them roam?"

Leigh looked at her watch. "Better do another round. Pickup isn't for a half hour, and if we cut them loose, they'll want more tokens."

"They used all their tokens already?" Warren asked in disbelief.

"Are you kidding? A bunch of sixth-grade boys in a room with machines that light up and make loud noises? They spent the wad in five minutes."

"We'll do another round," Warren agreed. He leaned in close and threw her a smile of challenge. "You and me. Best of three?"

"You're so competitive."

"Winner gets a twenty-minute backrub."

Leigh smirked. "Deal."

Chapter 5

The Koslow living room was already a hive of activity when Leigh walked through the front door at 7:16AM the next morning. Her father and her Aunt Lydie were busily carrying boxes both up and down the stairs while Frances and another Floribunda pulled items out of some boxes and packed them away in others.

"Do come over here, Leigh, we need you!" Frances ordered. Leigh weaved through the boxes on the floor toward where her mother stood next to Virginia, a woman in her mid seventies whom Leigh had known forever and whom she had always unfortunately associated with the adjective "horse faced." The term was somewhat less apt now that Virginia's wild head of chestnut hair had thinned and turned to gray, but her jutting jaw, prominent brow, and bushy eyebrows still fit the image. Not that Virginia's appearance was objectionable — her unusual face was actually quite appealing in a charismatic sort of way. What made Virginia objectionable, aside from the fact that she was a hopeless gossip, was the fact that she was forever pestering both friends and acquaintances with intrusive personal questions.

"Look at these decorations," Frances instructed Leigh, holding up a half dozen plastic toy figurines of Dalmatian puppies playing with ribbons and packages. "You think these are from the seventies?"

Leigh shook her head. "No. Those came from McDonalds." She looked deeper into the box. It was full of similar offerings. "All these things came from kids' meals at fast-food places," she explained. "That whole fad didn't start until the eighties, at the earliest."

Virginia sighed. "Well, I'll swear, Frances, I thought Angie played with them when she was a girl. I guess I'm remembering wrong. They must have been the grandchildren's." She dropped the toys back into the cardboard box, which judging by its markings had once held cases of whiskey. Having heard plenty about the escapades of Virginia's husband, Leigh was not surprised.

"That's all right," Frances declared as she sealed the box back up. She picked up a sharpie marker and squeaked out a series of precise letters across the lid. *REJECTED.*

"Well, what about these, then?" Virginia asked, pulling over another box and opening its lid. "I *know* they're from the seventies. Angie and I did all the cross-stitching before she left for— Oh, my. Oh, dear. This is terrible."

Leigh leaned over to take a look for herself. The mess of jumbled fabric inside had probably once been a very nice set of placemats and napkins. But judging from the jagged hole on the lower corner of the box, the pile of fluff that had replaced a good part of its contents, and the abundance of scattered brown pellets throughout, it had long since been repurposed as a mouse nest.

"Well, that's that, then," Frances said decisively, reclosing the lid and taping it shut. She put an extra piece of tape over the hole on the lower corner, then called out to Leigh's father. "Randall, could you take these two boxes back to Virginia's car, please? And bring in the tree from her trunk? We're ready for it, now."

"Oh, yes," Virginia said happily. "At least we saved that!"

Randall Koslow, VMD, walked over and picked up the boxes. He nodded a wordless greeting to Leigh, but the expression on his face spoke volumes. *Thank God you're here, because if I had to stay in the house with all these women the rest of the day I'd lose my ever-loving mind.*

No problem, Dad, Leigh's own expression answered.

"Leigh, darling," Virginia began, her attention refocused as soon as the boxes were out of sight. "Have you been having any more of that gall bladder trouble your mother was telling us about?"

"No, I haven't," Leigh replied as politely as she could fake. The gall bladder incident had been nine years ago, but Virginia never forgot a juicy bit of medical information. And you couldn't avoid direct questions from her either — the woman simply repeated them, using more detail each time. The only way to handle Virginia was to give as short an answer as possible and move the hell on. "How are you and Harry doing these days?"

"Oh, well Harry just did the radiation implant for his prostate, you know," she said with enthusiasm. "We thought about the surgery, but we decided to go with the implant because…"

The rest of Virginia's answer flitted through Leigh's brain

without impact as she studied the room around her. Frances had been very busy indeed since yesterday afternoon. Apparently she had gone about the entire house removing any items or decorations from the walls that did not appear authentic to the seventies. Those must have been in the boxes that Randall and Lydie had been carrying up to the attic. Leigh recognized a few of the boxes coming down as being the Koslows' own family Christmas decorations.

She hoped there were more Christmas decorations in those boxes than she remembered, because with the family's personal pictures gone from the walls, along with virtually every other knickknack that had been added to Frances's collection since the early 1980s, the house currently looked rather bare. And most of the boxes on the floor looked like they had been opened and "rejected" already.

Leigh moved to help Randall bring in the tree, and the two of them carried the long box between them and sat it down in the middle of the room. Frances eagerly popped open the lid.

"See what I told you!" Virginia cried with delight. "It's in perfect condition!"

Leigh looked down to see the disassembled parts of a shiny aluminum Christmas tree. The center trunk was white metal, while each of the branches was a perfectly straight rod, covered like a bristle brush with shimmering "needles" of bright pink.

"Doesn't that take you back?" Virginia cooed.

"It's perfect!" Frances exclaimed. She turned to Leigh. "Here, dear. You and Virginia can start setting this up in the corner. We've no time to lose!"

"I'm off to the clinic," Leigh's father said mildly, so mildly Leigh suspected he was hoping that no one would hear him.

"So soon!" Frances said with a shriek, whirling around. "But the attic! We've got—"

"It's all taken care of," Lydie interrupted, removing her work gloves as she walked down the last few steps. "Let him go, Frances. We're good."

Frances hesitated.

Randall disappeared.

Lydie looked down into the box and immediately handed Leigh her gloves. "Here. You'll need these."

"Lord, yes!" Virginia proclaimed. "The times I drew blood trying to put ornaments on this darned thing! It's like giving your fingertips a biopsy!"

Leigh put on the gloves. She couldn't remember ever working with a tree quite like this one, although she'd seen pictures of them. The tree she'd grown up with had been artificial also, but it was green and lifelike. Hadn't that been in the seventies?

She propped up the center rod in its stand, and Virginia began to hand her the limbs — very carefully. "So you think you're over the gall bladder issues, then?" Virginia inquired.

"Definitely. Do you remember when you got this tree?"

"No. And how is your little one? She's had it so rough, poor thing. I thought they'd never let her out of the neonatal intensive care unit. Is she doing better?"

Leigh jammed a branch in its hole on the trunk. The tip of it was indeed sharp. How did kids not poke their eyes out on these things? "Allison will turn twelve tomorrow," she answered, wishing she could hurry up without hurting somebody.

"Oh my," Virginia said grimly. "What an age. Has she started her monthlies yet?"

Leigh was saved by the doorbell. She looked up hopefully as Frances ushered in another Floribunda, but although almost any distraction would have been welcome at that moment, the arrival of Lucille Busby was an arguable exception. The arrival of Lucille Busby was unpleasant under any circumstances.

"Lucille, dear, come on in," Frances said gamely, holding open the door and gesturing for the older woman to move directly to the couch.

"Well, I'm sure as hell not standing out on your porch all the damn day!" Lucille squawked, shuffling forward with her walker. Leigh watched the woman's slow progress with surprise, then wondered at that reaction. She supposed that subconsciously, she had always viewed Lucille as eerily immortal. Lucille was the oldest of the Floribundas, and she had been complaining about some ailment or other — and predicting her own demise in increasingly macabre detail — for as long as Leigh had known her. And yet the woman had persisted in torturing and depressing those around her for decades without ever showing the slightest sign of age-related deterioration. Until now.

Lucille stood a good foot shorter than Leigh remembered as she slouched over her walker and shuffled across the carpet. Her back was hunched, her hands were shaky, and a tube ran from her nose to a portable oxygen tank. She wheezed with every breath and her complexion was sickly pale.

"Hurry up, idiot!" Lucille rasped to the space behind her. "What kind of lazy bones can't keep up with the likes of me, I ask you?"

A short, plumpish woman who looked like she was somewhere in her fifties hustled in the front door and rushed to Lucille's side. She was dressed in scrubs like a medical assistant, but she didn't wear a nametag or carry any medical gear. Her short, graying brown hair was bedraggled, she wore large out-of-style glasses, and she appeared extremely nervous.

Lucille turned around to sit on the couch, and the assistant clumsily helped her maneuver into position with the walker.

"Ouch!" Lucille squawked. "If you're going to kill me, woman, the least you can do is suffocate me in my sleep. Not break my bones while I'm standing!"

"I'm sorry, Ms. Busby," the assistant squeaked.

"Leigh," Frances said smoothly, pretending as she always had that Lucille spoke and acted like a normal person, "you remember Lucille. And this is her personal assistant, Bridget."

Leigh and Bridget exchanged nods, but Lucille merely glared at Leigh, as she did most people. Leigh could never fathom why Lucille chose to be a part of the garden club, given that she appeared to detest everyone in it. Then again, it was equally unfathomable why the other members put up with her. Lucille had loomed large as a specter of negativity even in Leigh's childhood; her earliest memories of the woman were of conflating her with Dr. Seuss's sour kangaroo. And that was before Lucille got really cranky.

"I sent you a wedding present," Lucille said fiercely, staring at Leigh through cold blue eyes. "Never got a thank-you note."

"Oh for heaven's sake, Lucille, not *that* again!" Frances rebuked. "We've been through this before. Leigh sent the note. It got lost in the mail. Now, this is serious, women! We have to *focus!*" She clapped her hands, and all the women, including Leigh, snapped to attention. Frances had always been irked by Lucille's now nearly fourteen-year-old lament over the missing thank-you note, but Leigh had never heard her mother shut the old witch down so succinctly. Usually the standard, repeated accusations and denials went on for at least five minutes.

Go, Mom!

"Did you bring any decorations from your house?" Frances asked, looking from Lucille to Bridget.

"I sent this brainless numbskull up to the attic for them," Lucille replied, gesturing to Bridget. "But she said she couldn't find any old stuff. I don't know. Maybe she's blind. But I'm sure as hell not going to go crawling around up there. I'll die soon enough in my own bed without having to be dragged down feet first from the rafters with cobwebs in my hair!"

The assistant lowered her voice and spoke to Frances. "There's hardly anything left in that attic. Her son's been going through it for a while now — I think he's selling stuff online."

Frances's perfect poise gave way a little. Her shoulders sagged. "Oh dear. But I thought..." She took a seat herself. "Well, I do hope the others have more luck."

Noticing that Lydie had wisely slipped out of the room at some point, Leigh turned back to the Christmas tree and stuck in another branch. Risking bloodshed on a mechanical task was one thing, but engaging socially with three Floribundas at once was beyond her call of duty.

"You can't use that!" Lucille sputtered.

Leigh looked over to see Lucille's reptile eyes staring at the growing Christmas tree.

"Why ever not?" Virginia said resentfully. "It's vintage!"

Lucille sniffed. "Vintage sixties, maybe."

"We used it in the seventies!" Virginia argued.

Lucille shook her head stubbornly. "You may have still had it in the seventies, but if you put it up, you were as out of fashion as a poodle skirt! Don't you remember the cartoon? With the fat-headed little boy and the snarky dog?"

The women looked at each blankly for a moment.

"Oh," Frances said finally. "You mean *Peanuts?* The Christmas show with Charlie Brown?"

Lucille pointed a crooked finger. "That's the one. Where the boy wraps a blanket around some pathetic little twig and everybody starts singing and what all. Don't you remember how that show made fun of trees like this? Pretty much said flat out that they were part of everything that was wrong with Christmas!"

"Oh, dear," Virginia moaned, sinking into a chair. "That's right. I'd forgotten that."

Lucille nodded smugly. "It got so you were embarrassed to have an aluminum tree in your house. Everybody wanted real trees."

Frances stood up again. "But when was that, exactly?"

Leigh took off a glove, pulled out her phone, and looked it up. *"A Charlie Brown Christmas* first aired in 1965," she reported.

Frances sat back down. Her eyes were getting the glassy look that made Leigh's heart skip.

"Mom, it's okay," Leigh said quickly. "We still have the tree we had when I was a kid up in the attic. What's wrong with that one? It's definitely vintage seventies, even if it's not so different from the ones you buy today."

"Well," Frances said uncertainly, "I suppose if we used our old ornaments and you decorate it like you remember when you were little, it *would* be authentic."

"Oh, but green trees are so mundane!" Virginia opined. "Can't we use the pretty pink one anyway?"

"They were out of fashion I tell you!" Lucille huffed, beating her walker on the floor for emphasis. "I will not allow us to be the laughingstock of the regional organization!"

Leigh tried to tune out the bickering as she quietly deconstructed and repacked the offending tree. She had no doubt who would win the argument. Anyone meeting Lucille for the first time might attribute her crustiness to dementia, assuming she'd lost her normal ability to self-edit. But Leigh knew better. Lucille might have declined physically since the last time Leigh saw her, but mentally she was as sharp — and ready to draw blood — as ever.

The Floribundas were still arguing when Leigh finished the task and silently excused herself to the kitchen. Lydie was sitting at the table with a tiny light bulb in her hand, meticulously switching it out for every other bulb on a long string of multicolored tree lights. Leigh dropped into the chair next to her. She spied another string of lights on the floor that were tangled into a ball and pulled it into her lap. "Mom's getting nervous."

Lydie nodded. "The house itself is in fine shape, and there won't be any problem with the refreshments. But they're definitely short on decorations."

Leigh glanced at her watch. "Has Mom been checking her blood pressure? Do you know?"

"I checked it," Lydie replied. "It's not bad. But it's early yet."

The sense of foreboding that had plagued her yesterday hit Leigh again with full force. "Aunt Lydie," she asked in a hushed tone, "what happened at your sixteenth birthday party?"

Lydie's wrists dropped down on the table with a thud. "Shhh!" she ordered, throwing a glance over her shoulder towards the doorway. "You didn't say anything about that to your mother, did you?"

Leigh was taken aback. She looked into the eyes of her ordinarily mild-mannered aunt and found them ablaze. "Um... no," she answered. "Why?"

"Don't you breathe a word of it!" Lydie insisted sharply. Then she softened her tone and leaned closer. "I know that Mason put his foot in his mouth yesterday, but you'll just have to forget he said anything. Believe me, now is *not* the time to bring up old ghosts. Later, after all this is over with, we'll talk. But for the rest of the day, mum's the word. All right?"

Leigh didn't have a chance to respond. Someone was tapping on the back door. She looked up to see another of the Floribundas, Anna Marie, balancing a limp-looking cardboard box over one hip. Leigh rose, opened the door, and removed the unwieldy box from the older woman's arms just as one corner of it collapsed. A mass of jumbled exterior Christmas lights spilled onto the ceramic floor, along with a shower of dust, loose bulbs, and shards of previously broken ones. Anna Marie, a stick-thin, wig-wearing blonde whose face was always plastered heavily with makeup, looked at the mess and laughed lightly. "Oh, fiddle! Hello, Leigh. Hello, Lydie. It's so nice to see you both again! Where is everyone?"

Leigh set down the collapsed box. "Hello. They're in the living room."

"Thanks, love!" Anna Marie replied. Then she sauntered out the doorway.

Leigh and Lydie looked from the mess on the floor to each other. Then Leigh grabbed her mother's broom. They both knew what would happen with Anna Marie. She would find the most comfortable chair in the house, repose in it as if she were Cleopatra, then not bestir herself the rest of the day. She had come to the back door instead of the front, no doubt, because the kitchen was fewer steps away from wherever she'd parked.

"Finally!" Lydie said with triumph as the string of lights in her hands burst into color. "One down, fourteen to go!"

Leigh stopped sweeping. "You've got to be kidding me. Don't any of these lights work?"

"Not yet," Lydie replied stoically.

Leigh looked down at the pile of exterior lights at her feet. They looked older, dustier, and even more hopeless than the smaller interior ones that Lydie was fussing with. "Do we have to use vintage lights?"

"Well, they're made differently today, you know," Lydie explained. "In the seventies, everyone used plain multi-colored lights, inside and outside. And the outside lights were simple strings with big bulbs, not like these fancy hanging icicle ones we have now."

Leigh watched with a wince as her aunt painstakingly began plugging a test bulb into every socket on the next string, having no guarantee it would light up even if all the bulbs were good. Leigh couldn't stand it. She was sure she could drive to a drug store right now and buy a nearly identical string for two dollars.

"Put those away, Aunt Lydie," she announced. "I'm buying new lights. Retro is in — I'll find ones that look close enough, and I'll be back before you know it."

Lydie's hands paused in mid air. Leigh expected an argument, but she didn't get it. Lydie's eyes darted into the living room. "Slip out the back then, and be quick about it," she whispered conspiratorially. "We'll need both exterior and interior strings. I'll clean up that mess and hide these in the attic."

Leigh smiled. She dashed out to grab her coat under cover of another loud squabble from the living room.

"You can't tell me Hummel figurines weren't popular in the seventies!"

"Well, of course they were, but not that one!"

"What's wrong with her?"

"That's 'Spring Cheer!' We're supposed to be decorating for Christmas, you moron!"

"Well, maybe she's 'Christmas Cheer!'"

"I used to have a dozen Hummels, but one night, Harry —"

"Those are spring flowers! We're not using it, I say!"

"But her dress is green!"

Leigh escaped again unnoticed, shaking her head. The Floribundas didn't get along with each other any better than they got along with anyone else, but for whatever reason, they didn't seem to *mind* each other, either. If you asked them tomorrow about today's decorating party, they would tell you they'd had a fabulous time.

She never had understood it. Perhaps they had their lighter moments when Leigh wasn't around. Perhaps even Lucille had a kinder, gentler side.

She shrugged on her coat. As she opened the back door she could hear the oldest Floribunda still ranting, as loud as her obviously impaired lungs could bluster.

"That Hummel will go on the mantel over my stinking, maggot-ridden corpse!"

Or maybe not.

Chapter 6

Leigh returned with two armfuls of Christmas lights just as her husband and kids arrived, bringing her nephew Mathias with them. Technically, Matt was her first cousin once removed, but she and her cousin Cara had grown up next door to each other and had always felt like sisters. Besides which, it was easier to have each other's children call them "aunt," an illusion which allowed the kids to share both grandmothers as well. "Awesome timing," Leigh proclaimed, stopping them in the street and then walking them around to the kitchen door. She held out the shopping bags containing the exterior lights. "Take all these out of the boxes first, then collect all the trash and stash it in your trunk. We want everyone to think these lights are vintage."

"Done," Warren said cheerfully. He took the bags from her arms and handed them off to the boys, who accepted them with simultaneous yawns. "How's the decorating coming so far?"

"Don't ask," Leigh replied.

Warren smiled. "Floribundas showing their thorns this morning?"

Leigh answered him with a grimace, then shot a questioning look at her daughter. The boys were headed for the back door, but Allison was moving toward the front. "Where are you going?" Leigh asked her.

Allison stopped and turned around. "To find Grandma."

"Aren't you supposed to help hang the lights?" Leigh questioned. With all the chaos of Ethan's party, she had neglected to find out what Frances had asked of Allison on the phone last night. But now that she thought about it, her petite daughter was the last person in the family Frances would send up a ladder.

"No," Allison answered. She started walking again.

Leigh looked at Warren, but he merely shrugged. "I'll go get your dad's ladders," he said, moving off.

Leigh caught up to her daughter at the bottom of the porch steps. She had the distinct feeling she was missing something a better mother would know about. "What *did* Grandma ask you to do?"

Allison's shrewd brown eyes studied her, even as the girl's slight figure squirmed a bit. She cast a glance toward the house and lowered her voice to a whisper. "I'm on surveillance."

Leigh blinked, disbelieving. "Surveillance of whom?"

Allison didn't answer for a moment. "Do you think the Flying Maples are anything like the Floribundas, Mom?"

"I have no idea," Leigh answered. "Why are you asking? What exactly is Grandma worried about?"

The creases in Allison's already serious little forehead deepened. She lowered her voice another notch. *"Sabotage."*

"Sabo—"

"Mom!" Allison shushed her with a gesture. "Grandma said she's just being cautious. She doesn't want to get any of the other Floribundas all worked up."

Leigh managed to stifle herself. *That,* at least, sounded like a great idea.

"But Grandma does worry that maybe these other women are upset enough to try and get revenge somehow. And it can't hurt for me to keep an eye out," Allison argued. "Crazier things have happened, you know."

Leigh knew. "Fine," she agreed. "But if you see anything, just tell somebody, okay? Don't try to do anything about it yourself."

"Oh, there you are!" Frances said, popping open the door. She smiled indulgently at Allison, then looked out beyond them expectantly. "Where are Warren and the boys?"

"They went around back," Leigh explained.

"And did you find the extension cords you needed?" Frances asked, eyeing the bags as they walked inside.

"I did," Leigh said honestly, happy that she had, incidentally, purchased an extension cord. She was also glad that her aunt had covered their tracks so smoothly, although Lydie's skill as a liar was disturbing in other contexts.

Leigh looked around her mother to see the same three Floribundas parked in the center of the living room. They were still sorting through decorations and still arguing, but the number of dilapidated boxes at their feet had multiplied.

"Delores and Jennie Ruth came by," Frances answered the unspoken question. "They dropped off all the decorations everyone

NEVER MESS WITH MISTLETOE 53

else could find. They couldn't stay, of course — they're on baking detail."

"Ah," Leigh acknowledged. Delores and Jennie Ruth were the odd couple of the Floribundas, the former being very small and the latter quite large. Delores, a multiple divorcee, owned a stately older home near the golf course in West View, and Jennie Ruth, who was widowed at a young age, had moved in decades ago to serve as her companion. Leigh had never heard that either of the women were particularly skilled at baking, but if their efforts lowered Frances's stress level by relieving her of the duty, Leigh was all for it.

"Lydie's upstairs in the sewing room finishing up the lights," Frances continued. "Why don't you start setting up our old artificial tree? I pulled out the photo album to help you remember how we used to decorate it. Now, I'd best go outside and —"

"Oh, no, Mom," Leigh interrupted, thinking quickly. The boys couldn't have all the evidence of her crime hidden away yet. "The women obviously need you in here!" She quickly handed her bags to Allison. "Could you take these upstairs to Grandma Lydie?"

Allison nodded and dashed off, and Leigh turned back to Frances. "Don't worry, I can put up the tree and supervise outside, too. I'll have them string the lights all around the porch roof just like Mr. Rudzinskas across the street always did. I remember exactly what it looked like."

Frances's brown eyes looked ever so slightly watery. "Thank you, dear," she replied. "That would be marvelous."

Leigh could barely hear her mother's last words over the shouting.

"The Muppets won't do!" Lucille declared.

"That show was on in the seventies, I'm telling you!" Virginia argued. "I think I know how old my own children are!"

"But the Muppets aren't Christmassy enough!'"

"Miss Piggy's dressed like Mrs. Claus!" Virginia screamed.

A knock sounded on the door, and Olympia swept into the room. She was wearing a long, dated-looking fur coat and she towered over the rest of the women by at least a head. She looked flushed and excited as she greeted everyone, but as her eyes took in more of the bare walls and empty surfaces around the house, her good cheer fizzled. "But... where is everything?" she asked with alarm.

"This is all that we can agree upon," Frances reported, pointing to the coffee table. "And a few things we can't. But there's no hope for the rest of it."

Olympia cast a critical eye over the pile of acceptable decorations. There were three glass tumblers that showed Santa Claus enjoying a Coca-Cola, a Little Golden Book of Rudolph the Red-Nosed Reindeer, the plush Miss Piggy doll, a calendar tea towel from 1975 (decorated with fruit), some glass perfume bottles shaped like stockings, a poorly done hook rug of a snowflake, a plastic snowman wearing a Steelers' jersey (number 75), a foot-tall angel made of burlap, and a "Great Songs of Christmas" album courtesy of Goodyear tires.

"Oh, dear," Olympia said dourly. "Oh, my."

"But what are we going to do?" Anna Marie cried from her chair. "The tour starts in *hours!*"

Frances was looking pale again, and Leigh resisted a strong urge to pull her own hair out. This ridiculous house tour was certain to be one of the most wonderfully exciting, gloriously memorable days of her mother's life.

If it didn't give her a stroke first.

"I told you we'd be laughingstocks!" Lucille said snidely, banging her walker again. "I told you all!"

"Mom! Grandma!" a high-pitched voice shrieked as footsteps pounded down the stairs two at a time. Allison skipped the last three steps altogether and sailed into the living room, then dashed across it to the door. "They came and left a— And now they're driving off!"

Leigh raced after her daughter onto the porch, but saw only the briefest glimpse of an SUV as it sped around the bend at the end of the block. "They who? Left what?" The second question was a dumb one. In stepping out to see the car, Leigh had practically tripped over a giant rectangular plastic bin set squarely in the center of her mother's porch. Attached to its lid with clear tape was a sheet of notebook paper, folded in half.

"I saw them through the window," Allison explained as she gave up the chase and returned. "They just double parked and carried it up... I never thought they'd ding-dong-ditch! I figured Grandma was expecting them!"

Warren and the boys came around the corner just as Frances and Olympia appeared on the porch.

"What's this?" Frances asked. She leaned over and pulled off the note.

"It was two women in a silver SUV, Grandma," Allison reported.

"How old were these women?" Olympia asked brusquely. "What did they look like?"

Allison looked at Leigh. "Around Grandma's age, I guess," she said uncertainly. "They were both medium height, medium build. One had blondish hair and the other gray. They were both wearing dark leather coats, and jeans with boots."

Virginia, who was now standing in the doorway, brought her hand to her heart and breathed in sharply. "Biker chicks!"

No one had any response to that.

"Read the note out loud, Frances," Olympia ordered.

Frances adjusted her glasses on her nose and complied.

To our fellow gardening enthusiasts,

We've collected a few things it appears we have no use for, and we thought you might like to borrow them. Please take good care of them and return them to this bin and we will send someone to pick them up early next week. Have a lovely day!

Cheers,
The Flying Maples

The last words hadn't left Frances's lips before Olympia began to pop off the top of the red plastic bin.

"Wait!" Virginia cried, slamming her hands down violently over the lid. "What if it's a bomb?"

"Then you would have just exploded it, you featherhead!" Lucille wheezed from the doorway. All of the Floribundas had now made it to the porch, although Lucille was breathing heavily from the effort and leaning on her assistant as well as her walker.

"It isn't a bomb," Olympia said impatiently, throwing off Virginia's hands and setting the lid aside. "It's —"

The women let out a collective gasp.

"It's exactly what we need!" Olympia finished in triumph. She reached in and lifted out a giant macramé wall hanging in the shape of a Christmas tree. "Oh, course! Macramé! Everyone had these!"

"Ooh! And look at the Santa!" Anna Marie cooed, picking up the flat plastic decoration beneath it. Leigh recognized the cartoonish figure immediately. The chubby, smiling Santa holding a Christmas tree was one of a set of three "melted popcorn" decorations that had once hung on the wall of every elementary school classroom in America, as well as in many family rooms. "They have all of them!" Anna Marie cried with delight, pulling out a prancing Rudolph with yellow antlers and a Christmas tree decorated with a candy cane and a star on top.

"Look at this garland with the little plastic pine cones!" Olympia exclaimed, digging deeper. "Oh, Frances, it's perfect to run up the stair rail! And here's molded wax candles, and a sleigh centerpiece, and plastic candle lights for outside, and a cardboard Advent calendar! Oh, this is precisely what we need! And so clean! It's all just perfect!"

"There's even a red and green lava lamp!" Anna Marie effused. "And look at all the macramé! I always hated that nonsense, but I love it today!"

Leigh looked around to see that Warren and the boys, as well as Allison, had disappeared. No doubt the boys had lost interest in the bin as soon as the bomb threat was dispelled, but Allison's whereabouts were more concerning. The child's natural curiosity was dangerous enough without her grandmother giving her delusions of employment as a private security officer.

"Don't you think this is all just a little too suspicious?" Virginia insisted.

"Don't be ridiculous," Olympia chastised. "They're just being thoughtful. They must have been collecting all these decorations for months! They clearly realized, even if we didn't, that it would be impossible for us to collect the equivalent overnight."

Leigh watched as her mother stood still with her lips pursed, staring thoughtfully down into the box. Frances had yet to say a word.

"It's exactly what we need!" Anna Marie insisted, blinking awkwardly as one of her false eyelashes came loose.

"But why would they want to help us?" Virginia asked. "We all know the Flying Maples only started up their chapter to shut ours down!"

"Have none of you illiterates ever heard of a Trojan Horse?" Lucille spat.

Leigh resisted the impulse to roll her eyes. An interesting shape in the bottom corner of the bin caught her eye, and she reached down and pulled out a giant bottle of cognac with a green and red plaid ribbon tied around its neck. The women fell silent again, gaping.

"Here's another note, Mom," Leigh announced, holding open the cardboard tag so that Frances could read it.

Frances's face creased with concern. "It just says, 'Celebrate!'"

"Poisoned!" Lucille barked.

Virginia's hands flew to her mouth, muffling her own scream. Then her eyes widened and she turned to Olympia. "You don't think—"

"No, I do not," Olympia said firmly, taking the bottle from Leigh's hands and replacing it in the bin.

"I don't either!" Anna Marie said petulantly, crossing her arms over the bulky layers of necklaces adorning her thin chest. The dangling eyelash had fallen off and now stuck to the front of her sweater. "And I'm not going to run all over this town looking for more decorations when we have everything we need right here!"

"Ha!" Lucille snorted. "You wouldn't *run* anywhere if the hounds of hell were chasing you!"

Anna Marie turned to Lucille and stuck out her tongue.

Leigh looked around for an escape route, but she was hemmed in.

"Ladies!" Olympia said loftily. "I really must insist."

"I say we put it to a vote!" Lucille rasped. "Who trusts those drunken upstarts?"

"Well, I don't!" Virginia cried, her eyes beginning to tear. "I'm sorry, but I just don't think they're up to any good, and I don't think we can take a chance on trusting them when we have so much riding on this!"

Olympia made a growling sound. "Fine! Let's put it to a vote then! You two say no, Anna Marie and Frances say yes, and as the president I break the tie, and I say yes, *so there.* We use the decorations!"

"Now hold on a minute," Virginia argued. "Frances didn't vote!"

All eyes turned toward Leigh's mother, who stood pensively, studying them all in turn. She might be keeping the rest of them in suspense, but Leigh never had any doubt what her answer would be. Frances was a born worrier, and when it came to contriving drama from nothing, she could conspire with the best of them. But she was also unfailingly practical. And making a success of this house tour truly was the stuff of her dreams.

Frances's back straightened. She cleared her throat and broke into her fiercest voice of authority. "We will use the decorations," she proclaimed. "All of them. This is *my* house, and I say so. Now, I want everybody to get back in the house, get over it, and get busy!"

Leigh smiled to herself as every one of the Floribundas, even the sour Lucille, dropped their arguments and followed directions. Frances, Virginia, and Olympia all carried the bin inside the house while Leigh held open the door for them.

"Hey, Mom," Ethan called as he rounded the house's corner again, this time with his arms full of lights. "Where are we supposed to put these?" Mathias and Warren followed him, each carrying a ladder.

Leigh shut the door behind the women and stepped down off the porch, then explained to the three of them how her neighbor across the street had always decorated his nearly identical house when she and Cara were growing up. The cheap plastic exterior lights she'd bought weren't quite as big and gaudy as the old glass-bulbed teardrop ones, but once they were strung up, she was hoping no one would notice. If they plugged in the big plastic Santa light she'd seen in the bin and put it up on the porch rail, the effect would be complete. Less than classy, maybe, but authentic.

"Did you see where Allison went?" Leigh asked when she had finished.

Warren gestured with his head as he climbed. "She's right there."

Leigh turned to find her daughter standing quietly at her side. She really hated it when Allison did that. "Where have you been?" she asked.

"I got the license plate number of the SUV," Allison replied. "Just in case."

Leigh stared at her. "Wasn't it already driving off before you could get downstairs?"

"Well, yeah. But I thought they might circle back around to watch. And they did. They stopped just up the street there." She turned and pointed. "They didn't notice me. Nobody ever does. So I wrote everything down in my notebook. What was in the bin?"

Warren and Leigh exchanged a look. Allison had insisted since she was a toddler that she wanted to be a veterinarian when she grew up, just like her grandpa. But her interest in less savory affairs had become increasingly disturbing. Crime-fighting, in Leigh's well-informed opinion, was neither a healthy nor a desirable preoccupation for an almost twelve-year-old. No matter what Leigh's long-time best friend Detective Maura Polanski thought.

Leigh refrained from saying what she was really thinking, however, and instead answered her daughter's question.

"Interesting," Allison replied. "Maybe the Flying Maples really are just trying to be nice."

"I'm sure they are," Leigh agreed, sounding more certain than she felt. Half the Floribundas were paranoid drama queens who created their own reality, true. But given the bizarre staging of this morning's gift, the Flying Maples appeared to be a bit more "spirited" than your average garden club, themselves.

Still, they had just saved the Floribundas' bacon. Leigh glanced down at her watch. The Holiday House Tour would officially open in a little over four hours.

"Who was yelling about poison?" Mathias asked as he climbed. The fourteen-year-old's eyes were slightly more open to the light now. Like most high schoolers, he did not believe that life began before noon on Saturdays. Leigh was surprised that her mother had managed to convince him to come, and she wondered exactly what bribe had been offered. Leigh's children and Cara's used to be together so much that the families referred to them collectively as The Pack, but those days were disappearing. Mathias and Ethan were still good pals despite the age difference, but Matt and Allison bickered constantly, and the high schooler wanted nothing to do with his own little sister.

"Nobody," Leigh answered shortly, finding herself irritated by a second mention of the word "poison" in a matter of minutes.

The blaxe you brew for your adversary...

STOP THAT.

Leigh gritted her teeth. Why, oh why, could she not seem to shake this unjustifiable sense of impending doom? Perhaps she would already have forgotten the silly fortune if Mason hadn't brought up whatever the heck had gone wrong at Frances's sweet sixteen. But Lydie's response to her question about the incident had hardly been reassuring. *Now is not the time to bring up old ghosts!*

The ghosts of whom?

"Sure they did," Ethan said innocently. "I heard it, too. One of them yelled, *'poisoned!'*"

The boy's imitation of Lucille's malevolent rasp was so dead on, even Leigh couldn't help laughing. "Well, they were imagining things," she said. "So forget about it." She started toward the front door. "If you guys think you have the outside under control, I'll head back in. I believe I have a date with a six-foot artificial tree and a bunch of forty-year-old ornaments that will probably disintegrate when I touch them. Allison, you want to help me?"

The girl's forehead creased with concentration. "No," she said finally. "I have some other things to do."

Leigh walked on into the house, trying hard not to worry what her daughter meant by that. She had barely cleared the threshold when Lydie grabbed her arm.

"Leigh, dear," her aunt said in a low voice. "We have a problem."

Chapter 7

"Of course we do," Leigh responded with a sigh. "To which problem are you referring?"

"I just answered a call from Sue Turner," Lydie explained. She spoke softly to avoid being overheard, but none of the nearby Floribundas were paying attention. They were having too much fun fussing over a macramé owl wearing a Santa Claus hat. "With all the commotion, I don't think Frances heard the phone ring."

Leigh shook her head. She hadn't heard the phone ring, either.

"Sue's sick," Lydie reported. "Lying in bed with a temperature of a hundred and three. Her daughter's come over to sit with her and thinks she has the flu. Sue's normally hardy as a mule, so she's not taking it well."

Leigh could imagine. She didn't know Sue as well as she knew most of the Floribundas, but she remembered a frightening woman built like a drill sergeant who was always complaining about how weak and out of shape everyone else was. When the other women complained about arthritis and plantar fasciitis, Sue would tell them it was all in their minds and advise them to lift free weights.

"Unfortunately, the Floribundas were counting on Sue to provide the beverages," Lydie explained. "Namely, her famous sweet-cider punch. And as reliable as she always is, no one dreamed of bothering with a backup plan. But Sue was planning on going shopping first thing this morning, and of course she never made it out of bed."

Leigh's brain searched for a Plan B. "You want me to go buy some premade punch or something?" she offered, selecting her words carefully.

Lydie looked thoughtful. "No, I'm afraid that won't do. You have no idea how much... *discussion* went into planning the refreshment menu at the emergency meeting yesterday."

Leigh glanced over at the Floribundas, who were now bickering over whether a midnight blue wax candle embedded in plastic greenery and dusted with fake snow was "Christmassy" enough. "I can imagine."

"Let's just say that every single baked good was carefully chosen to balance the flavors in Sue's special recipe," Lydie went on. "And those treats are being baked even as we speak. I spoke with Sue's daughter and I'm sure I can make the punch myself, but it will take a while. I'll have to head out right now to round up the ingredients, and I'll need to mix it up in the kitchen here in order to get it chilled in time."

Leigh relaxed a little. As long as she herself wasn't being asked to cook, bake, or otherwise produce anything consumable by the public, all problems were solvable. "You go then," she said. "I can handle everything here."

"Good," Lydie replied, although the worry lines in her forehead remained. "For now, I'll just tell Frances that Sue needs help with the punch. That shouldn't cause her too much concern."

"Aunt Lydie," Leigh pressed, "are you sure Mom's blood pressure is going to be able to take a day like this?"

"She'll be fine," Lydie answered. "Her new medication is definitely working. It's just that…"

Leigh had the distinct feeling that she was missing key information. "This has to do with that sixteenth birthday again, doesn't it?"

Lydie's eyes fixed on hers. "I hope I'm just being overprotective," she said after a moment. "Almost certainly I am. That was all a very long time ago. Just please, if you can…"

Leigh watched with bated breath as her aunt nervously nibbled on her lower lip. "Yes?" she urged.

"Just try to keep your mother out of the kitchen once the food starts coming in," Lydie ordered, lowering her voice. "But for heaven's sake, don't let her realize you're doing it!" She shrugged on her coat, grabbed her purse, interrupted the Floribundas' current argument to say a few words to Frances, then hurried out the door.

Leigh remained standing in place, staring after her aunt, until she heard her mother's shrieking "suggestion" rise above the din. "Leigh, dear, that tree isn't going to put itself up, you know!"

Leigh couldn't disagree. She decided to buckle down and get to work.

Three hours later, she was still working. After countless interruptions for squabbles among the Floribundas over which decorations should go where, blown circuits, shedding sequins, a "messy" lunch break, an overflowing toilet, the extensive cleanup operation necessitated by said overflowing toilet, a Floribunda resigning her membership, the chipping of a glass grape, one lost hearing aid part, and the reinstatement of a Floribunda membership, Leigh was finally hanging up the last of the family ornaments.

"Thirty minutes and counting!" Olympia shouted as what seemed like an army of people scurried everywhere throughout the Koslow home. In addition to the actual Floribundas, spouses and other family members had been coming and going in a steady stream.

Cara and her daughter Lenna had arrived mid-morning with their homemade star-shaped cookies, which they had iced into adorable miniature Christmas trees by stacking smaller cookies atop progressively larger ones. Cara had left again to get back to her freelance project; but Lenna, who had only just turned twelve herself, remained to help her grandmother Lydie with the serving. Allison had been flitting about everywhere helping various Floribundas hang, rehang, move, switch, dust, tie, untie, and fluff. Leigh still wasn't completely sure what role Frances expected Allison to play, but as long as she stayed busy inside Leigh figured the child couldn't get into too much trouble.

Warren and the boys had finished all the "high" work in record time and had left immediately afterwards, easily making them the MVPs of the male auxiliary. Lucille's son Bobby, whom his doting mother had always spoken of in terms somewhere between the pope and Jesus, had honored all present — in his mother's view — by dropping off a surprise load of fresh greenery and mistletoe from the garden store he managed. Unfortunately, he had carried the whole business into the house wearing his muddy work boots, and if Frances had been holding anything heavier than a feather duster at the time, he would have suffered a concussion. Virginia's lush of a husband Harry had been even less helpful. He had arrived just as Bobby was leaving, picked up an armload of the mistletoe, and proceeded to tack it up at various unexpected and awkward locations in order to "liven up the place." His next move was to wander into the kitchen and hassle Lydie about how much fun it would be if she "accidently" spiked the cider.

Olympia's husband Melvin was much more productive in his task of bringing lunch for the workers, but even his efforts fell short of Frances's approval. With the Koslow kitchen booked to capacity with refreshment setup, the plan was for the women to eat a quick meal on paper plates while standing around the dining room table. Poor Melvin had not been aware that, according to Frances, there was "absolutely no meal on God's green earth" that was messier to eat standing up than a catered taco buffet. But once the food arrived, she had little recourse besides waiting for everyone to finish and then vacuuming the entire carpet one more time. Which, of course, she would have done anyway.

The last two Floribundas, Delores and Jennie Ruth, arrived just before noon with mountains of cookies in tow. Both women were on the far side of eighty, but they had baked up a storm all morning and now were anxious to join in the last of the decorating. Anna Marie, on the other hand, had returned to a seated position after the Flying Maples delivery and had not budged since, other than to consume a taco. Her entire contribution to the decorating process consisted of lifting ornaments out of a box at her feet and handing them to Leigh to put on the tree.

Leigh reined in her drifting thoughts as a pair of plastic mice covered with a velvety fuzz began to dance in the air in front of her. "Oh, how precious!" Anna Marie gushed. Leigh smiled back as she took the mice and hung them in the topmost branches. She had always loved the boy and girl mouse. But like most of the velvety ornaments, the poor things were shedding fuzz as if they had the mange. Leigh's parents hadn't put up the big tree with all the old family ornaments in decades, preferring a smaller tree decorated with a more curated selection instead. There were a few staples, like the shiny metal tree topper and the bird's nest, that were still brought out every year, but the box she was unloading now was full of more childish and sentimental oldies that hadn't made the cut.

Anna Marie held up a Styrofoam ornament. It was round in the back and flat in the front, with an inset for a picture. The outside was covered with shiny sequins held in place by push pins. Leigh winced slightly as she recognized the photograph that was glued inside. It was her school picture from kindergarten, when her hair was in a pixie cut. Frances thought the style was cute and "so easy to take care of!" but Leigh was constantly asked by the other children if she was a boy or a girl. She shook her head. "Oh, no. That one can go back in the box."

"Oh, but you look so cute!" Anna Marie insisted. She whipped her head around as if seeking a second opinion.

"All right, fine," Leigh capitulated quickly, snatching the ornament. She hung it on the back side of the tree in the least conspicuous location possible, as she had been doing ever since she was six.

"Quiet now!" Olympia ordered from the staircase landing. "We need a group meeting. Everyone gather around, please!"

After several minutes of murmuring and shuffling, everyone managed to move where they could see the Floribundas' president. Leigh hoped that part of the master plan was to control the entry of traffic into the house, because the Koslow home was not large by any measure, and bottlenecks were a distinct possibility.

"Is everyone clear on their assignments post-opening?" Olympia began. "I hate to even bring it up, but we all know that, in this day and age, petty theft is a possibility against which we must be constantly vigilant!"

"World's going to hell in a handbasket!" Lucille squawked.

Leigh felt a strong desire to point out that petty theft was not strictly a new thing, but as the Floribundas all murmured their agreement with "amens" as reverent as a prayer service, she decided to keep her mouth shut.

"I'll run through the assignments again," Olympia continued. "Delores and Jennie Ruth will watch the upstairs bedrooms. Anna Marie, you stake out the sewing room. Virginia will stay at the top of the stairs and keep an eye on the bathroom and the hall. Lucille will sit in the dining room, Frances will watch the living room, Leigh will keep the music playing, and I will float. Lydie will keep the refreshment table stocked in the kitchen, and the regionals will be handling the ticket-punching on the front porch. Any questions?"

"Have you ever run a Fortune 500 company?" Virginia's husband Harry called out facetiously. He sounded slightly tipsy.

"Why yes, I have," Olympia replied with complete sincerity. "Three of them. Any other questions?"

Delores politely raised her hand. The tiniest of the Floribundas wore her snow-white hair in a perfect ballerina bun, always had glowing spots of warm peach in her dimpled cheeks, and was so petite she looked as if she bought her dresses in the children's section. There was an almost ethereal air of grandmotherliness about Delores, a saccharine veneer lifted straight from a Norman Rockwell painting. But appearances could be deceiving.

"Yes?" Olympia called.

"I demand the master bedroom," Delores said with a sweet smile.

"Oh, no, you don't!" Anna Marie shouted. "I want it! No one can expect me to sit on that hard stool up in that sewing room for six straight hours!"

"Well, what else would you do? Get *off* your lazy bum?" Lucille scoffed.

Leigh tuned out the rest of the "discussion" and went back to her box of ornaments. She smiled to herself as she hung up a skiing snowman made of peppermint candy, a Santa Claus holding a football, and two fuzzy red reindeer with gold chain collars and eyes of smeared black ink. Then she lifted out a series of ornaments that brought back not-so-pleasant memories. They were made from a kit, consisting of assorted shapes of hard Styrofoam onto which she and her mother had painstakingly pinned hundreds of different colors and styles of sequins into symmetrical patterns. They were pretty enough to look at, but while the years had not dimmed their gaudy beauty, they also hadn't dimmed the memory of the aching pain in her fingertips caused by all those blasted straight pins.

The Floribundas were still bickering when Leigh finished with the last of the ornaments. The argument ceased only when Harry noticed that someone was putting a sign up in the Koslows' front yard.

"The regionals are here!" Frances exclaimed with excitement as everyone rushed to the front windows. "Oh, look! Do you believe it? We're *official!*"

The women all sucked in a collective breath of awe. It might have been a moving moment if Lucille hadn't broken into a coughing fit. "I'll get more water," Bridget's small voice piped up as she hurried toward the kitchen. The other women watched the personal assistant go in silence, and Leigh wondered if they, like she, had entirely forgotten Bridget's presence. It was easy enough to do. Although Lucille had kept her employee at her side all morning, the pugnacious older woman so dominated any space that her meek assistant seemed to melt into the background as nondescriptly as the walker or the oxygen tank. Given Lucille's sparkling personality, Leigh doubted that Bridget's camouflage was accidental.

Bridget returned with a glass within seconds, and Lucille snatched it from her hands. "You wouldn't need to run if you'd kept my glass full in the first place!" she berated.

"Sorry, Ms. Busby," Bridget said in a low voice, fading into the background again.

"Oh, just look everyone!" Olympia said, sweeping her hands over the living room. "Take a moment and look at what we've accomplished, will you?"

Leigh glanced at her mother and smiled. Frances was beaming. Despite the chaos and the drama, their little house did look amazing. She couldn't say it looked exactly like it had when she was a child — there were far too many decorations for that. Frances had never strung garlands because they were "impossible to dust," extra lights "wasted too much electricity," and real greenery of any kind "dropped those nasty needles everywhere." But today the Koslow home sported all of the above and then some, and it looked magnificent — like a vintage seventies snapshot or a scene from an old Christmas movie. But one thing still seemed to be missing...

"Oh, no!" Leigh exclaimed. "I forgot the icicles!" She rushed back to the ornament box and began to dig.

"Good heavens!" Frances agreed. "We can't have that!"

"We're opening in five minutes!" Olympia announced.

"Found them!" Leigh said triumphantly. The cheap tinsel usually tangled into massive clumps when stored, which is why most people threw it out every year. And why, when it fell out of fashion, it also disappeared. But since Frances had always slavishly packed away each individual strand, the Koslow family supply was still intact.

"Everyone come by and take a handful," Frances ordered as she moved to the tree. "We can make it a group project!"

The mood turned festive as everyone — with the exception of Anna Marie — filed by Leigh and then draped their quota of shiny silver icicles over the branches of the artificial tree. Leigh loved icicles. When she was a child, she used to pull them off the tree and tie them around the wise men to make electric fences for the sheep in her nativity set. She would hold a strand in her hand, walk across the carpet in her fuzzy slippers, and then charge the fence with a zap of static electricity.

When everyone had finished hanging their tinsel, Frances did what she always did. She said "let me just fix this one little clump..." and then proceeded to rearrange every strand. But by that time, everyone else was too busy to notice. Final cleanup was underway, and then it was off to the battle stations. Leigh took her place by the turntable and cued up the top album on her stack of vintage vinyl records, courtesy of the Flying Maples.

"It looks beautiful, Mom," Leigh praised when Frances finally stepped back to admire her artwork. "The whole house looks absolutely perfect. You should be proud."

Frances smiled back, her dark eyes sparkling as strains of *Osmond Family Christmas* carried through the air.

"I see our first guests!" Olympia called excitedly from the front window.

"Here we go!" Frances said gleefully, bouncing in her practical low-heeled shoes. "I do hope nothing goes terribly wrong."

She threw out her chest and strode purposefully toward the door.

Leigh's jaws clenched. She did not, and never had, considered herself a superstitious person.

But she really wished her mother wouldn't say that.

Chapter 8

"Seven o'clock," Olympia whispered to the workers gathered in the kitchen. There were no guests within earshot at the moment, although Leigh could hear several people walking up the stairs. "The first house is shutting down now, so we've less than an hour to go. And so far everything has gone *perfectly!*" Olympia gave a little clap and smiled her gummy smile.

Leigh wondered if it were possible to tempt fate with a claim that was patently untrue. She decided to be optimistic and say no. Not that the previous five hours had been a disaster; the Koslows' 1970s-styled 1930s house was being quite pleasantly received. The guests seemed delighted with its "everyman" authenticity and true Pittsburgh feel, and comments to the regionals were uniformly positive. But "absolutely perfect" was pushing it. One woman had tripped down the stairs and sprained an ankle, a little girl had thrown up her lunch on the porch, and Leigh had been called to plunge the powder room toilet twice. Not to mention that Virginia's husband Harry seemed to think he had been billed as entertainment. He wandered around like a game show host giving nonsensical speeches, scoping out attractive women, and making a nuisance of himself under the mistletoe. He had even tacked up a sprig of it in a corner above a trash can, only to get himself slapped by an unsuspecting millennial he attempted to ambush underneath it.

All in all, though, things were going about as well as Leigh could have expected.

"Hey, honey," Olympia's husband Melvin said upon his sudden reappearance in the kitchen. Unlike Harry, Melvin had removed himself from the premises right after serving lunch. "Are you all getting hungry yet?"

"Oh, no!" Olympia cried. "You're early! Dinner shouldn't arrive until the guests have stopped coming!" Her exasperation was obvious, but she attempted to smooth it over by turning to the women with a lighthearted smile. "Men! They do try, the poor dears."

Dr. Pepper, as he was unfortunately named, was an unassuming, shrimpy-looking soul, but his calm, unflappable demeanor did suggest he would have an excellent bedside manner. He didn't act in the least insulted. "Dinner will be delivered at the appropriate time," he replied in a deep voice, his tone soothing. "I just wondered if you'd like something to tide you over."

"No, thank you," Olympia answered tightly. "I'm fine."

Melvin, who had to look up at his wife by at least half a foot, nevertheless stepped up close to her, squared his shoulders and stared her down. "I'd like to make sure of that," he said quietly.

Olympia glared back at him furiously for a moment, but then she blew out a frustrated breath, retreated to a corner of the kitchen, and rolled up a sleeve. "Just get it over with and get out of here, would you?" she snapped, whispering a little too loudly.

Melvin withdrew a blood pressure cuff and stethoscope from his jacket pocket, wrapped the cuff around his wife's upper arm, and proceeded to take a reading.

Oh, dear, Leigh thought with foreboding. *Not her and Mom, too!*

Everyone else politely averted their eyes.

"How is the cider punch holding up?" Leigh asked. The liquid level in the glass bowl seemed to be getting low.

"It'll be fine. I've got more in the fridge," Lydie answered, turning around to fetch it.

"You want some, Aunt Leigh?" Lenna offered, picking up the ladle.

Leigh shook her head. She liked cider, but it was rough on her stomach, and she didn't need any additional stress in that organ. "It's getting rave reviews, I must say. And the cookies, too!" She looked over the now-dwindling array of 3D Christmas trees, gingerbread men, cookie-press treats decorated with colorful crystals and shiny metallic sugar balls, and strawberry-shaped date cookies with green-frosted leaves.

She couldn't eat any of them, dammit. Not until the tour was over and all the guests had been served. She had sworn on her life, as had they all. If she was starving, there was always that ancient, squished-flat granola bar in her purse.

Sigh.

"What's Allie doing?" Lenna asked, sounding slightly miffed.

"She says she can't help in here because she has another job, but she won't tell me what it is!"

"She's on a secret security detail," Leigh answered in a whisper. "Your Grandma Frances doesn't trust Mrs. Busby to keep a sharp enough eye on all the little stuff in the dining room, so she's got Allison stationed in there for backup."

"Oh," Lenna muttered, seeming appeased. No doubt Allison's job sounded even more boring than her own.

"Oh, for heaven's sake!" Olympia voice carried angrily from the corner. "I'm perfectly fine! I used to compete in triathlons! I was a world class cyclist!" She threw her arms over her head, and without another word to the women she left the room, nearly colliding with Bridget in the process.

"Oh, I'm sorry," the personal assistant apologized. Olympia merely humphed and kept going, and Bridget slunk up to the table like a dog afraid of a beating. "I... um..." she said to Lenna in a small voice. "I wondered if I could have a small cup of punch?"

"Sure," Lenna answered with enthusiasm, ladling out a large portion.

Melvin approached the table also. "I'd like a cup of that too, please," he said grimly.

Leigh watched with surprise, but no small amount of amusement, as Bridget covertly swept several cookies off the table and into a napkin in her palm. "Oh, thank you," she said, taking the cup Lenna offered. Then she turned and left, tasting a sip on her way. Lenna handed another brimming cup to Melvin and he also thanked her and left the room.

"Oh, shoot!" Lydie exclaimed. One of the pitchers of cider had slipped from her hands and splashed drops of liquid across the shining orange countertop and floor. "Is anyone coming?"

"Not yet," Leigh assured as she grabbed a mushroom dishtowel from a drawer and helped to sop up the spots.

"I'll do that," Lydie insisted, handing Leigh the pitcher of fresh punch instead. "Here, you go ahead and pour this."

Leigh took the pitcher and moved to the table. The first stream of liquid had just trickled into the existing punch when a strange sight caught her eye. She lifted the pitcher again and set it down. "Aunt Lydie?"

"Yes?"

"What fruit is in here besides cranberries?"

"You mean juices?"

Leigh stared at the translucent white berry that bobbed up and down on the still-rippling surface of the amber-colored punch. The berry was round, with a yellowish spot on one end and tiny white veins running along its sides. She'd never seen a fruit quite like it before. "No, I mean fruit. What is this thing?"

Lydie's head appeared over her shoulder. "Oh, good Lord!" Lydie cried, plunging her fingers straight into the bowl and extracting the fruit. She stared upward, and her face colored purple. She said something very uncomplimentary about someone. "I can't believe he did that!" she fumed. "Right smack over the serving table!"

Leigh's eyes followed her aunt's. Tacked up on the ceiling with a piece of scotch tape, directly over the punch bowl, was a cluster of fresh mistletoe.

Lenna giggled.

"What was he *thinking?*" Lydie fumed. She climbed on a chair to pull the offending plant down, then carried the punch bowl to the sink. "Is the man insane?"

"Harry strikes again," Leigh said with resignation.

"That odious man has been in here pestering us all day!" Lydie exclaimed as she tilted the punch bowl and poured the rest of the liquid down the sink. "Holding that mistletoe over Cara's head and mine both, begging us for kisses... that SOB's got the busiest hands north of Pittsburgh. I never have been able to stand him!"

"But when could he have put mistletoe up there?" Lenna asked. "I didn't see him!"

Lydie sighed as she began to wash out the bowl. "I didn't either, but we've had plenty of distractions, and he's tall enough to stick a sprig up there with one hand. Probably he did it the last time he was in here a few minutes ago, and he's planning to come back in and catch some unsuspecting woman in the next group while she's leaning in to take a cup."

"But," Leigh interjected, feeling slightly queasy as she watched her aunt vigorously scrub the sides of the bowl. "Isn't mistletoe... poisonous?"

Lydie looked at her oddly. "Well, I suppose it is, if you eat it. But no one's going to do that!"

"Then why are you scouring that bowl?"

"Because I don't like anything falling off the ceiling into my beverages!" she replied. She finished scrubbing, gave the bowl a good rinse, and set it back on the table. "Now, let's refill it."

Leigh's uneasy feeling was not so easily assuaged. "But… we already served people from the bowl when it had the berry in it," she pointed out.

"No, I didn't!" Lenna defended. "The berry only just fell in, Aunt Leigh. Otherwise I would have noticed it."

Lydie threw Leigh a meaningful look. "Of course she would have. Now pour the punch. Everything's fine."

Translation: *You sound like your mother.*

Leigh searched for her inner rational side. Everything they were saying made perfect sense. She was only borrowing trouble. "You're right, I'm sure," she agreed, although her voice sounded unconvincing, even to her own ears. Loud squeaking noises indicated that the group of guests she'd heard earlier was coming back down from the bedrooms, and she excused herself. The usual flow of traffic was for people to enter through the front door, see the living and dining rooms, make a loop upstairs, then finish off with a treat in the kitchen and exit out the back. Leigh slipped through the kitchen doorway just ahead of the people entering. Then she walked to the turntable, switched out Johnny Mathis for Nat King Cole, and wandered into the dining room.

All afternoon, Lucille had been parked in an armchair in the corner, and Bridget had been hovering nearby. Leigh stepped to where she could see Lucille's lap, and was not at all surprised to see a crumpled napkin resting there. Allison was leaning against the side of the china cabinet, half hidden by a large dieffenbachia. "So," Leigh whispered as more new guests filed in the front door. "How long till Lucille broke the oath?"

Allison giggled. "She made Bridget sneak them to her. And she won't let her have a single bite!"

Leigh shook her head. While the rest of the Floribundas had at least some charm to counterbalance their psychoses, Lucille's positive attributes were more elusive.

"We're on pace for a record crowd!" Olympia reported, popping in. "Oh, but it's been marvelous, hasn't it?"

Leigh looked over as Lucille began to cough again. Bridget

tapped absently on her back, but Lucille pointed to a glass of water that sat on the floor beside her chair. "Oh, of course," Bridget replied, flustered. She reached down, but misjudged the location of the glass and accidentally knocked it over onto the carpet. "Oh, dear! Don't worry. I'll get you another one!"

Lucille continued to hack as Bridget fled from the room, and Olympia quickly stepped over and extended her own cup of punch. "Here, dear," she said.

Lucille reached for the cup and took a sip. Her coughing began to ease.

"Did something spill?" Frances demanded, her voice rising in pitch as she rushed up. "It wasn't punch was it? It will stain the carpet!"

Leigh thought she heard a tapping noise at the front door.

"Here's more water," Bridget cried, practically knocking over everyone else to get back to her employer. "You're not choking to death, are you?"

Lucille stared daggers at her assistant, making no move to take the glass. She made no move to give Olympia the rest of her punch back, either. "No thanks to you," she said acidly. "I swear you'll be the death of me yet, girl. Just put that down!"

Bridget set the glass down on the floor next to the spilled one and slunk back to her position by the wall.

"Was it punch that spilled?" Frances repeated, unable to see for herself.

"No, just water. I'm sorry. I'll go get a towel," Bridget apologized, sounding near tears as she took off again.

Leigh looked toward the front of the house. She couldn't figure out who would be tapping at the door. It was a mild day for December, and two of the regionals had been stationed at a card table on the porch all afternoon, greeting the public and punching tickets. Once the guests were verified, they were invited to walk straight inside, no knocking necessary.

Leigh stepped out around her mother, went to the door, and opened it. One of the regionals was standing just outside, smiling with one of the most obviously faked smiles Leigh had ever seen. Next to her stood a fully uniformed West View Borough police officer.

He wasn't smiling at all.

Chapter 9

"Can I... help you?" Leigh found herself saying uncertainly. She was at a loss. For all the feelings of impending doom she'd suffered this weekend, this particular development seemed out of order. The police were supposed to show up *after* a disaster. Had she missed something?

"Are you the owner of the house, ma'am?" the officer asked.

"No," Leigh replied. "My parents are the owners. My mother is just inside. Why?"

"Could you ask her to come out here, please?" he asked.

Leigh would really prefer not to do that. But she had no excuse for refusing. She exchanged a glance with the two thoroughly panicked, broadly smiling regionals, then pushed the door closed again and whirled around. Her mother and Olympia were standing right behind her. Their newest guests had moved into the dining room and were exclaiming over the glass grapes just a few feet away. "Mom," she whispered. "A policeman wants to talk to you. I think it might be better if you went outside."

Frances's eyes bugged. She went stock still. Olympia reached out and clutched Frances's arm with her long, bony fingers, clenching tight. "What's all this about?"

The unexpected assault seemed to jolt Frances out of her stupor. She looked down at the claws that had latched onto her, then brushed Olympia off as if she were a fly. "I have no idea," Frances replied loftily. "But I certainly intend to find out. How dare they send an officer here, interrupting our event and frightening away the guests! The very idea!"

Frances pushed past Leigh and swung open the door. She introduced herself to the officer out on the porch and he asked to speak to her in relative privacy. They walked down the steps and around to the side of the house, and Leigh and Olympia followed.

"Please do tell me what this is about, Officer Wright," Frances demanded as soon as the four of them were out of earshot of any wandering guests.

The policeman, who appeared no more than twenty-five or so, seemed somewhat embarrassed. "I'm sorry to distress you, ma'am. I'm sure this is all nothing to worry about. But we've had a 911 call in regards to this location, and we have to check these things out as a matter of policy, you understand. You're hosting some sort of party here?"

Olympia could not control herself. Seemingly in disbelief that anyone could be unaware of the importance of the Holiday House Tour, she informed the young gentleman of the nature of the event in her usual superior tone, including several whoppers detailing the involvement of local celebrities and sports heroes.

The young officer did not seem impressed. He turned back to Frances. "If this is a commercial venture, I'm afraid I'm going to have to ask you to shut it down, at least temporarily."

"*Shut it down?*" Frances and Olympia both screeched.

"A 911 call about what?" Leigh asked.

The officer shuffled his feet. "Well, now. I'm sure it's all just a hoax, ladies. The dispatcher seemed to think the voice was muffled on purpose and when the chief heard it he said the same thing — that it was almost certainly some kids or maybe an upset neighbor trying to make trouble. But we have to check these things out, just the same."

"Check out what?" Frances demanded.

"An anonymous caller gave emergency services this address," the officer answered finally. "They said we'd better clear this house out quick, because inside it was 'snowing anthrax.'"

No one said anything for a moment. They all seemed to be digesting the absurdity.

Finally, Leigh released a pent-up breath. "Anthrax!" she repeated, practically cheerful with relief. He could have said *so* many worse things. So many more plausible things! "Well, of course it's a hoax! Good grief, where would anybody get anthrax? Who even talks about it anymore? That's crazy!"

"I got you, ma'am, believe me," the officer agreed. "And the way it was stated, it wasn't framed as a threat — it came off more like a concerned citizen report, if you know what I mean. But still, I do have to ask the homeowner a few questions."

"Of course! I understand." Leigh turned to her mother. But the homeowner had gone deadly pale. "Mom?" she asked anxiously.

"Mom? Are you okay?"

Frances made no response.

"Anthrax..." Olympia murmured in a low, wispy tone. Her normally florid complexion had gone as pale as Frances's.

Holy crap. What was wrong with the two of them?

"But this is nothing!" Leigh insisted. "It's nonsense! Just some jerk pulling a prank! *'Snowing* anthrax?' Give me a break! There's nothing whatsoever to worry about!"

The women turned even paler.

Olympia snaked out a hand and clutched Frances's arm in another pincer grip. "Without treatment, the inhalation form of anthrax is 90% fatal," she muttered tonelessly.

"What?" Leigh cried, baffled. "No! This isn't—"

"I knew I shouldn't do it," Frances mumbled, her voice sounding equally lifeless. She appeared not to notice that the Floribunda president was cutting off the circulation in her arm, much less pay any attention to what Olympia was saying. "I knew it was too much to ask. But I wanted this so badly..."

"Mom!" Leigh said loudly, peeling off Olympia's claw. "Mom, what are you talking about? Everything is fine. The tour has been fabulous!"

Frances's eyes focused on Leigh, but the look in them was sheer mania. "That's the way it always seems at the beginning. But then everything goes wrong, and people get sick, and it's *all my fault!*" Her last words turned into a choking cry as she turned from Leigh and raced toward the front of the house.

"Ma'am!" the officer called, sounding baffled. "Ma'am? I just need to ask you a few—"

"Come on!" Olympia cried, grabbing at Leigh's arm now. "We've got to stop them!"

"Stop who? From what?" Leigh demanded as she pushed Olympia's hands away and dashed after her mother. "Mom, will you stop? Calm down!"

Frances slammed her hands down on the card table on the porch. "We're closing early," she told the regionals. "It's for public safety, but don't tell them that. Tell them... tell them the house is on fire!"

"Mom!" Leigh protested, but hurricane Frances was gone already. She blew past the confused regionals through the front door and headed straight for the kitchen as Leigh followed.

"Get rid of the food!" Frances yelled to Lydie. She hoisted up the punch bowl and swung it toward the sink. "Throw it away! All of it!"

"Frances!" Lydie exclaimed. "Whatever has gotten into—"

"*Just do it!*" Frances ordered, dumping the entire contents of the punchbowl down the drain.

"Mom," Leigh tried again, lowering her voice. "Remember your blood pressure. You've got to calm down."

Frances set the empty bowl on the counter and whirled to face her. "I will not calm down when people are being poisoned under my roof!"

"Who's being poisoned?" Lydie demanded.

"Nobody!" Leigh answered.

"You don't know that!" Frances screeched.

"Frances," Lydie said calmly, "why on earth would anybody try to poison anybody?"

"Ask him!" Frances wailed, pointing to the police officer, who stood blinking in the kitchen doorway, looking as confused as everyone else. "I don't know, but I can't let it happen all over again. I just can't. I never should have taken the chance!"

"It was the Flying Maples!" Virginia screamed as she appeared behind the policeman. "I told you they were out for revenge! And they put something in the punch? Oh, Lord have mercy! I knew I didn't feel well! We're all going to die!"

"*Nobody is going to die!*" Leigh said firmly. "*There was nothing in the punch!*"

"Keep your trap shut, Virginia!" her husband Harry chastised. "There's people upstairs, still!"

"Who died?" Anna Marie yelled at full volume from the top of the steps.

"Oh, for Pete's sake!" Leigh heard Harry say as he peeled off from the group and pounded up the steps. "I'll take care of it!"

Leigh's attention remained focused on her mother. Frances was in full freak-out mode, and Olympia was freaking out right along with her.

"Was it in the punch or in the cookies?" Olympia demanded, looking at the police officer.

The poor man appeared completely overwhelmed.

Virginia pushed her way forward. "Maybe it was neither! Maybe there was poison on the decorations! I told you it was a trick! Those Flying Maples want us dead! All of us!"

"Who are the Flying Maples?" the policeman demanded, rediscovering his voice at last.

"Their imaginary enemy," Leigh assured him, still trying to keep her voice calm, even as she contemplated stuffing a whole Christmas tree cookie into Virginia's gaping mouth. Frances looked terrible. She was pale as a ghost and breathing heavily. Even by "Frances standards" of nutty behavior, this panic rated as an overreaction. And what was Olympia's excuse?

Leigh looked over to see Melvin making his way to his wife's side. "Olympia, dear," he said softly. "You cannot afford to upset yourself like this. Come out to the living room and —"

"Oh, do hush up!" Olympia snapped. "Did you not hear what the man said? He said we'd all been poisoned with anthrax, Melvin. ANTHRAX!"

"No, I did *not* say that!" the officer insisted, whipping his hat off in frustration. A sheen of sweat had broken out across the frontier of his prematurely receding hairline, and his complexion was flushed. "All I said was that we had a citizen report of a possible danger here. In the department's judgment, it was almost certainly a prank call, but regardless, our job is to —"

"You see!" Olympia crowed.

They all heard Harry's voice echoing loudly down the stairs, followed by multiple footsteps. "Terribly sorry about this... medical emergency... family member... hopefully nothing serious..."

The crowd seemed to collectively hold their breath as Virginia's husband led the remaining guests down the stairs, through the living room, and back out the front door. "Yes, right out this way... Merry Christmas, to you, too... You enjoy the rest of the tour, now!" A door slammed shut, and everyone breathed out again.

Thank goodness none of them had to see this, Leigh thought to herself, proud to have one positive thought in the midst of utter inanity. Frances had moved from the counter and was scrambling around the kitchen trying to dump the rest of the food into the trash can while Lydie tried to rescue it. Olympia was shoving off her husband while he attempted to put a cuff on her arm, and Virginia was essentially spinning around with her hands in the air. All of which proved very distracting for the unfortunate police officer, whose goal of getting Frances's attention long enough to answer his questions still eluded him.

"If it was in the box of decorations, we could get the inhalation *or* the cutaneous form!" Olympia moaned to no one in particular. "The skin type isn't as deadly, but those horrible black spots... Oh, dear!"

"Who died?" Anna Marie demanded again, pushing into the kitchen.

"It's anthrax!" Virginia shouted.

Delores and Jennie Ruth, who were now listening from outside the doorway, screamed in horror.

Leigh had had enough. "STOP THIS!" she yelled louder. "There is no anthrax! No one has died! And no one has been poisoned. This is all a FALSE ALARM!"

The house went quiet for a moment. Virginia stopped spinning and took a step closer to Leigh. "How do *you* know that?" she accused.

"Because there isn't one shred of evidence to show that anything has actually gone wrong here!" Leigh pointed out. "The only thing that's happened is people misunderstanding what they've heard and jumping to conclusions!"

"Thank you!" the officer agreed, replacing his hat with authority. Leigh felt another wave of sympathy for the man. No doubt the police academy had prepared him well for stealthy burglars and brawling streetfighters, but a gaggle of hysterical Floribundas likely fell outside the basic curriculum.

"I need everyone to *stay calm,*" he said forcefully. Then he turned to Frances. "Ms. Koslow, do you have any reason to believe that anyone in particular has any reason to threaten you or your household with bodily harm of any kind?"

Frances straightened a bit. She was still holding an empty cookie tray over the trashcan. She looked back at the officer, then at everyone who was clustered around staring at her. A tinge of red returned to her cheeks, and Leigh began to relax a little. All of a sudden Frances looked more embarrassed than frightened. When at last she answered, her voice was slow and thoughtful. "No, I suppose not. Not... bodily harm." Then her eyes flashed fire. "But an attempt to disrupt this happy event? Absolutely!"

"Hear, hear!" Virginia agreed.

"Oh, no," Delores's small voice purred. Leigh was surprised to see the diminutive woman standing right next to Virginia, considering that she must have elbowed her way through half a dozen people to get there. "I'm sure the Flying Maples would never do anything like that. I believe they are all really good and wonderful people inside, no matter how horrible and vicious they may act." She smiled and batted her long gray eyelashes with innocence.

When Leigh was a child, she used to think that Delores was sweet. As an adult, she found her pretty damned scary.

The policeman turned to Leigh. "Will someone please tell me who the Flying Maples are?"

Leigh opened her mouth to answer, but Virginia beat her to it. "They're the garden club chapter that were supposed to have *their* house on the tour tonight. But they had black mold, so we got their spot. And now they can't *stand* that everyone who's anyone in Pittsburgh has seen this house and knows that the Floribundas are the original and legitimate garden club chapter of the West View area!"

A smattering of applause broke out as Frances, Olympia, Anna Marie, Delores, and Jennie Ruth all signaled their approval of Virginia's statement. Lydie and Harry merely stared at them.

The officer stared at them too. Then he turned to Leigh. "Are they serious?"

Leigh nodded. "I'm afraid so."

The officer sighed and pulled a notebook from his breast pocket.

The gesture gave Leigh a sudden twinge of panic. Where was Allison? The child was never far away when disturbing things happened. Leigh looked in the most likely place — right behind her elbow — but her daughter wasn't there.

Seeing that Lydie had managed to get Frances to sit down at the table with the officer, Leigh pushed her way out of the crowded kitchen. She was relieved to catch sight of Allison in the living room, standing with her cousin Lenna by the Christmas tree.

"Thank goodness," Leigh gushed, rushing up to them both. "Are you two okay?"

Allison frowned. "Why wouldn't we be, Mom? You just said it was a false alarm."

Leigh was spared the indignity of answering by her hypochondriac of a niece.

"I've had a stomach ache all afternoon!" Lenna whined, tears just starting to pool in her pretty baby-blue eyes. "What exactly is anthrax?"

"Something cows get in Africa!" Allison said with exasperation. "I already told you, you just drank too much punch!"

"But she's sick, too!" Lenna argued, pointing.

Leigh looked up to see Jennie Ruth shuffling across the living room, holding her stomach. At gatherings of the Floribundas, Jennie Ruth was the easiest to overlook, because she almost never said anything. Yet she was invariably present, very much like a bump on a log. In fact, Jennie Ruth was like a log in a lot of ways. She was wide, heavy, dull, and seemingly devoid of content. The only actions Leigh could ever remember Jennie Ruth taking at past Floribunda meetings in the Koslow home were to belch, complain that the food was gone, and insist on planting more tulips.

Jennie Ruth reached the couch, sat down with a plop, and curled up on her side.

Oh, no.

"Jennie Ruth!" Leigh cried, hurrying up to her. "Are you feeling all right?"

The least objectionable of the Floribundas opened her eyes and looked up with a dazed, slightly annoyed expression. Then she belched.

"We'll be leaving now," called an irritated voice from the front door. Leigh whirled to see the regional representatives, binders and boxes in hand. "Your mother and your president appear to be 'otherwise engaged' at the moment, but all the checked-in guests have now cleared this stop, so your portion of the tour is over. You may tell them that we're not at all pleased at whatever has caused this undignified chaos and we shall discuss it in much more detail at a later time. At the moment, however, we're cold." Both women tugged their coats more snugly around them. "It's been a long day and we're going home. Good night."

"Good night," Leigh said pleasantly.

There really was nothing else to say.

Lucille's personal assistant Bridget popped out of the dining room and scurried up to Leigh. "What's happening?" she asked, looking down at Jennie Ruth. "Is she sick?"

Leigh honestly didn't know how to answer that question. Was

hypochondria a sickness? She looked over Bridget's shoulder into the dining room and saw that Lucille's chin was planted in her chest. Now that Leigh thought about it, one cranky voice had been missing from the mayhem. "Is Lucille all right?" she asked.

"Oh, she's fine," Bridget replied, waving a hand dismissively. "She nodded off a while ago. And a good thing, too! With all this excitement..." She stepped closer to Leigh and lowered her voice to a whisper. "Because she's not *really* fine, you know. Miss Lucille's much worse off than she wants anyone to know. Even if she does talk about dying all the time."

Leigh lifted a questioning eyebrow at the unrequested flow of information, but Bridget's lips flapped on. "She's got congestive heart failure. She was a smoker from way back. And her kidneys are shot, too. Did you know she has a DNR? That means 'do not resuscitate.' Says she's ready to go and she doesn't want any fancy-pants doctors young enough to be her grandkids keeping her alive just to boost their own egos. But she's bad. Really bad. She drops off to sleep like that all the time now. Sometimes at night she'll get where she can't hardly breathe. Her lungs are like wet cotton. Why, just last week—"

Leigh was spared further medical details by another knock at the door. Out the window she could see a pizza delivery man holding a stack five pies high. "Excuse me," she said, moving towards the door. But before she could open it Olympia rushed into the room, her shorter, rounder husband hot on her heels.

"Stop!" the president called out to Leigh, palm raised. "We cannot bring any more food into this house until we know exactly what is going on!"

"Olympia, precious," Melvin begged. "Would you let me handle this? You need to sit down a minute. Have you been keeping yourself hydrated?"

Olympia turned on her husband as if he were a biting fly, all pretense of marital harmony forgotten. "Oh, go drink prune juice, you nagging little fool!"

Under other circumstances, Leigh would have been amused to hear that particular line flung at a proctologist. But she was not in a laughing mood.

"The food will stay on the porch!" Olympia continued to rant. "Until the police are certain this was a false alarm."

Melvin did not give up. "All right, all right, dear," he said soothingly, pulling out his wallet. "I'll pay for the food and just set it down outside. I promise. Now you go back into the kitchen and sit down, all right?"

"Leigh," Olympia ordered, ignoring her husband. "Does your mother have a computer? I need to look up first aid for biological warfare! Quickly!"

"All of the electronics are hidden away," Leigh answered. Behind Olympia in the dining room, she could see that Lucille had begun to slump in a rather uncomfortable-looking manner. She glanced around for Bridget.

Melvin had gone out to pay the pizza guy. Lenna and Jennie Ruth were still holding their abdomens and moaning. "I'll go get Grandma's pink stomach pills," Allison announced as she headed up the stairs. Everyone else appeared to be either in the kitchen or standing just outside of it, where a general argument had erupted over whether the Flying Maples did or did not have access to deadly bacteria. Bridget was nowhere in sight.

"Oh, no!" Olympia cried. "Why did you do that?"

Leigh fought an urge to shove the unhelpful chapter president out of her way. Up to now, aside from the pesky pathological lying thing, Olympia had seemed more emotionally stable than your average Floribunda. Why was she going bonkers over a silly phone prank?

"Because there were no personal computers in the seventies, of course!" Leigh reminded as she hurried around Olympia and into the dining room. If Lucille fell over any further she was almost certainly going to slip out of her chair.

The toilet flushed in the half bath, explaining where Bridget had gone. Leigh reached Lucille, put a hand on her shoulder, and gently attempted to shake the older woman awake. If she was as ill as her assistant claimed, surely she'd "worked" long enough today and should be taken home. "No!" a returning Bridget called out from the doorway. "Don't wake her up!"

Leigh froze. All the chaos in her mind was organizing and swirling down into one ominous black tornado. She looked back at Bridget, whose expression could only be described as peeved.

"She's such a witch when she's awake!" the assistant whispered as she rushed forward. "Just leave her be! She'll sleep for another half hour if you let her!"

"Bridget," Leigh said breathlessly, trying to guide the other woman's gaze downward with a subtle flick of her eyes. Surely, dense as the assistant was, she could see the ashen pallor of her employer's face, the unnatural angle at which the woman's head now bobbed on her neck? The complete and utter stillness of the usually laboring chest?

"She's gone," Leigh whispered.

Chapter 10

Bridget stared down at Lucille for a full three seconds. Then her eyes rolled back in her head, her knees buckled beneath her, and she went down like a collapsing toy. "Help!" Leigh called to Olympia in a loud whisper. The last thing she wanted to do was to call everyone else's attention to the dining room. The unexpected sight of Lucille had nearly given her a heart attack; giving the same jolt to a houseful of Floribundas risked mass casualties.

Leigh made a grab for Bridget. She managed only to snag the end of the assistant's shirt, but it was enough to keep the unconscious woman's head from slamming against either the china cabinet or the floor. Leigh dropped down and patted the woman's cheek. "Bridget! Are you okay?"

Where the hell was Olympia? The dining room was only partially separated from the living room; most of the space in between was an open doorway, and Olympia had been standing in the middle of that space not two seconds ago.

Bridget began to stir. The front door opened and closed.

"Olympia!" Leigh heard Melvin cry.

Leigh looked over to discover why Olympia hadn't responded. The Floribunda president had also passed out flat.

Bridget struggled up, and Leigh helped her into a chair. Melvin roused Olympia and got her to a sitting position on the floor. Out in the living room, Jennie Ruth and Lenna still lay on the couch, evidently oblivious. There was so much noise coming from the kitchen that both Leigh and Melvin's cries of distress had apparently gone unnoticed.

"Dr. Pepper!" Leigh said none too patiently. "Could you come here, please?" She didn't care if Olympia's husband were a proctologist or a podiatrist. If he worked anywhere in the human medical field he was more qualified to handle this situation than she was. At least in the eyes of the law. Her real-world experience, she chose not to think about.

"Dr. Pepper!" Leigh called again, more firmly this time. Not until

Olympia started shooing her husband away did the balding doctor finally look up in Leigh's direction. But when he saw Lucille, his pale eyes widened instantly.

"Good Lord," he murmured, scrambling to his feet. As soon as he reached Lucille, Leigh stepped over to grab her mother's trifold screen. She stretched the seventies vintage wood and brass-mesh contraption across the doorway, blocking off sight of Lucille's chair from anyone in the living room. Olympia, who was sitting on the floor just outside the dining room doorway looking woozy, barely noticed as Leigh erected the barrier right in front of her. Leigh then collapsed into a dining room chair herself.

If she were a normal person, she might expect the doctor to start CPR, or at least to call an ambulance. But Leigh Koslow Harmon was not a normal person. Leigh Koslow Harmon was an individual cosmically cursed to attract the no-longer-living like flies to honey. And there wasn't a doubt in her layperson's mind that Lucille Busby was no longer living.

Melvin finished his examination, then turned troubled eyes toward Leigh. He shook his head. "How long since…" he asked.

Leigh shrugged helplessly. She couldn't remember how long it had been since she'd seen Lucille awake, but she had felt no pulse beneath the papery skin of the woman's neck, and the frail body was already cool to the touch.

"Ohhh…" Bridget moaned from her chair. She sniffed, then started to blubber. "This cannot be happening again. Not to me!"

Again?

Leigh filed the disturbing comment away in her brain. She already had too much to think about.

Melvin took hold of the blanket that was laid across Lucille's lap and pulled it up and over her head. "There's nothing I can do," he said to Bridget. "I'm sorry." His voice was calm and wholly professional, but to Leigh's eyes, he looked quite shaken. "She's been gone for some time now, I'm afraid."

Bridget blubbered louder.

Melvin turned to Leigh again. "Ordinarily I would call emergency services, but under the circumstances… I suppose we should summon the officer in the kitchen?"

"I suppose we should," Leigh said limply, having no desire to get up again. Her legs felt like jelly. Yes, Lucille was terminally ill and chronically unhappy and by Bridget's account, at least, was ready to go. But for the woman to take her last breaths in the Koslows' dining room, peacefully or otherwise, in the middle of the Holiday House Tour was bad.

It was very, very bad.

Frances was not going to take this well.

Leigh forced herself up and slipped around the screen. Olympia was still sitting on the floor with a dazed expression on her face. Leigh skirted around her, too. She had to elbow several people out of the way to get into the kitchen, since eavesdropping on the policeman's interview with her mother had clearly become prime entertainment.

"It's the garland with the fake snow on it, I'm telling you!" Virginia insisted stubbornly. "How do any of you know that isn't powdered anthrax right out there on the railing? Hmm?"

"Excuse me," Leigh said quietly, near to the officer's ear. "Could I talk to you privately for a moment? It's important."

It was a strange request, and Leigh expected to meet some resistance. But the officer practically shot up out of his chair. "Of, course," he said briskly. "Thank you very much, Ms. Koslow and uh… ladies. I'll be in touch."

Before anyone else could question the interruption, Leigh led him quickly out of the kitchen and into the dining room. She hoped no one would follow them immediately. But she knew it was only a matter of time. "Mrs. Busby passed away at some point, sleeping in her chair," Leigh said in a whisper as the policeman moved around the screen. He caught sight of the covered figure and stopped short.

"I'm a medical doctor," Melvin introduced, his voice equally hushed. "And I can assure you that Ms. Busby is indeed deceased. From what her personal aide tells me of her medical history, sudden death is probably not unexpected. But under the circumstances…" He looked awkwardly from the still-sobbing Bridget to Leigh and then back to the policeman. "I thought you should be the first to know."

The officer stepped forward, pulled down the blanket a moment, then put it in place again. "I'll call backup," he said, sounding very much like a man in physical pain. Leigh felt for him. He was a small-force, suburban rookie cop who thought he'd been dealing with a simple prank call. By the end of this evening with the

Floribundas, he'd be wishing he'd drawn vice duty.

"I'm afraid I'm going to have to ask everyone to stay put for the moment," he said as he placed his call.

"We understand," Leigh answered.

"Leigh?" Frances's voice rang out suddenly. "What's going on in there?"

Leigh hustled to block her mother from coming around the screen and found herself suddenly face to face with every other person in the house. Even Lenna and Jennie Ruth had gotten off the couch to join the semicircular throng of people who now stood staring at her.

"Yeah," Harry pitched in. "What's going on, cutie pie?"

Leigh bristled, but let the indignity pass, since Harry had been covertly chugging the Flying Maples' gift of cognac all afternoon. It should be the policeman, not her, who was making this unpleasant announcement — or at the very least, the doctor. But the officer was talking on his phone, the doctor made no move to appear, and if she didn't say something in the next three seconds her mother was going to plow right past her. However poorly Leigh explained the situation, her words had to be better for Frances's blood pressure than *that*.

"I'm afraid that Lucille has passed away during a nap," she said simply. "I'm sorry, everyone."

The faces that looked back at her were dumbstruck. No one said anything. Seconds ticked by. Leigh watched in dismay as all remaining color drained from her mother's face.

"She died of natural causes. Of course," Leigh added, breaking the awkward silence.

She shouldn't have to say that. It should be assumed. They all knew that Lucille was dying. So why did every single Floribunda look so... nervous?

The blaxe you brew for your adversary often burns you more than him.

STOP!

More tense silence.

Finally, a red-faced Virginia stepped toward Leigh, her eyes narrowed to a menacing look. "And how do *you* know that?"

Leigh's face turned equally red as she stared down the older woman with annoyance. True, Leigh had no idea what had happened to Lucille. But she *was* certain that her mother had no reason to feel guilty about it, which was exactly what would happen if Virginia or anyone else so much as suggested that—

"It's a cover-up!" Virginia shrieked. "Lucille was poisoned! I knew it!"

"It's *anthrax!*" Olympia screamed.

Melvin came flying around the screen. "No, no, dear," he said, fussing over his wife like a mother hen. "It wasn't anything of the sort! You must calm down! Please, remember your—"

"Oh, hang my blood pressure!" Olympia snapped. "What does it matter if we're all going to die?"

Anna Marie pushed her way to the front of the crowd. "Oh, hush up, Olympia!" she said fiercely, planting both hands on her bony hips. "I've got a great-grandchild on the way and it's supposed to be a girl and after two sons and three grandsons I'll be damned if I'm going anywhere until I get to buy little pink baby dresses!" She stamped her foot furiously. "And as much of a shame as it is for Lucille to go like this, we all know she's been hailing that sweet chariot with both thumbs and a whistle for months now. What I want to know is what finally pushed her over the edge, because I'm telling you right now, I for one *refuse* to go with her!"

"Nobody's going anywhere, because no one has been poisoned!" Leigh tried to say again, painfully aware that she had no credibility with any of the Floribundas, in whose eyes she still wore pigtails, jumped rope, and overwatered violets. But she had to give it a shot. "We all know that Lucille was terminally ill. The only thing that's gotten everyone upset is that silly prank call, but we have no reason to think the two things are related!"

Delores stepped out in front of her. "My dear Leigh," the tiny figure said melodiously. "I'm sure you're right. You and your mother wouldn't have any reason to try and hide any foul play that occurred here. Oh, no! Your homeowner's insurance is up to date, I'm sure. Isn't it? And besides, even if Lucille was poisoned in your house, we all know that it wasn't intentional. It would have been entirely a matter of negligence, and my word, that could happen to anyone who wasn't taking appropriate precautions in their kitchen."

Frances moaned.

Stifling an urge to strangle the passive-aggressive Delores's skinny little neck, Leigh deliberately ignored her instead. "I repeat," she stated. "We have no reason to believe that anyone was poisoned."

"But Aunt Leigh," Lenna whined. "My stomach aches! And you know that mistletoe berry fell in the punch!"

Oh, crap.

The room erupted in gasps and cries of horror. "Mistletoe?"

"Mistletoe berries in the punch!"

"Good Lord, they're deadly!"

"I had the punch!"

"So did I!"

Frances swayed slightly on her feet, and Leigh swooped in to steady her.

"Now just a minute!" Lydie said forcefully, coming forward from the back of the pack. "Lenna March, you said yourself that you didn't serve a single person after that berry fell in the bowl. This man here," — she threw a venomous look at Harry — "tacked some mistletoe up on the ceiling of the kitchen not an hour ago, and yes, a berry did drop off, but of course we saw it right away. We dumped that punch and scoured the bowl and refilled it with fresh punch and that was the end of it. And I'll have no more nonsense about that!"

Lydie's firm, rational voice and easy logic calmed the crowd for all of about ten seconds.

"But Jennie Ruth's stomach hurts, too!" Virginia insisted. "And Olympia passed out!"

All eyes moved to Olympia, who was still sitting on the floor.

"That's four people down!" Virginia continued. "Who knows how long it will be before the poison starts to take effect on the rest of us!"

"The room is spinning a bit," Harry admitted, staggering to a chair.

"Oh, that's just because you're drunk as a skunk!" Virginia chastised her husband, undercutting her own argument. "You think we didn't see you guzzling on the sly all evening, you fool?"

"But, wait..." Olympia muttered, rising to her feet at last. "I don't understand. Anthrax doesn't strike nearly so quickly. Why, even if you inhale the spores, you don't get sick for days!"

Leigh had no idea if Olympia knew what she was talking about, but it sounded promising. "Of course not!" she echoed. "Anthrax is impossible. So can we all please forget that and calm down?"

"I've been so foolish," Olympia continued, her voice sounding stronger. "Why, even the Ebola virus has a two-day incubation period!"

"*Ebola!*" Virginia cried.

Leigh gave up. The Floribundas were on their own. She was worried about her mother, but at the moment, Lydie seemed to have Frances in hand and was leading her away from the crowd. Leigh took the chance to make a beeline for the girls.

Lenna was sitting on the couch again, holding her stomach and looking miserable. Throughout the communal freakout that had just taken place, Allison had been sitting on the arm of the couch, scribbling furiously in her pocket notebook. "Are you girls okay?" Leigh asked, worried about both of them, but for entirely different reasons.

"My stomach really does hurt," Lenna said tearfully. "But Allie says I just drank too much punch. And I did drink a lot. And apple cider does always give me a stomach ache."

"Well, I'm sure that's all it is, then," Leigh said comfortingly. "Did you take a pink tablet?"

Lenna nodded. "I'm sure I'll be better soon," she said bravely.

Allison was still scribbling. "Allie?" Leigh repeated. "Are you okay?"

"I'm fine, Mom," the girl answered. "I just want to write everything down before I forget it. In case it's important later."

Leigh's heart thudded in her chest. This was exactly the kind of nonsense she'd been afraid of. A normal preteen girl would find the events of the day both saddening and scary. She would not focus on documenting them for investigative purposes. Leigh and the esteemed Detective Maura Polanski were going to have words later.

"Why would it be important?" Leigh asked. "Honey, Lucille was in very poor health. I don't know if she got overexcited by all the craziness going on or if the timing was just coincidence, but I'm sure she died of natural causes."

"Probably, Mom," Allison answered tonelessly. "But it won't hurt for me to write things down."

"EMS and additional officers will be arriving any minute," Leigh heard the policeman announce. "If everyone would make yourselves comfortable, please. It's important that nobody leaves the house just yet. Thanks for your cooperation."

His words were met with a cacophony of moans, groans, and wails. "We'll be trapped here together for *days!*" Virginia lamented.

Leigh could not express how much she hoped not.

She looked around her. There were way too many people in the Koslow house, especially considering that no one wanted to be anywhere near the dining room. Lydie had quietly spirited Frances off up the stairs. Jennie Ruth and Anna Marie remained seated in the living room, while a smiling Delores informed her dearest friend Jennie Ruth of how well equipped emergency rooms were these days. A still-shaky Olympia had moved to the wingback chair by the window. Bridget had left the dining room also and was now pacing back and forth, rubbing her face in her hands and muttering. Virginia was running around holding a cloth over her nose and mouth. Harry idled by the turntable, where he made the brilliant decision to cue up the Mormon Tabernacle Choir's *Joy to the World.*

Leigh steeled herself for a very long night.

Chapter 11

Lucille's body had only just been removed from the house when her son Bobby, the garden store manager, blew through the front door and stomped into the middle of the living room. Bobby was around fifty, had an enormous potbelly, talked in a very loud voice, smelled like cigarette smoke, and was still wearing the same muddy boots he'd gotten in trouble for wearing into the house that morning.

He looked around the room, red-faced and wild-eyed, until his gaze landed on Bridget. The fretful personal assistant was standing by the Christmas tree at the time, and when she saw him she made a pathetic mewling noise and tried to slip behind the branches.

"You did this!" he shouted at her, pointing a finger. "What happened? What did you do to my mother? She was perfectly fine this morning!"

The longtime Floribundas who were in the living room looked at Bobby with the same "dear me, what a bother" look they had been giving him since he was a ten-year-old making flatulent sounds with his armpit. Those who didn't know him gaped with open astonishment. Leigh, who considered herself to fall somewhere in the middle, wasn't surprised that Lucille's not-so-bright troublemaker of a son was upset and yelling. But his fixation on the trembling personal assistant was bizarre.

For a moment everyone in the room remained perfectly still except Allison, who pulled out her notebook and started scribbling again. Then the three police officers who had been conducting interviews in the dining room, kitchen, and master bedroom reappeared.

Bobby did not seem surprised to see them. "I want her arrested!" he demanded, still pointing at Bridget, who slunk even further behind the tree. She had already toppled a wise man; now she knocked off two Styrofoam ornaments and snagged icicles in her hair. "For negligence! I don't know what she did wrong, but I'm damned well going to find out! You stupid, incompetent—"

Bobby's tirade was interrupted by the local police chief, who stepped forward with a raised palm and quietly suggested that Bobby follow him into the kitchen to discuss the situation. Bobby, surprisingly, obliged without complaint. The two men left the room, and a moment later Melvin was dismissed from the kitchen and came to join the rest of the restless in the living room. The officers interviewing Frances and Lydie in the dining room and upstairs went back to their tasks, and hushed chatter broke out once again among the Floribundas.

Leigh's peripheral vision caught sight of her daughter moving stealthily around the outskirts of each gossiping group. It was obvious to her that the girl was eavesdropping, but Leigh realized that Allison was right — no one paid much attention to a small, dark-haired child with glasses. Nor did anyone seem to notice that the deceased woman's beleaguered personal assistant was still quivering behind the Christmas tree.

"Bridget," Leigh assured, "I really think you can come out from there. Nobody's going to hurt you in a house full of police officers."

Bridget didn't move. "Why is Bobby being so mean?" she sniffled. "He knows how sick his mama was. Why would he blame me?"

Leigh wasn't sure how to respond. It seemed crass, so soon after the death of his mother, to give her honest opinion on either the character or the intellect of Bobby Busby. But not doing so made it impossible to answer that question.

"You're perfectly safe, here," Leigh repeated. "Come on out, please."

Slowly, in a series of jerky, uncertain motions, Bridget made her way back around to the front of the tree. Three more ornaments fell, but this time Leigh was able to move the sheep and the other two wise men to safety. Shiny icicles stuck to Bridget's frizzy hair and trailed behind her head like cobwebs.

Leigh pulled them off and returned them to the tree. "Don't take it personally. Bobby's upset."

"I know, but—" Bridget looked genuinely confused. "But he seemed to like me well enough when he hired me. And I haven't made any horrible mistakes. Really! I haven't!"

"I believe you," Leigh said, looking into the woman's miserable pale eyes and meaning it. If Bridget *had* done something to hasten

Lucille's inevitable demise, Leigh didn't think she was aware of it. Her level of defensiveness, however, was interesting. "Why would anyone think you'd made a mistake?"

Bridget shot a suspicious look at Leigh, and her body tensed. "No reason," she said sharply. "I'm going to go sit down somewhere." She moved out of range of any further questioning, then leaned awkwardly against the arm of a chair, pretending to be part of another conversation.

Leigh got the message. She had not forgotten the comment Bridget had muttered upon realizing that Lucille was deceased: "this cannot be happening *again.*" Did Bridget even realize she had said it?

Leigh couldn't help but wonder how Bobby and Lucille had come to select her. Perhaps they had a difficult time finding someone willing to take Lucille's steady stream of verbal abuse. Or maybe they were penny-pinchers who hadn't tried that hard to find someone competent in the first place. Either way, Leigh suspected the personal assistant's past record of achievement in the field was less than stellar.

She looked over to see that Allison was now alone with Virginia near the bottom of the stairs. Virginia was carrying on an animated monologue, and Allison was taking notes.

No, no, no…

"So, what are you two up to?" Leigh interjected shamelessly.

Virginia ignored her. " — the healthiest of all of us, wouldn't you know it. Anna Marie's so lazy she sends Eugene out for the mail and he can't hardly breathe with the emphysema, but she's fit as a fiddle. And their house! Good Lord 'a mercy their house is like a pigsty. She hires a woman to do for her, you know, always has, never mind that they can barely afford it. Now I do remember she had some thyroid troubles a few years back, but — "

"Virginia," Leigh interrupted again, "have you been interviewed yet?" She knew the answer already. Only Lydie, Frances, Bridget, and Melvin had been interviewed so far. Why the police were delaying Leigh's own torture when she had technically been first on the scene, she didn't know. But she was anxious to get it over with. When it came to being grilled by cops over her involvement with the nonliving, practice did not make perfect. It only pushed a person one notch closer to needing psych meds.

"No, I haven't," Virginia answered, sounding miffed. "And they had better reserve a good amount of time for me, because I have quite a bit I'd like to tell them!"

"Oh?" Allison encouraged in her most innocent voice.

Leigh shot her daughter a look of disapproval.

The cause was lost. Virginia was entirely too delighted to have an attentive audience. "Well, don't get me wrong, you know I think the Flying Maples are behind all this. But that doesn't mean there isn't something fishy about Little Bobby storming in here and popping his cork like that. I always did say it was just a tad bit suspicious how grand that family lived after Big Bob passed. Lucille got the insurance, you know. Family didn't have two dimes before that — Big Bob spent it all on his booze and his motorcycles. He had diabetes and heart disease both, but when he passed don't you know it wound up being an 'accident.'"

Virginia leaned in closer and lowered her voice. "That's what pays the most, you see. The 'Accidental Death and Dismemberment.' Can't get squat in regular life insurance for a man with a bad heart, but you can buy the accidental kind, because they figure if you can't breathe, you can't get in too much trouble. But they didn't know Big Bob, I guess, because he was always banging himself up on that bike, and sure enough he spun out on a wet road and bought the farm and made his wife a millionaire!"

Leigh caught both herself and Allison casting an involuntary glance toward the dining room. Lucille? A millionaire?

"Oh, you wouldn't know it to look at them now," Virginia continued, seeming to understand the unspoken question. "By the time Lucille settled Big Bob's debts and bought that nice house of hers, there wasn't a whole lot left for fripperies. Little Bobby flunked out of college and she spent another bundle setting him up in a business that failed. But she got some money. Oh, believe you me, she did."

Leigh believed her. She couldn't remember ever thinking of Lucille as rich, but she'd never thought of her as poor, either. In Leigh's memory Lucille had simply been a cranky widow friend of Frances's who was best avoided. And when Leigh was a kid and "Little Bobby" had appeared at Floribunda events, he was best avoided too.

"Lucille had one of those policies on herself," Virginia said, lowering her voice further. "She told me she did. Said if she was going to croak anyway, she might as well line her kid's pockets while she was doing it. I told her it wouldn't work — you know those policies don't pay out if you do yourself in. They'll pay if someone else whacks you, since it's still a 'non-natural' death, but they sure as hell won't pay your beneficiary if he's the one who did it! I told Lucille that, but she just sniffed and told me not to worry. So, I bet you two shakes of a lamb's tail that Little Bobby's going to try and cash in somehow. No matter how Lucille really died, he's going to try and make it *look* like an accident. An accident he had nothing to do with!"

Leigh breathed in sharply. For all her paranoid ravings, Virginia raised a valid point. Why else would Bobby storm in the house and essentially accuse Bridget of criminal neglect?

Leigh felt her cheeks flame with annoyance. She knew she should give Bobby's outrageous behavior a pass, given the circumstances, but still... what kind of opportunistic weasel starts planning his pay-out strategy within an hour of his mother's death? And at an innocent woman's expense?

"How long is this going to take?" Harry asked, breaking into their conversation.

His wife scowled up at him. "Let the police do their jobs, Harry. What's the matter, don't you have a bottle in the car?"

He shook his head, and Leigh noticed that the ordinarily suave Casanova seemed nervous. Beads of sweat had broken out on his forehead, his face was flushed, and he fidgeted with his hands. "No," he said with a sulk. "And the cognac's all gone."

Virginia drew back in horror. "The cognac! You weren't... You mean that bottle you've been carrying around was the *Flying Maples'* cognac?"

Harry dropped his head and nodded, guilty as a little boy.

"*Oh, my God!*" Virginia screamed.

All three police officers popped out of their rooms again.

"Help! You've got to help him!" Virginia continued to scream. "He's been poisoned!"

"No, I haven't!" Harry insisted, still looking distinctly guilty. "I'm fine! Really, I am!" He turned to his wife and put his hands on her arms. "Calm down, honey. Look at me! I'm fine!"

The officers exchanged looks among themselves, which Leigh

interpreted as variations on "Can we go back to traffic duty, please?" Finally, the upstairs policeman who had been speaking with Lydie started down the stairs and motioned for Lydie to follow him.

Virginia was fussing over Harry, feeling of his forehead. "Are you feverish? Do you have a headache? How's your urine stream?"

"Oh, good Lord, Virginia, will you hush?" Harry said peevishly.

The three officers formed a huddle and began talking quietly among themselves. Leigh stepped to Lydie's side. "How did it go?"

"I didn't have much to say, I suppose," Lydie answered with a shrug. "But I'm worried about your mother. Is she still in the dining room?"

Leigh nodded soberly. They couldn't see Frances; the officers had left the screen in place for the interview process. "How was she doing before?"

Lydie blew out a breath. "Her pressure was okay. But she's very upset. She can't stop thinking that she's done something wrong. That she's responsible for Lucille's death in some way."

"But—" Leigh protested.

"Don't tell me," Lydie interrupted, holding up a hand. "It's nonsense, of course, but you know how stubborn your mother can be. She has this ridiculous idea that somehow she deserves all this misfortune by tempting fate."

Another sick feeling rose in Leigh's middle. She did not want to think about, much less hear spoken out loud, those last two words. "Why is that?"

Lydie started to speak, then shook her head. "I told you," she whispered, too low for the still nearby — and obviously listening — Allison to overhear. "It has to do with... the incident. But I can't get into that now. We just need to keep reinforcing that none of this has anything to do with her."

"Will do," Leigh promised.

The police officers broke their huddle, then turned to face the crowd in a grim-looking line. The chief cleared his throat. "I'm afraid that we're going to have to ask for everyone's cooperation here. Now, most likely, nothing's wrong and Mrs. Busby died of natural causes. But we've got enough, uh... suggestion of... irregularities, say, that we think it's best to have a medical team come in and check everyone out before any of you leave the premises."

A smattering of groans was punctuated by several ear-piercing screams.

"You mean we're all going to die?" Virginia screeched.

The chief threw her a long-suffering look. "No," he said firmly. "Of course not. All we want is for EMS to take a look at anyone who's having symptoms of stomach upset, or who has passed out, or who feels funny in any way. You've all been through a traumatic emotional experience, and that can cause a lot of symptoms on its own. We just want to make sure that's all we've got going on here. All right?"

Delores stepped out of the crowd toward the officers and offered a beatific smile. "Will a stomach pump be necessary, do you think, Lieutenant?" she asked sweetly.

Somewhere in the back of the room, Jennie Ruth moaned.

"Um..." the chief said uncertainly. "We'll leave that to EMS. They should be here soon. In the meantime, please just relax, and we'll try to keep these interviews moving."

The chief returned to Bobby in the kitchen, and the officer who was interviewing Frances slipped back around the screen and into the dining room.

Leigh's heart began to pound. She didn't know what to make of the chief's announcement. She supposed that Lucille's death happening so soon after the bizarre prank call might make the authorities choose to err on the safe side. But she had to wonder if there was something else going on. Was it something that Bobby had said? Surely they wouldn't take seriously all of Virginia's ravings about the Flying Maples!

"Excuse me, Ms. Leigh Harmon?" asked the officer who had just interviewed Lydie.

"Yes?" Leigh answered.

"You're the person who first noticed that Mrs. Busby was deceased?"

She nodded.

"Could you come upstairs and answer a few questions for me, please?"

She started up the steps with legs that felt like lead.

Chapter 12

Leigh made her way through the play-by-play fairly well, she thought. She laid out for the officer everything she could remember happening between the last time she'd seen Lucille alive and the moment she'd found her deceased in the dining room. Leigh's short-term memory, which had taken a hit during the twins' early days and which she was convinced had been deteriorating at double speed ever since her fortieth birthday, served her surprisingly well, and she was able to answer all of the officer's questions. The not so aimless chit-chat that followed was slightly trickier.

"Are you feeling all right yourself, Ms. Harmon?" the policeman asked. Officer #2 was an unassuming man in his mid thirties, and Leigh was quick to notice the contrast between this "regular" local officer and the county detectives who worked with her friend Maura. This guy not only acted friendly, he appeared to actually *be* friendly, which was to say he did not automatically assume that everyone he met was capable of murder.

He also didn't seem to recognize her name. That was always nice.

"I'm feeling fine," Leigh answered.

"Did you have any of the punch or the food in the kitchen?" he asked.

"I had a little of the punch. But I didn't eat anything."

"When was the last time you drank any of the punch?"

Leigh didn't like that question. She felt defensive of her mother and her Aunt Lydie both, but she tried to keep the pique out of her voice. "Earlier this afternoon. I'd say it's been at least four hours now. Why?"

The policeman smiled and shrugged. "We're supposed to ask everybody that. Now, did you see anything else today that seemed suspicious to you in any way? Anything else you want to tell us about?"

Leigh couldn't help but smile. What an adorable rookie he was.

No self-respecting detective would ever assume those two questions had the same answer. "No," she said simply, answering the second one.

Not that she meant to be unhelpful, of course. But her duty as a mother came first. Allison had already been drawn into this unfortunate spectacle way more than was healthy, and so had Lenna. What purpose would be served by Leigh's bringing up any of her own half-baked thoughts and observations? No purpose at all, except further delay.

"Well, thank you, then," the officer said politely, writing something in his notebook. "That'll be all. Could you send up Harry Delvecchio, please?"

"I'd be delighted to," Leigh agreed. Then she took herself gratefully out of the bedroom and down the stairs.

She was greeted by a sea of anxious faces. "They'd like to talk to you next, Harry," she explained, trying to keep her voice light.

Evidently, she failed. Harry's face went pale and he sank down on the back of the sofa. "Oh, Lord," he moaned. "They *know!*"

"Know what?" Virginia hissed, coming close and making a shushing gesture. Not everyone in the room was paying attention, but they could have heard him if they chose to.

Harry looked up at his wife with sad, bloodshot eyes. He looked like a hound dog that had gotten caught raiding the garbage can. "I didn't mean anything by it," he mumbled. "It was just a bit of fun."

"What did you do?" Virginia demanded in a harsh whisper. "Tell me!"

Harry's hang-dog head hung down farther. Leigh could barely hear his mumbled answer. "I kind of... well... juiced up the punch a little."

Virginia put a hand to her mouth to stifle her own shriek. "You what? Oh, you old fool! When? And with what?"

Harry lifted his head and gave her a look.

"The cognac?" Virginia mouthed, her eyes wide with horror. This time, she stuck her entire fist in her mouth. She looked around the room to see who was paying attention and seemed relieved that only Leigh, Lydie, Allison, and Lenna were close enough to hear. Everyone else was clustered around the front of the room, where Olympia was telling some ridiculous story about a role she'd played as an extra in a Bollywood flick.

"It was just a little dribble," Harry defended miserably. Gone was the cocky flirt of earlier in the afternoon. The man Leigh saw before her now was regretful, scared witless, and could have passed for about ten years old. "And it was late. We were about to shut down anyway."

Leigh became suddenly aware that her aunt, standing on her left, was giving off a significant amount of radiant heat.

"Harry Delvecchio," Lydie growled, "you tell me, and you tell me *right now,* exactly what you put in my punch bowl and when!"

Leigh fought a strong urge to shrink in her shoes. Her mild-mannered aunt didn't use her mama-bear voice very often, but when she did, someone was in serious, *serious* trouble. In her peripheral vision, Leigh could just see Allison and Lenna slink quietly out of range.

Harry looked like he was about to cry.

"Answer me!" Lydie demanded.

"It was just a couple gurgles!" Harry moaned. "There was enough punch left in the bowl that it couldn't possibly have given anyone so much as a buzz, I swear! I thought you'd taste it and it would be funny, that's all!"

Virginia swore and gave her already subdued husband a swat on the head. "What were you thinking? You know people have medical conditions! Some people can't handle *any* alcohol!"

"Oh, now, that's nonsense," Harry protested, bucking up a little. "A little spirits never hurt anybody. Besides, it's Christmas!"

Lydie quickly deflated him again. "When, Harry? When exactly did you cause this organization to start illegally serving alcohol to the general public?"

"Um..." he mumbled miserably, "Sometime around seven, maybe? I swear, Lydie, I don't remember. You were fussing with something in the cabinet and your pretty little granddaughter wasn't looking. I tipped the bottle and tacked up the mistletoe. I was going to wait a minute and then come get some punch myself and pretend—" He broke off suddenly and shot a glance at his wife, whose presence he seemed momentarily to have forgotten. He cleared his throat. "Well, but then a bunch of people came up and I suppose I forgot about it."

Lydie's face was steaming with heat and she was breathing heavily. Leigh found herself glad the police were present. Lydie had never been a violent person, but for an obnoxious married playboy to pester her all day begging for kisses and then commit the ultimate indignity of contaminating her cooking? *Oh, my.* Harry was lucky to be in one piece.

"You," Lydie said acidly, "are going up those stairs right this minute. And you are going to tell that officer every single thing you did, *in detail.* And believe me, if you don't, I will! Do you understand me?"

Harry rose to his feet with a nod. He sniffed once, like a sulky child, and headed off up the stairs.

"Was that really necessary?" Virginia said to Lydie, striking a confrontational tone.

Lydie whirled on her. "Yes!"

Virginia shriveled, then pursed her lips into a pout. "This is all because of those Flying Maples, I'm telling you. They called in that anthrax threat just to upset us. Even if they didn't actually have any of the powder, they figured the fear of it alone might be enough to put one of us over the edge — and look what happened! At the very least, they wanted to shut us down and bring shame on our chapter in front of the whole regional organization... the whole city! I wouldn't be half surprised if they poisoned that cognac while they were at it, just out of spite. Why, anyone who drank that punch in the last hour could get violently ill at any moment!"

It seemed obvious to Leigh that if the cognac had been poisoned, the man who had drunk the majority of the bottle straight up had a hell of a lot more to worry about than anyone who had sipped the liquid diluted in punch. But she refrained from pointing that out. Given the look of horror on little Lenna's face, there had been more than enough talk of poisoning already.

"Oh, honey," Lydie said gently, turning to her trembling granddaughter. "Don't feel bad. It's not your fault. If Mr. Delvecchio was bound and determined to play childish games in the kitchen, there was nothing you could do to stop him."

"But," Lenna stammered, tears glistening on the lids of her cornflower-blue eyes. "He said I wasn't paying attention!"

"Well, clearly I wasn't either," Lydie rebutted, hugging the girl to her side. "And it was my responsibility, not yours. Neither of us had any idea we were watching a hen house with a fox about."

"The cognac wasn't poisoned, Lenna," Leigh added. "I'm sure of it."

Virginia humphed.

All of the women startled to attention as Frances emerged from the dining room. Although she walked with her usual perfect posture, Leigh could see that her mother was still badly shaken.

"Ms. Virginia Delvecchio?" the young policeman behind Frances called. "Can I speak with you a moment?"

Virginia threw back her bony shoulders. "You most certainly may, young man, and I do hope you have a good deal of time!"

The police officer's own shoulders sagged. "Yes, ma'am."

Frances joined her family. "Oh, my, but that was unpleasant," she said, attempting a fake smile as she looked at her granddaughters.

"Everything is going to be fine," Lydie said firmly. "Like I said before, if there's any fault to be had in the kitchen, it's mine." To Leigh's surprise, Lydie then told her sister all about Harry's confession. The tale did have the effect of turning part of Frances's guilt into good old-fashioned rage, but only for a minute. Then Lenna asked an unfortunate question.

"Grandma Lydie, could Lucille drink alcohol? Or was it bad for her?"

The women all went silent and stared at each other. Leigh tried to remember what Bridget had babbled about Lucille's medical condition, but her input wasn't required. Allison was already on the case. The girl flipped through a few pages of her notebook, then cleared her throat.

"Lucille had congestive heart failure and kidney failure," Allison read, "according to Virginia. Bridget also mentioned that she had trouble with anemia. They both said she was on a lot of different meds, although they didn't say what." She looked up at Leigh. "Isn't alcohol a contraindication for a lot of meds, Mom?"

Leigh's heart started to pound again. Aside from the fact that most normal, happy twelve-year-olds did not throw around words like "contraindication," she did not care for where her daughter's mind was going. "It can be," she answered vaguely. "Do we know that Lucille had punch?"

Even as Leigh asked the question — which she had hoped would put the unpleasant line of thought to bed — a memory of Lucille coughing popped into her head. She had needed something to clear her throat...

"I saw her drink it," Allison answered confidently. "Bridget always kept a glass of water nearby, but Lucille had punch, too. She had at least two cups that I saw, one not long before she died."

Lenna started to tear up again, and the women let out a heavy, collective sigh. Allison's stark view of logic and reality could be painfully inconvenient.

"Allie, honey," Leigh reasoned, "I suppose it's possible Lucille got a little bit of alcohol. But it's extremely unlikely she got a significant enough amount to matter. She had much more serious problems going on, any of which could have ended her life. Unless the medical experts tell us otherwise, there's no reason to chase down other possibilities."

Allison's dark eyes studied her mother critically. "Okay," she agreed, unconvinced.

"Is anyone else hungry?" Anna Marie appealed, bestirring herself from the couch for the first time in over an hour. "It's ridiculous that we're all sitting in here starving to death when there's a mountain of cold pizza out on the porch!"

"But we don't—" Olympia began.

"Oh, get over yourself!" Anna Marie said rudely, practically knocking Olympia out of the way as she opened the front door. "The Flying Maples couldn't possibly have done anything to this pizza and I'm going to eat it!" She flung open the door, reached down, picked up all five boxes, and wrestled them inside. Then, visibly panting, she peered over the top box and searched across the room until she found Frances. "They're cold. How about warming them up a bit for us?"

Leigh looked at her mother, but Frances didn't move. Her face had gone pale again, and she had the same distant, shocky expression that had been frightening Leigh ever since the police showed up.

"Potato salad," Frances murmured, her words barely discernable.

"Oh, for heaven's sakes!" Lydie tutted as she urged Frances into a chair. "If you're capable of operating an oven, Anna Marie, go do it yourself!"

Leigh blinked at her aunt with surprise, as did the girls. Lydie was never waspish. But then Frances also never stared into space with a haunted expression while babbling about deli products.

Anna Marie stood still. She looked from the pizza boxes toward the kitchen and back with a puzzled expression on her face. Then she started to move back toward the couch again.

"Oh, let me do it," Leigh offered, stepping over and taking the boxes out of the helpless woman's bejeweled hands. "It will take a couple minutes. But I agree there's no reason we shouldn't eat something while we're waiting."

She'd taken two steps into the kitchen before remembering one reason: the police chief was conducting an interview inside. "I'm sorry," she apologized quickly. "Would you mind if I put these in the oven to warm? Everyone's getting pretty hungry out there."

The chief made a vague gesture with his hand that Leigh took as a yes. She set down the boxes and turned on the oven.

"You don't understand," Bobby said with frustration. "I didn't know anything about that when I hired her. She seemed all right, and my mother liked her."

The chief didn't reply, and Leigh got the idea he was waiting for her to leave before resuming the interview. But Bobby was not so patient. Although she popped the pizzas in the oven and departed straightaway, she couldn't help but overhear more.

"When I found out she'd pretty much murdered the old guy, of course I wanted to fire her! But my mother thought it was an honest mistake, and they were getting on well enough, and she's so damned hard to please... I tried to talk to her, but she just wouldn't have it, I tell you!"

Leigh walked out of the kitchen.

He's making it up, she told herself. *Virginia was right. He's making Bridget look as suspicious as humanly possible... because he wants the insurance money.*

She felt her legs wobbling beneath her. Her gaze moved involuntarily toward where Bridget now stood by the front window, fidgeting with the curtain pull. She was twisting it first one way, then the other, staring at it with a bug-eyed glare.

Delores appeared at Leigh's side. "She's such an odd creature, isn't she, poor thing?" the tiny woman said, following Leigh's gaze to the personal assistant. "Lucille used to liken her to a hamster, you know. Said she was brainless and was always running about in circles. But I always thought of her more like a fox. A fretful, demented fox that's been kept in a tiny, airless cage all her life…"

Delores's voice turned wistful as she finished, and the hair on the back of Leigh's neck rose. How her mother could plant crocus bulbs beside these women for thirty years was beyond her. Twelve hours in the company of most of them was enough to do her in, and she'd had enough of Delores's particular wacko syrup by noon. She would rather hear Jennie Ruth belch all day.

"Yes, well…" Leigh said vaguely, by way of excusing herself. Lydie was trying to prop up both a pale Frances and a distressed Lenna while Allison — much to Leigh's chagrin — was back in action eavesdropping.

Leigh looked at her watch. It wasn't nearly as late as she felt like it should be. "What can I do?" she asked her aunt as she approached. "Mom, are you okay? You want a glass of water or something?"

"No, thank you, dear," Frances replied dully, still seeming as if she were only half present in the room. "Is your father back yet?"

Leigh and Lydie exchanged a glance. They both knew that any function at the Koslow house involving the word "Floribunda" would be enough to ensure Randall's absence for the duration. He might have had appointments at the clinic during the day, but where he had gone afterwards was anyone's guess.

"No, he's out still," Leigh answered. "You want me to try and call him?"

"Never mind. If he were home he'd just go hide in the basement, anyway." Frances looked more like herself when she scowled.

Leigh smiled. Maybe her mother would be all right after all.

"Melvin, would you stop fussing!" Olympia shrieked from the other side of the room. "What has gotten into you?"

Leigh looked up to see the diminutive proctologist slinking off to an empty chair. The rest of the room fell quiet.

Jennie Ruth belched.

Frances startled as if the grim reaper himself were chasing her.

A brisk pounding on the front door was followed by its immediate opening. "EMS!" a chipper woman in white called out. "Who's the patient?"

Chapter 13

The pizza was gone. All the cookies were gone, too. The Koslow house was more of a disheveled, crumb-laden wreck than it had been for forty years, and the fact that Frances wasn't bustling about trying to vacuum under people's feet worried Leigh as much as her mother's ghostlike pallor. EMS had come and gone, diagnosing only a few mildly upset stomachs and other symptoms of anxiety. Everyone had been interviewed except the two girls; Bridget was in the kitchen with all three officers now. The Floribundas and their spouses camped in the living room near the door, half falling asleep as they waited for permission to leave. It had gotten so late Randall had even come home.

Leigh slouched by the record player, musing over what response she might get for cuing up a rousing track from *John Denver and the Muppets.*

"Mom!" Allison whispered urgently, tugging on Leigh's sleeve.

Leigh looked to find her daughter's face fraught with distress. "What is it?"

"My notebook!" Allison cried, her voice nearly cracking. "It's missing!"

Leigh's adrenaline shot up. The words made no sense, but a mother knew her own child. Allison could have said "I want chocolate, not vanilla," and the effect on Leigh would have been the same. Something was terribly, desperately wrong. "What do you mean?"

Allison took a deep breath, obviously trying to calm herself. That action in itself upset Leigh further — the child had always been calm as a cucumber. Allison reached a hand in her back pocket and pulled out the miniature flip notebook she always carried. "I brought this one with me," she began to explain. "You know I always keep it in my pocket. But it was mostly full when I got here. After Lucille died, I went and got one of Grandma's. A bigger one."

Leigh nodded in understanding. She had seen the upgrade.

"But it wouldn't fit in my pocket," Allison continued. "And

when Lenna got examined she wanted me to be with her, but I didn't want to carry the bigger notebook with me because that would be weird, you know? So I hid it away. And now it's *gone!*"

Leigh's tired brain struggled to process the information. Allison was very attached to her notebooks, but this reaction was over the top. "Honey, anyone could have picked it up. Moved it somewhere without thinking —"

"Mom!" Allison stamped her small foot with frustration. "How stupid do you think I am? I didn't just lay it down somewhere! I hid it! I opened up Grandma's secretary, the third drawer down, and I slid it in underneath some of the family albums. And now it's *not there!*"

Leigh felt something cold and slithery wrap itself around her heart. Allison's notebook. The girl had been wandering around all afternoon, eavesdropping, taking notes. Everyone in the house had seen her do it — or could have, if they'd bothered to pay attention. Anyone could have watched her put the book in the secretary. And if Allison was sure the book was gone now, its disappearance was no accident. Someone had indeed noticed what she was doing. And someone didn't like it.

"I see why you're upset," Leigh answered finally. She looked at the crowd by the door. All of the women had purses. Melvin had a small medical-type bag and even Harry had an overcoat with big pockets slung over his arm. Any one of them could easily be concealing a notebook the size of Allison's.

Bridget came running out of the kitchen bawling. "I didn't do anything!" she cried out to everyone and no one at the same time. "I didn't, I didn't, I didn't!" She raced around and into the powder room, slamming the door after herself, and the three police officers walked out of the kitchen behind her. The younger two stood solemnly, watching, while the chief addressed the crowd.

"Well, everyone, I appreciate your patience," he announced. "I know it's been a long day for you and a long night, too, and it's probably way past some of your bedtimes."

Jennie Ruth made a very loud, rude, harrumphing sound. Several people turned to look at her, but her expression was utterly impassive. She could be a partying night owl offended by his assumption about her bedtime, or she could have been randomly clearing her throat. With Jennie Ruth, it was impossible to tell.

"I have some good news and some bad news," the chief continued. "The good news is, most of you can go home now. We've finished our interviews and gotten what we need."

"Well, hallelujah!" Anna Marie said sarcastically, grabbing up the coat that was already waiting on the arm of the couch beside her.

"The bad news," the chief went on, "is that as much as I'd like to assure everyone that Mrs. Busby died of natural causes and that there won't be any need for more questioning, we have had some concerns raised that are going to require us to bring in additional law enforcement. So some of you may be contacted again. For now, though, the following people can leave..." He rattled off a list of names, then stopped abruptly. His chin lifted. "Leigh Harmon?"

Leigh made a faint waving gesture, and he met her eyes.

"Leigh *Koslow* Harmon," he confirmed.

Crap. She was afraid the chief would recognize her name. She'd gotten lucky only dealing with the two newbies so far. But after the nightmare at that empty church building down the road last spring...

"I know you," he said soberly.

Leigh favored him with a small, self-conscious smile.

The chief gave his head a shake and finished his list. "Everyone whose name I mentioned can leave."

The reminder was unnecessary. The people mentioned first were long gone, and even those at the end were half out the door already.

The chief turned to Frances and Randall. "Mr. and Mrs. Koslow, I'm afraid we're not quite done here. We do have some additional personnel on their way over to take a quick look around your house."

"That's perfectly all right, officer," Frances said blandly, not meaning it.

Remembering the missing notebook, Leigh looked down at her daughter. Allison's small face had changed from distraught to furious. "Allie, honey," Leigh attempted to soothe. "I'm sorry about the notebook. But short of demanding that everyone open up their purses and—"

"They're not going to interview me?" Allison said with disbelief. "Or Lenna, either? Did no one even tell them I was *in the room* when Lucille died?"

Leigh sucked in a breath. Mother that she was, she'd never even thought of Allison or Lenna being interviewed. The idea was as horrifying as it was preposterous. The girls were minors. They were merely innocent bystanders. Right?

"He must not know. I'll have to tell him," Allison said with determination.

"Allie, honey, I don't think—"

Allison marched up to the police chief and waited patiently to get his attention while he spoke with the other officers. After being ignored for a solid minute, she boldly tapped on the man's arm. "Excuse me, Chief Graham?"

Leigh held her breath.

"I'm Allison Harmon, Frances Koslow's granddaughter. I was in the dining room with Lucille Busby the whole time, and I took notes about what happened. I was wondering when you were going to interview me? I have some information that I—"

"Oh, that's all right, sugar plum!" the chief said affably, giving Allison a pat on the head. "I think we've got all we need for tonight. We won't have to bother you or your little friend either one." He looked up at Leigh, then dropped his hand behind Allison's shoulders and gave the girl a push toward her mother. "You can take the girls on home now, Mrs. Harmon. Have a good night!"

Dismissed.

Allison's petite body stiffened, and her face reddened. Not with embarrassment, but with rage.

Contrary thoughts warred in Leigh's brain. The overprotective mother in her was delighted. The new mother who had sat by an incubator in the NICU for weeks, praying that the tiny, struggling preemie inside would someday be strong enough to go home and play with her strapping twin brother — that woman was so happy she could do somersaults. Yes! The chief said go home! Now she could feed her daughter some warm noodle soup and put her to bed in her pretty pink room with her puppy dog!

But the other Leigh had problems. The Leigh that had, ever since she was Allison's age, bitterly resented the very same patronizing, paternalistic, sexist treatment that her daughter was experiencing now. The chief genuinely might not believe that either of the girls had any useful information to impart. He might also not want to unnecessarily stress a minor. But there was no question in Leigh's mind that if Allison were a male of the same age, and therefore a foot taller, her assertion that she been present when Lucille died and would like to talk about it would not have earned her a pat on the head and the designation "sugar plum."

Dammit.

The absolute last thing mother-Leigh wanted was for Allison to get embroiled in some ugly controversy over a life insurance settlement — which thanks to Bobby was clearly going to get ugly whether Lucille died of natural causes or not. But as she watched the small figure before her tremble with rage, it was middle-school-Leigh who grabbed her brain's control panel.

"Chief Graham," she said, interrupting the men's banter, which had moved on to Duquesne basketball. "I don't think you heard what my daughter said." *We both know you did, but I'm repeating it so you can save face. Appreciate it.* "She was actually present in the dining room, with both Lucille and Bridget, for the entire afternoon and evening. Her job was to watch the dining room in case anything was stolen. She got the job because she's very observant. So if you're wondering about anything that happened between Bridget and Lucille around the time of her death, you would be wise to ask Allison what she saw. Not only does she have an excellent memory, but she has a convenient habit of writing things down."

The officers went quiet. They looked down at Allison, then at each other. The chief seemed mildly confused. "Uh… well, thank you, Mrs. Harmon. But the thing is —"

Leigh smelled blood. It was one thing to dismiss her when she was standing up for herself. Dissing her when she was trying to set an example for her daughter was like waving bacon in front of a corgi.

"What you should also know," Leigh interjected, "is that after Lucille died, when everyone was gathered around in little clusters bemoaning and speculating, Allison was listening in and taking notes. And *someone* evidently found that threatening, because someone watched where she hid her notebook and then removed it. So if one of the people you interviewed thought that Allison had jotted down information important enough to steal, don't you think maybe that information is important enough for you to listen to?"

The police chief's jaw went slack. Leigh's tone was perfectly polite, of course. She'd spent more than enough of her life accidentally getting on the bad side of law enforcement, and she preferred not to go there again.

"Uh…" he began again, removing his hat and scratching over his ear. "Well, I suppose that could be useful information, yes. And I'll be sure to pass that along. But you see—"

Leigh couldn't believe she could not get through to this man. Pass along to whom? The West View police could handle most minor crimes, but major criminal investigations got kicked up to the county level. Had Bobby pushed the insurance angle so far they were already calling in the county to investigate fraud? Or worse yet, had they actually believed his claims of negligence by Bridget? What reason did the police have to think that the death of a terminally ill woman with a standing do-not-resuscitate order was anything other than a naturally occurring event?

"Why can't you—" Leigh began, but didn't finish. A much calmer looking Allison was tapping on her arm.

"It's okay, Mom," Allison said, her voice oddly hopeful.

Leigh followed her daughter's gaze toward the kitchen, where a newcomer had entered through the back. Standing in the doorway, obscuring most of it with her large frame — and wearing a thoroughly disgruntled expression on her face — was Detective Maura Polanski, Allegheny County Police Department.

Homicide Division.

Chapter 14

Leigh sat at the Koslows' kitchen table with her parents and her Aunt Lydie, sipping at a cup of candy-cane flavored herbal tea. The house was quiet now, and they were alone. At least temporarily.

As soon as the police chief had confirmed that Detective Maura Polanski and the county homicide squad would indeed be taking over the investigation, Leigh had managed to convince Allison that she could go home and go to bed in good conscience. Allison not only had the utmost respect for the abilities of her "Aunt Mo," but she knew that the detective would take Allison's own input seriously. So while Detective Polanski proceeded to debrief the West View officers, survey the area, and interview the still-distraught Bridget, Allison had found another blank notebook and set herself to the task of recreating as much as she could remember of the one that was lost. She had still been writing furiously when Leigh walked her and Lenna out to Cara's car and waved them all goodnight.

Maura was outside now, helping Bridget secure a ride home after the kindly Bobby had stranded his mother's employee by removing Lucille's car from the premises. Maura was expected to come back inside and speak briefly with Randall and Frances before they turned in for the night. Leigh's mother was still far from herself.

"Frances," Lydie said calmly and tenderly, for about the fortieth time. "You have got to snap out of this. I know that everything that's happened this evening has brought back... bad memories. But be sensible. No matter what nonsense has been said, you and I both know that Lucille simply passed. And that's *all* that happened."

Frances sat staring blankly across the table. Her face was pale, and her eyes not only looked glassy but were growing increasingly bloodshot. She reached for her steaming mug of tea, lifted it, then set it down again.

Lydie sighed. "I give up. Randall, you try."

Leigh's father watched his wife with a concerned frown. Finally he leaned forward and took her hand. "What is it you're not telling us?" he asked.

Frances's eyes reddened even more. Then they began to water. She expelled a heavy, shaky breath, then looked at her twin. "I'm not so sure Lucille did just pass. I'm not sure of that at all."

Leigh's eyes met her Aunt Lydie's. Frances wasn't just "talking drama" about the Flying Maples anymore. They remained silent, watching while Frances gathered her nerve or came to a decision. Leigh wasn't sure which.

"You know that Lucille has always been obsessed with death, and by that I mean with death in general. It was simply her personality," Frances began. "If she was a teenager now, she'd be one of those goth kids with black clothes and skull tattoos and a metal stud in her nose. But for the last year or so, all she talked about was her own death. Her husband's passing made her rich, you know. At least for a while. The way she crowed over that insurance policy..." Frances pursed her lips, then shook herself with disgust. "Unseemly is what it was. She and her husband were never a love match, but you would have thought she won the lottery, not lost the father of her children. And practically in the prime of his life!"

Frances stopped talking and took a sip of tea. Her dark eyes now looked annoyed, rather than vacant, and her color was returning. Leigh breathed a silent sigh of relief. She would take judgmental Frances over haunted Frances any day.

"Lucille was healthy as a horse practically her whole life," Frances continued. "But when she did start to have some serious problems, the things she was saying became truly disturbing."

"Virginia was saying that Lucille had a policy on herself," Leigh said. "A policy she wanted her son to cash in on. It was an accidental death policy, but she thought Bobby would push the issue and try to collect no matter how Lucille died."

Frances raised an eyebrow. "Virginia said that? To whom?"

Leigh tried to remember. "I think just to Allison and me. Why?"

Frances didn't answer for a moment. She seemed deep in thought. "Virginia has always been a gossip. But still, I'm surprised she would say that."

Now Leigh was confused. "Is it not true?"

Her mother's dark eyes bore into hers. "Oh, it's true all right.

That's the problem. Don't you understand?"

Leigh looked across the table at her father, then at her aunt. She did not understand, and apparently neither did they.

"Oh, for heaven's sake!" Frances burst out. "Lucille has been plotting her own demise for months now!"

Leigh coughed on the sip of tea she was about to swallow. Lydie dropped the cup she'd just picked up. And Randall, who had been tipping back in his chair, let its front feet crash down onto the ceramic tile with a thud.

"Are you saying that this woman planned ahead of time to commit suicide in our house?" he asked, not sounding at all pleased. His voice was not raised, but for Randall, it qualified as a shout.

"No," Frances replied calmly. "No, that's not what I mean. Not the way that you think, anyway. But... well, I can't be sure."

Leigh was still confused.

"Talk sense, Frances," Lydie ordered.

Frances dropped her hands on the table with a clunk. "Lucille was terminally ill, and she knew it. But she didn't want to die the old fashioned way, which is to say naturally — and with dignity. She wanted to defraud the insurance company so her son could get some money out of her death, just like she did when her husband passed. She said so explicitly, on multiple occasions. All the Floribundas knew that."

Frances paused, grabbed a paper napkin from the center of the table, and began to sweep up crumbs as she talked. "Surely you noticed how... well, how awkwardly the announcement of Lucille's passing was received by everyone? It was hardly a normal grieving reaction. It's upsetting to lose someone so suddenly when you've known them half your life... never mind whether you really liked them or not. But we all knew that Lucille *wanted* to die, which made us feel conflicted. And if that weren't enough, I'm sure that every Floribunda in that room — well, except Olympia perhaps — was thinking the same, horrible thing that I was thinking!"

Frances's voice cracked, and her face started going pale again. She batted furiously at the crumbs.

"Tell us what that was, Frances," Lydie goaded gently. "What were all the Floribundas thinking?"

Frances stopped fidgeting. She drew in a ragged, sniffling breath.

"We were wondering who gave in!"

Leigh leaned forward. "Gave in? Explain what you mean, Mom."

Frances's eyes had taken on the glassy tone again. "Lucille couldn't do it by herself. She needed help to set things up. A plan solid enough to fool the insurance company. And she... well, she asked for help. From the Floribundas."

Peppermint tea soured in Leigh's stomach.

"From the whole chapter?" Lydie asked with disbelief. "Are you joking? She brought this up as new business?"

"No, no!" Frances protested. "Lucille is smarter than that. She asked people one by one, outside of the meetings. And one by one, they told her no. We were all horrified at the mere thought of it!"

"She asked you, too?" Randall inquired.

A queer mixture of both pride and annoyance distorted Frances's face. "No. She did not ask me. I believe she knew in advance what my position would be."

"So she asked everyone else individually, but you all compared notes after?" Leigh asked.

Frances waved a dismissive hand. "Essentially. Virginia finds these things out. We all knew what was happening. Lucille offered money. Her son was supposed to make compensation, although it couldn't happen until well after the case was settled, to avoid suspicion. Lucille was adamant that the plan would be brilliant and that there was no way any Floribunda would ever be implicated."

Holy crap. Leigh definitely felt sick now. "Mom," she said heavily. "Do you really think that what happened to Lucille here today could have been a setup? That one of the Floribundas could have helped her and Bobby to do it?"

Frances looked truly miserable. "I don't know. As much as I hate to think of it, I can't say it's impossible that one of them changed her mind. I can't imagine why, what could make any of them so desperate, but... Or maybe I'm completely wrong. Maybe Bobby found another way. Or maybe Lucille really did simply pass! I don't know!" Frances covered her face with her hands, and Randall wrapped a comforting arm around her shoulders.

Leigh swallowed a lump in her throat. Her parents weren't usually affectionate types.

After a few seconds, Frances lifted her head. "I wish I could believe she passed on her own, but I can't. I can't make myself believe it because of the grand exit. Don't you see? Her dying right at the end of the greatest, most glorious event ever in the history of the Floribunda chapter? In public view? With all the publicity and hoopla and wringing of hands and gnashing of teeth sure to follow — and with no regard at all to whatever effects such a tragedy might have on the rest of us? It's so... *Lucille!*"

Leigh digested the concept slowly. Then she thought a bad word.

"I see what you're saying," Lydie offered. "But I still don't think we should assume the worst. You said it yourself: the woman was terminally ill."

Randall cleared his throat. "Lydie's right. A lot of people talk about ending their lives, but when it comes right down to it, most people can't. It goes against basic human instinct."

No one said anything else for a moment. "Mom," Leigh asked finally, her voice hesitant. "Did you tell the officer any of this during your interview?"

Incredibly, the faintest of smiles spread across Frances's lips. "Would you believe he didn't ask?"

Leigh believed it. "Yes, but Mom, you know Maura will. And you have to tell her the truth."

Frances's lips pursed with blessedly normal disapproval. "Did I ever say I wouldn't? I have the utmost confidence in Maura's ability to handle this situation," she defended. "But that doesn't mean I'm looking forward to it."

"Of course not," Randall said soothingly. "Tell her what you know, and you'll be done with it. What happens after that won't be your concern."

Frances harrumphed. "Easy for you to say. *You* won't have to attend future meetings of the Floribundas!"

Lydie, Leigh, and Randall all exchanged a look. None of them commented.

A gentle rapping sound on the back door alerted them to Maura's return. Leigh jumped up and let the detective in, then gestured for her to join them. Having been Leigh's friend since their college days, Maura was treated as one of the family. The imposing detective folded her large frame into a kitchen chair and relaxed. Maura's gruff demeanor and tendency to explode like a volcano over Leigh's imagined misdeeds could be scary, but the detective's baby-blue eyes and apple cheeks betrayed her underlying good nature. Besides which, being happily married and having her first baby at forty-two this past spring had definitely had a mellowing effect.

"Do you want to interview us officially now?" Frances asked.

Maura shook her head. "That won't be necessary, no. I have your statements. I will have some additional questions after I sort through everything, but that can wait until after you've had a good night's sleep."

"Excellent news," Randall declared, rising. "In that case, off we go."

"Wait, Dad," Leigh insisted. If there was anyone who could get a good night's sleep content with roughly fifty-fifty odds that a death and not a murder had just occurred in his dining room, it was her no-nonsense father. But her own nerves on one particular point were not so easily soothed, and she wanted his input as well as Maura's. "Before anyone leaves," Leigh said, "I want to know what Maura thinks about Allison's notebook disappearing." She explained the situation as completely and concisely as she could.

"Oh, merciful heavens," Frances wailed. "This is all my fault. I should never have assigned that poor child to the dining room!"

Oh, no. Leigh wanted to smack herself. The last thing she wanted was to make her mother feel guilty.

"Do stop that nonsense, Frances," Lydie demanded. "I think we all need to take a breath and remind ourselves that we are talking about the Floribundas, here! We all know how ridiculously paranoid some of these women are. Not a one of them would be above sneaking a peek at what that child had written. Any perfectly innocent party could have had second thoughts about something they'd said, or worried that they'd been misquoted. Maybe they wanted to see what else Allison had overheard. Maybe they were bored and merely wanted to cause a scene!"

Leigh took a deep breath and let it out slowly, following her aunt's advice. Lydie was right. The disappearance of Allison's notebook was not a good thing. But there were reasonable explanations besides the targeting of her daughter by a deranged insurance-defrauding murderess.

"I will definitely look into it, Leigh," Maura said, writing a line in her own notebook. Then she shut it and returned it to her pocket. "And we'll talk more tomorrow morning. But for now, Dr. and Mrs.

Koslow, I suggest you evict the lot of us, take your house back, and get some sleep."

Randall stood up again, and this time, so did everyone else. A heavy cloud still hung over the household, but everyone was exhausted, and for now, there was nothing more to be done. Goodnights were spoken, Lydie went back to her own house, and Maura and Leigh walked out to their cars.

"Maura," Leigh said quietly as she opened her door and got in. "Tell me straight. Am I just being an overprotective mother? Or should I be worried about Allison?"

Maura's answer came a beat too late for Leigh's satisfaction. "It's highly unlikely she's in any real danger. Look, Koslow, I haven't even read all the reports yet. But you know I'll do everything I can to keep everybody safe. Even if I get pulled off the case."

Leigh groaned aloud. It was only so much help to have a friend who was a police detective when certain higher-ups kept declaring conflicts of interest. "Not *again!*"

"And whose fault is that?" Maura returned crossly.

Leigh shut up. Arguing her innocence when it came to her statistically improbable involvement with homicide never got her anywhere.

"You're looking nearly as rough as your mother, by the way," Maura continued. "I suggest you get some sleep yourself. I promised little Eddie his second-ever taste of cake at your house tomorrow, so we expect this party to be first rate."

"Oh, my," Leigh moaned. "The twins' birthday. How could I almost forget that?"

Maura cracked a grin. "Ah, sweet parenthood. It's amazing what age and a little sleep deprivation can do to you. This morning Gerry squirted diaper rash cream onto his toothbrush." She slammed the car door shut behind Leigh. "Drive safe."

Chapter 15

Pet therapy.

It was best stress antidote Leigh knew of. Within ten minutes of her sitting on the couch, she had a geriatric cat purring in her lap and a well-fed corgi asleep on her feet. Now she never wanted to move again.

Her tasks for the kids' twelfth birthday party had been completed. She had wrapped the packages, performed her standard perfunctory cleaning pass, set the table, and put up the few low-key, gender neutral decorations both kids had been willing to agree on. Her duties in the kitchen, thank God, were nil. Ethan and Allison, in their infinite wisdom, had specifically asked their father if he would fix all their favorite foods, so the meal was Warren's problem. She always enjoyed these yearly family get-togethers for the kids, and she was determined that everyone would enjoy this one, too, despite the awkward timing. This moment was the most relaxed she'd felt in days. But her respite was doomed to be brief.

"She *is* coming before the party, isn't she Mom?" Allison asked in a voice underlain with tension. The girl was standing at the window again. She'd been watching out of it and pacing in front of it for the last forty-five minutes.

Leigh tried hard to maintain her zen. "Allison, if Maura said she would interview you today before the party, she will interview you today before the party. I really wish you would stop thinking so much about it. It's your birthday! Wouldn't you like to do something else while we're waiting? Something fun?"

Allison turned from the window and regarded her mother with a sober expression. As she reached up and adjusted her glasses, she looked so much like her grandfather Randall it was uncanny. "Mom," she said firmly, "this is serious. I have things I need to tell her."

Leigh sighed and sat up a bit, much to the consternation of Mao Tse, who dug in her claws as her bed shifted sideways. Leigh's feet moved as well, but the loudly snoring Chewie was oblivious. "I don't suppose I can convince you to forget about everything that happened yesterday, just for the next few hours?"

Allison stared back at her. "You know what I really want for my birthday, Mom?"

For a second, Leigh felt a faint flicker of hope that she was about to hear a request for a shiny new phone or a bedroom makeover or maybe even a bicycle. But then she got real. The girl's only request to date had been for subscriptions to boring software services, which Warren had thought perfectly sensible. Leigh had thrown a new comforter set into the mix anyway, just to give the girl something solid to unwrap. But she doubted it would be received with much enthusiasm. "What's that?"

Allison stepped closer to her. "I want you to talk to me about this case. Like you would if you didn't still think of me as a little kid."

Icy terror gripped Leigh's heart. *No.* Allison was her baby. She'd only been born a few weeks ago, after all, and it was Leigh's job to protect her from all that was evil in the world. Her brother was so much easier. Ethan had always had a cheerful disposition and naturally gravitated toward the positive in life. What's more, he was in absolutely no hurry to grow up. But this child, this dark-eyed, serious-minded little girl, seemed intent not only on growing old before her time but running into a flaming inferno with a mini fire extinguisher in one hand and a notebook in the other.

"This case?" Leigh repeated stupidly.

Allison frowned. "Never mind." She began to stomp off.

"Wait," Leigh said, feeling lousy. She'd been feeling lousy for a while now, wracked with mother guilt over a truth she hesitated to admit, even to Warren. But the fact was, dammit, she didn't particularly *want* the twins to turn twelve. Not that the alternative was preferable, of course. But twelve was one of those milestones a mother had mixed feelings about. Eleven was the last year that kids could be kids, while thirteen was full-blown teenagerhood. The only thing that was certain about age twelve was that it was an awkward year for boys and pure hell for girls, and both genders responded by taking their frustrations out on their parents.

Leigh enjoyed being a kids' mom. Many times over, she had wanted to freeze her happy little family just the way it was. Why must time rock the boat so viciously?

Allison stopped. She crossed her bony arms over her skinny

middle and looked at her mother expectantly.

Get a grip, Koslow, Leigh ordered herself. Would *you* like to be frozen at the age of five, still skipping around your parents' house in a pixie cut and a polyester dress?

She shuddered.

"All right, Allie," she said boldly, patting the couch beside her. "Let's talk. What did you find out yesterday?"

Allison stared at her mother suspiciously for quite some time before a warm smile spread across her face. She stepped over the snoozing corgi, pulled yet another notebook out of her back pocket, and sat down. "Well," she said brightly, "I found out a lot of things." She opened her notebook and flipped to a particular page. "The way I see it, there are three options. Either Lucille died of natural causes, she committed suicide, or she was murdered. Right?"

Leigh didn't feel as though the sparkle in her daughter's eyes was appropriate for the subject matter. But she nodded.

"The first one is probably the most likely," Allison continued matter-of-factly, "because she was really sick, and it must have been a stressful day for her. I wrote down everything Virginia said was wrong with her—" she stopped and looked at her mother. "You don't mind if I use their first names, do you? I know I'm supposed to say Mrs. So-and-So, but nobody else uses last names when they're talking, so it's kind of awkward when taking notes."

Leigh fought back a grin at Allison's earnestness. The girl was trying so amazingly hard to sound mature. "That's fine."

Allison smiled. "Anyway, I was thinking about how often older dogs and cats die when they're being boarded, even if they seem fine when they come in. Grandpa says it's the stress. They can be managing okay with a chronic problem, but then stress puts them over the edge and suddenly it's a crisis."

Leigh felt a twinge of pride. Allison had a good mind for medicine. If only she would stick with wanting to be a veterinarian!

"The Holiday House Tour had to be really stressful for Lucille," Allison theorized. "Bridget said that before the Floribundas' emergency meeting on Friday, she hadn't been out of her house for a week. So for Lucille to have a natural heart attack or a stroke wouldn't be that surprising. *But...*"

Leigh braced herself.

"If that's what happened, then every other weird thing that happened was a total coincidence," Allison finished, frowning again. "And you know how I feel about coincidences, Mom."

"Yes," Leigh agreed, pushing from her mind several previous examples she didn't want to think about.

Allison ticked off numbers on her fingers. "The anthrax call, for one. That was just plain weird. If someone wanted to disrupt the tour, they should have called earlier, when we had bigger crowds. Calling at the end like that, what did they get out of it? Nothing really, except sending the Floribundas into hysterics and making the police show up. Think about that, Mom."

Leigh thought about it. She still liked the kids-down-the-street theory. Never mind that kids still young enough to enjoy prank calls would also be too young to remember the 2001 anthrax scare.

"Second," Allison went on, "when Lucille's son showed up, he couldn't possibly have known about his mother's death for very long. He must have come straight from wherever he was when the police called him to Grandma's house. But the first thing he did was start blaming Bridget. I've read about the stages of grief, and it just seems like he blew through the 'denial' one pretty fast and got straight to 'anger.' I know he knew how sick his mother was... but if he *expected* her to go at any time, why flip out on Bridget like that at all? Strange, Mom."

Leigh did not disagree. Although, in her limited association with both Lucille and Bobby, she would not expect the son to mourn his mother's passing with any great sentiment. Lucille might have doted on Bobby, but the apple of her eye had always struck Leigh as a singularly self-centered lout.

"Third, somebody ripped off my notebook, which I don't need to tell you about," Allison said with a steely tone. "And fourth," She paused, then blew out a breath. "This one is harder to explain, but I know you'll know what I'm talking about. Let's face it, the Floribundas are weird. Even for old ladies. But the way they were talking after Lucille died..."

The girl's voice trailed off, and Leigh found herself leaning in. She couldn't imagine that any of the women would have talked openly, in front of Allison and the husbands and herself and Lydie, about Lucille's supposed insurance scam. But then again, Allison was right. They were weird.

"I could say that none of them were surprised," Allison finished. "And that's true. But that's not all of it. They were all just so nervous. Uptight. Almost like suspicious. And not of the Flying Maples, either, although they kept talking about them like they were superhero villains or something. But even though that's what they *said*, I kept getting this vibe like they were all really suspicious of *each other*. And as sick as everybody kept saying Lucille was, that made no sense. You know what I mean?"

Leigh cocked an eyebrow. Maura was right, dammit. The child did have amazingly good instincts when it came to criminal investigation.

"You're right," Leigh forced herself to say. She tried to stay calm by imagining an adult Allison wearing a white jacket and stethoscope and sitting in a nice, safe veterinary clinic surrounded by puppies and kittens. *There, that's better.* "They are suspicious of each other. Grandma admitted as much after you left last night." She briefly considered censoring the adults' conversation, but realized that doing so would be counterproductive. If Allison suspected information was being kept from her, her efforts at espionage would only increase, potentially putting her at risk. So Leigh bit the bullet and explained the potential for an insurance scam, as well as Frances's uncertainty over whether any Floribunda had played a role in it.

Allison listened with rapt concentration, making several new entries in her notebook. When Leigh finished, the girl's small face was practically aglow. "Death by natural causes is still possible," Allison said speculatively. "But it looks like I'm wrong about suicide or murder. If it's either, it's going to be both. Lucille would need at least one accomplice besides Bobby, don't you think?"

Leigh was uncomfortable. The word "murder" had come from her daughter's mouth twice in the last few minutes, and it rolled off her tongue all too easily. "Allison," she diverted, avoiding the question, "what exactly was in the notebook that disappeared?"

The girl's brow furrowed. But then her lips drew gradually into a sardonic smile. "That's the funny part, Mom. I started writing down everything that I could remember about Lucille as soon as you said she'd passed away. But I wrote all that in my pocket notebook. The one that got taken wasn't that one, it was the second one! All the stolen one had in it were my notes about what people were saying in the living room afterwards. That, and Virginia going on about people's medical conditions. So if somebody stole my notebook to see what I wrote about what happened in the dining room before Lucille died... Ha!" Allison crowed. "Epic fail!"

Leigh had a sudden, fierce urge to whisk the entire family away to Bermuda for a month. "Why were you taking notes about people's medical conditions?" she asked instead.

Her daughter looked at her as if the answer were obvious. "Poisoning, Mom. You know older people have bathroom cabinets stuffed full of prescription drugs!"

Leigh reconsidered. Bermuda was too close. Fiji, perhaps? She would check Warren's frequent flier account immediately after the party.

They heard the sound of something metal clattering to the floor in the kitchen, and Chewie leapt into action as if he'd been zapped with a cattle prod. A blur of sable-colored fur shot off after the sound while Ethan's voice drifted toward them. "Sorry, Dad. Slipped out of my hand."

Leigh reached down and rubbed her ankle where Chewie's toenails had excoriated her. Mao Tse, who did not appreciate being compressed, jumped from Leigh's lap with a mew of annoyance just as the doorbell rang. Chewie dutifully barked to alert them all of a visitor, but he could not be bothered to greet the individual in person. His greater responsibility lay with kitchen floor sanitization.

"Aunt Mo's here!" Allison cried with delight, jumping up and running to open the door.

"Happy birthday!" the detective greeted with a smile. She was wearing a bright red wool coat that made her look frighteningly like Santa Claus, particularly when she carried two wrapped packages.

"Hey, you weren't supposed to get us presents!" Allison reminded.

"I didn't," Maura assured, stepping inside. "These are from Eddie. He insisted. I think he's angling to make sure he gets something from the two of you when he turns one next spring."

Allison giggled.

Leigh wished her daughter did more giggling and less scribbling about poisons in notebooks. "Oh, Eddie will get presents from us," Leigh teased. "Lots and lots of really *noisy* presents."

Maura smirked. "Gerry and I will never be forgiven for that

toddler drum set, will we?"

Leigh smirked back. "Oh, hell, no."

"Can we talk now, Aunt Mo?" Allison begged. "We can go to my room. You want to interview me privately or does Mom have to be there?"

All lightheartedness drained from the atmosphere. "Mom will be there," Leigh answered, rising unwillingly to her feet. "Let's do this thing."

Chapter 16

Leigh had eaten way too much, and she blamed her husband. As usual, Warren had outdone himself. The dinner was scrumptious, the cake was amazing, and even the weird flavors of ice cream the kids had wanted ended up capping off the rest of the meal perfectly. Now that the presents had been opened and the birthday hoopla concluded, most of the crowd had gone outside. The weather was still pleasant for December, crisp and clear but not too cold, and both kids and adults alike were enjoying throwing around the new LED-lighted discs and watching Ethan fly his Millennium Falcon. Leigh remained inside, however, wallowing around regretting her third helping of dessert.

"The party's been lovely," Lydie congratulated from her position next to Leigh on the couch. "It's been nice to forget everything else for a few hours."

"Amen to that," Leigh agreed. Maura's "interview" with Allison hadn't been too horrible, since it was Allison who had done nearly all of the talking. Maura had easily deflected all the girl's attempts to draw information the other direction, though Leigh noticed the detective was far more polite about it than Leigh was used to. Maura's questions were dispassionate, her discussion of next steps was need-to-know, and she refused to participate in any group conjecture. If the detective was concerned about Allison's personal safety, she did a good job of hiding it, and Leigh found her fears relieved a little. Sooner than expected, Maura had pronounced the interview concluded and herself ready to party.

"Maura and Gerry do make wonderful parents, don't they?" Frances commented from the recliner. "They're both such calm, level-headed people. Towers of patience."

Leigh's lips twisted. Clearly, her mother had never been dressed down by Detective Maura Polanski in full flip-out mode. She certainly had never been falsely arrested by her bloodhound of a husband, Lieutenant Gerald Frank. But that was ancient history. "Yes," she agreed to the first part. "They are wonderful parents."

Mason entered through the patio door and came to sit down by Lydie. "That little drone is amazing!" he insisted. "You should go watch. Ethan's getting the hang of it pretty fast."

Lydie smiled and put a hand on his thigh. "I'll check it out in a minute."

"That was a nice basketball you and Randall gave him, too," Mason said to Frances. "Good quality. I would have loved one like that when I was his age."

Frances lifted her chin. Her gaze moved vaguely in Mason's direction, but she did not meet his eyes. "Thank you," she said politely.

The room fell quiet. Frances's socially acceptable response held no congeniality whatsoever. It was the way she always spoke to Mason. Unfailingly courteous, yet devoid of any warmth.

The same could not be said for the air temperature around Lydie. Today marked the first time in months that Leigh had been around both the sisters and Mason at the same time. Since Frances had decided not to openly protest her sister's upcoming Christmas Eve wedding, Leigh had hoped that the awkwardness among them would settle down. But all afternoon, the tension had been palpable. Leigh was convinced that Frances was actually *trying* to accept Mason as her future brother-in-law, but her attempts seemed to necessarily include either looking right through him or pretending he was somebody else. And although Lydie had seemed content with that level of acceptance at the time of her engagement, the closer the wedding drew, the more irritated she became with her sister's lack of progress.

Lydie puffed up with breath as if preparing to speak, but Mason quickly laid a hand on her arm. "Not now," he said softly. "It doesn't matter."

"It does matter!" Lydie insisted, her own voice at full volume.

"Not at the kids' party," Mason replied. "Go on out and watch the drone. You really should see it."

Lydie looked at her ex-husband and fiance a moment, then stood. "We will finish this discussion later," she announced to Frances. Then she grabbed her coat and walked out the patio door.

Leigh, Frances, and Mason were alone for only a matter of seconds before Frances stood up. "I wonder if Warren would like for me to start some coffee? That would be nice," she murmured, more to herself than to anyone else. Then she was gone.

Mason chuckled softly. Leigh turned to look at him. The look of regret on his face saddened her, but at the same time, she could see that he truly bore no ill will. "I think you're taking all this extremely well, you know," she praised. "I admire you for that."

He shook his head. "It's not a problem for me. Same old, same old. I just wish it didn't bother Lydie so much."

Leigh smiled at him. "That's big of you. I'm well aware of how it feels to be on the receiving end of one of my mom's super-chiller ice glares. And she loves me."

To her surprise, Mason smiled back. "She used to like me, too. Way down deep. That's why she got so damn mad at me when I hurt Lydie. She didn't admit it then, of course, and she'd sure as hell never admit it now. But I always knew. I could tell by the way she yelled at me."

Leigh's eyes widened. She'd always heard that Frances never liked Mason. She looked toward the kitchen and lowered her voice to a whisper. "She used to yell at you?"

He grinned broadly. "Oh, that was pretty much our primary form of communication, back in the day. She'd call me a hustler and a swindler and a two-bit snake oil salesman. And I'd ignore everything she said and pretend she adored me. Of course, that made her even more furious. Your dad never said a word about our back-and-forth, but I could tell he thought it was funny, and so did Lydie. So I just kept on. Frances would get so wound up at me that once or twice I even got her to curse." Mason chuckled to himself. "Oh, Lord. I wish I had a recording of that. One time, your dad was listening in, and I knew he was there because I could see him around the corner, although your mother couldn't. Well, she was letting me have it for some sin or other, I've no idea what. I was guilty of a lot of things, and whatever it was, she was probably right. But after she'd ripped me up one side and down the other and finally stopped to take a breath, I managed to squeeze a tear out of one eye and I said 'Francie, does this mean you don't love me anymore?' Hell's fire, I thought the woman would explode."

Leigh shook with muffled laughter.

"Yeah," Mason said with a chuckle of his own. "That's pretty much how your dad reacted. I heard words come out of your mother's mouth I haven't heard before or since. But I always figured if she really hated me, I wouldn't be able to get to her so much."

Leigh's mirth dampened a little as she observed the wistful glint in his eye. A pang of sadness struck her as she realized that for all of Mason's hard-won layers of thick skin, some part of him must still long for Frances's favor — even after all this time. And after everything she'd put him through.

"Yeah," he said more casually, relaxing back into the couch with a smile. "Those were the days. Between you and me, kid, I'd take the cursing and the yelling over this icy politeness any day. At least that was honest." His expression became concerned again. "But all that really matters is how Lydie feels."

"She was wonderful with my mother yesterday," Leigh praised. "The two of them were like peas in a pod again. Mom needed her desperately and Lydie came through, no matter how strained the last few months have been between them. But still, Mason, I've got to tell you... things are definitely different now. They always used to side with each other, no questions asked. But now, the second my mother dares to turn against her sister's man... Watch out for those claws!" Leigh smiled at Mason. "Methinks my Aunt Lydie is rather fond of you."

Mason's blue-green eyes twinkled, even as his smile seemed sad. "I wish my very existence didn't have to come between the two of them. Particularly at a family event like this. But I can't blame Francie for not making nice tonight. She's had a hell of a weekend."

"We've all had better," Leigh agreed.

Mason shook his head, his voice sympathetic. "It's worse for her. That whole 'Filthy Francie' thing really cut her to the bone. I didn't meet her till years afterward, and it still had a hold on her. I don't think she ever got over it, really. And everything about this just brings all that pain right back up. And believe me when I say — reliving the darkest stuff that's in your head, not being able to forget, having to go back over it in your mind... Well, that's some of the worst torture there is. I ought to know."

Leigh stared at him. She knew that Mason's past included misdeeds he might struggle to forget, but for him to draw parallels with her mother's squeaky-clean background was unexpected. She had never in her life heard the moniker "Filthy Francie." The very phrase was an oxymoron. "What are you talking about?" she asked.

He looked back at her a second, then dropped his head. "Aw, hell, I did it again, didn't I? I thought for sure Lydie would have told you that story while I was gone!"

Aha. The sweet sixteen thing again. Leigh shook her head. "No. She said she would, but... well, we haven't had a chance yet. So how about you enlighten me?"

Mason frowned. "You're determined to get me in trouble, aren't you?" He glanced toward the kitchen again, and kept his voice low. "Please don't tell anyone I let that name slip. Your mother hasn't heard it in decades and if she hears it this weekend it may well put her over the edge. Ask Lydie later and she'll tell you. But leave me out of it! Please, kid?"

Leigh was spared answering by Maura, who came back in the patio door with her son asleep on her shoulder. Seven-month-old Eddie was almost completely swallowed by a puffy turtle-green parka. The only part of him that was visible was a mohawk of cornsilk-colored hair on top of his head.

"He's out," Maura announced cheerfully, balancing the sleeping child against her chest with one strong arm. "We're taking off now; Gerry's bringing the car around. Thanks again for the invite. It's been fun."

Mason bid the detective goodnight and went back outside to find his fiance, and Leigh offered to walk her friend to her car. It was too cold to be out without a coat, which of course Leigh hadn't bothered to put on. "Thanks for coming," she said with a shiver. "And thanks for not dragging Allison into all of this any more deeply than you have to. You know how she can be. Show her a puzzle to be solved and she's like Chewie smelling popcorn."

Maura smiled. But only a little. The sight made Leigh four times colder.

"You know I care about your family like they were my own, and I'll always do whatever I can to keep them safe," Maura said quietly. "But you have to realize, this situation is a little different. It's not just a matter of Allie's having a healthy curiosity about what's going on around her. The fact is, she's a material witness to a suspicious death."

Leigh rubbed her arms briskly to warm herself. It didn't work. "Meaning?"

Maura was choosing her words with disturbing care. "Allison is a minor, and the testimony of a minor tends to get discounted in some quarters. Right now, that's good for us. Knowing Allie, it's important that you *not* frustrate her by withholding information, because if you do, we both know she'll try to find things out for herself. And we can't let her do that. Not this time."

Leigh agreed wholeheartedly. But she didn't like where the conversation was going.

"It's better for all concerned if no one outside the immediate family knows about Allie's 'special interest' in law enforcement. It may be too late, as close as all these women are to your mother, and as many people as saw her taking notes last night. But as much as you and your mother can downplay that, make her seem less of a threat than she actually is, the better. You get what I'm saying?"

Leigh nodded solemnly. "You mean that for a middle schooler, she's unusually observant, intelligent—"

"Yeah, that's the kind of thing you don't want to broadcast right now. In fact, just keep her away from the Floribundas altogether." Maura paused slightly. "If you can."

Leigh huffed out a rueful laugh. At least her friend understood the challenge. "Do you think Lucille's death could have been... foul play?"

Maura shrugged. It was the kind of official shrug that said she couldn't answer the question honestly, even if she wanted to. Leigh was used to that. But knowing what questions couldn't be answered never managed to stop her from asking them.

"We don't even have preliminary autopsy results yet," Maura said instead. "And it's doubtful they'll be conclusive. Toxicology will take weeks, maybe even months."

Leigh didn't how to respond to that. She hated uncertainty.

Maura's husband pulled their car up. He parked and got out to open the door to the back seat.

"The insurance policy in question is for a great deal of money," Maura said flatly.

Leigh shivered again. She could tell that Maura had more to tell her. Things she hadn't wanted Leigh to dwell on during the party.

"What I can tell you," Maura continued, "is that if we're dealing with insurance fraud, then our beneficiary has a major stake in making sure that Lucille's death looks like an accident, preferably criminal negligence. Murder would also do, so long as the finger of guilt doesn't point at him. But if he fails, he's looking at jail time."

Leigh's feet felt frozen to the ground. "I get that."

"Most likely he would need an accomplice, and the stakes are going to be high for that person as well."

Gerry took his sleeping son from his wife's arms and laid him in his car seat.

"I'm not saying that anybody involved necessarily has any reason to see Allie, or your mother, or you, as a threat to whatever game they're playing," Maura said firmly. "What I am saying is that they *could.* Which means the smartest thing for you all to do is to appear as unaware, as uninvolved, as uninterested, and therefore as nonthreatening as possible. Capiche?"

Leigh nodded mutely.

"I didn't want to get into this with Allie in the middle of her party, but I'll be happy to explain it to her myself if you'd like," Maura offered, moving to get into the passenger seat. Gerry had finished buckling in his son and was now behind the wheel. "She might take it better coming from me."

Leigh nodded again. "No question." *You should stop sticking your nose into this for your own safety* had never been a winning piece of motherly advice.

"I'll call her right after school tomorrow," Maura finished. Then she attempted a smile. "Stop looking like that, Koslow. Everything's going to be fine. Tell everybody I said thanks again and to have a nice night." She shut the car door, and then she and Gerry drove off with a wave.

Leigh remained standing at the edge of the drive. She could hear shouts and squeals of delight from the backyard, along with the happy yips of a corgi. It all sounded so wonderfully, blessedly normal.

But her limbs had no blood in them.

Chapter 17

Monday morning dawned bright, clear, and way too early. It was a gorgeous December morning, with sky the color of a robin's egg and frost shimmering on every blade and twig. Leigh watched out the window as Allison, Ethan, and Lenna hopped on the middle school bus. They were fortunate to have their own bus stop, right where the highway met the end of the private drive that connected the Harmons' house with the Marches' much larger farm. Leigh and Cara were no longer allowed to stand outside and wait with their offspring, however. That was entirely too "elementary school." Leigh still watched from the window, though. And Cara, who couldn't see that far from her own house, trusted that Leigh was watching.

Leigh took another drag of her pleasantly hot cup of coffee and managed a small smile. If she could excise anything and everything to do with Lucille Busby from her memory, her family had actually had a pretty stellar weekend. Ethan's laser-tag party on Friday night had been a blast. Frances had managed to get her house decorated authentically, and hundreds of paying guests of the regional Holiday House Tour had been delighted with it. And on Sunday, pretty much everyone in the family except for Leigh's Aunt Bess — who had given the kids her gifts early because a boyfriend had surprised her with a weekend Caribbean cruise — had enjoyed a scrumptious dinner and a laid-back evening of fun and frolic.

Her smile faded again. Unfortunately, the specter of Lucille Busby could *not* be excised. A looming threat still hung over them all, and it was going to hang there for an indeterminate amount of time. Never mind that Lydie and Mason's wedding was coming up and Christmas was in the air. She exhaled with frustration.

The school bus pulled away, and as Leigh gazed out over the front yard she caught sight of the green-plastic wrapping of the morning paper lying out in the grass. Warren was one of the last people in Pittsburgh who still paid for delivery of a printed newspaper, but this morning he'd had an early meeting and had left before the bundle arrived. Leigh put down her coffee and walked to the front closet. No sooner had she touched her coat than a corgi began circling her ankles. "No, Chewie," Leigh said regretfully. "I'm just going out for the paper. I'll be back in ten seconds. I'd love to trust you out front, but we both know you have zero control when it comes to squirrels."

The dog stared at her mournfully, his canine soul crushed. Leigh forced her eyes away and slipped outside. Chewie did guilt exceptionally well, the little beast.

She stomped across the crunchy grass and stooped to pick up the newspaper. Only then did she see the piece of trash. It was lying in the grass on the far side of a maple tree, which is why she hadn't seen it from the window. She frowned and walked towards it. Litter from the highway found its way into their yard all too often. People just opened their windows and tossed. It was infuriating.

She reached the mangled mess of paper, grabbed it by a corner with two fingers, and headed for the trash can. Half a dozen steps later, she stopped in her tracks. Warren's newspaper fell from her other hand. She stared.

The object she held was burned. Two-thirds of it was charred beyond recognition, and the rest was soggy with frozen dew. But Leigh could still tell what it was. The spiral binding was largely intact, and the cardboard cover wasn't so burned that you couldn't tell it was purple. The whole upper left corner still had white pages showing, and some of them even had scraps of writing on them. Familiar writing.

It was Allison's notebook.

Leigh's hands trembled. A large part of her wanted to drop the horror and simply start running. But she knew she had to think straight. *Evidence.* It's evidence. Be careful with it. She turned from the path to her trash bins and hurried back to the front door. Still holding the notebook with two fingers, she carried it inside and laid it on the table. Then she backed away from it, collapsed into a chair, and pulled a squiggling Chewie into her lap.

Allie's a material witness to a suspicious death, Maura's words tormented. *They could see her as a threat.*

Chewie snuffled out his grumpy sound, and Leigh realized she was holding him too tight. She relaxed her arms and let him down as a molten heat swelled in her chest. She stood again, scooped up the placemat on which she had dropped the remains of the notebook, and carried the whole mess to her bedroom. She hid it in a drawer, then walked back out and reclaimed her coffee cup.

"Nobody messes with my kids," she announced to the room with a growl, her face flaming. She downed the rest of her coffee, grabbed her keys, tossed Chewie an extra treat, and fired up her car.

Nobody.

"Where are you calling from, Koslow?" Maura's voice sounded from Leigh's cell phone. The detective sounded unnaturally calm. That was weird.

Leigh looked around. "The street outside my parents' house."

A beat passed. "Why are you there?"

Leigh thought about the question. "I don't know."

Maura heaved out a breath. "Listen, Leigh. I know you're freaked out right now. And you have every right to be. But I'm not sure this is a good time for you to be randomly driving around Pittsburgh."

"It's not random," Leigh defended. "I went to the school to make sure Allison was all right. Then I called and left the message for you. Then I called Warren and hung up before he could answer. Then I drove to the vet clinic because I always drive to the vet clinic. Then I remembered my dad doesn't go to work till noon on Mondays. Then you called back and the next thing I knew, I was here." She paused. "Okay, so maybe the last part was random."

"Maybe you shouldn't be driving anywhere right now."

"What else am I supposed to do?"

Leigh's nerves were on a hair trigger. She was antsy. She needed to move, to *do* something. There was no longer any question that Allison's notebook had been taken deliberately from its hiding place in Frances's secretary. Someone had seen Allison writing in it, become worried about what it might contain, snatched it, and removed it from the house. All that was bad enough. But taking that same notebook, burning it to the point of mutilation while leaving just enough intact to keep it recognizable, then tossing it where Leigh's family was sure to find it marked a whole new level of malice. Whoever did this was sending a message. A message to Allison, and to Leigh, and to anyone else who thought that what happened to Lucille might possibly be their business in any way, shape, or form.

Keep your mouth shut.

"I already told you," Maura said, again with the preternatural voice of calm. "You've reported what you found. Now you let me handle it. You don't need to do anything except what we already talked about. Keep Allie away from the Floribundas. All of them. She shouldn't even visit your parents' house, at least not right now. Go about your regular lives and keep Allie busy elsewhere. Act as if you've washed your hands of the whole business and have no interest in it. And if anything else troubling happens, call. Got it?"

Leigh's feet drummed on the floorboard of her car. "Yeah."

"Maybe you should go in and hang out with your dad for a while."

Leigh smirked. "How about my mom?"

Maura paused. "Spending time with your dad would be better."

Leigh almost laughed. She'd always known that Detective Maura Polanski possessed a professional "talk-you-off-the-ledge" demeanor for use on the job, but experiencing it personally was too bizarre. Leigh much preferred being sworn at.

"I need to burn off some energy," Leigh replied. "Call me if... Well, just call me."

"You know I will," Maura soothed. "And you keep in touch, too. I mean that, Koslow."

Leigh frowned to herself as Maura rang off with no signs of rancor. Being treated with such kid gloves could only mean the detective thought Leigh was on shaky emotional ground.

Well. If the shoe fits.

Leigh hopped out of her car. She really did need to burn off energy. She took in a lungful of the winter air, then set off running around the block. Since she was not, and never had been, someone who ran for exercise, the challenge was significant. The sidewalk was cracked and buckled by tree roots, she was out of breath before the first stop sign, and — most maddening of all — her body jiggled in all sorts of places it didn't used to jiggle. But she was antsy. And she was furious. And she ran all the way around the block and back to her parents' house despite the fact that by the finish line her ribcage was screaming with pain and she was gasping for air.

She sat down on the steps by her parents' back door and rested there until she caught her breath. Her body was exhausted, and she was no longer antsy. She was still furious, but her anger was no longer hot. She found that it was settling down to a more controlled, calculated simmer.

Excellent.

Leigh rose, then simultaneously knocked and turned the doorknob. "Dad?" she said. "It's me."

Randall Koslow would keep her head level. He always did, which is why in times of crisis her subconscious always led her to the vet clinic. But he should be home now, most likely sitting at the kitchen table enjoying the *Post-Gazette* with his morning coffee.

Leigh looked around the small kitchen. It was empty. But the rest of the house clearly was not. Multiple voices drifted in from the living room, loud and getting louder.

"Well, I don't trust her. She's still a newcomer!"

"What do we really know about her anyway?"

"Hear! Hear!"

Leigh froze in place. She'd know those scratchy, cranky, screechy voices anywhere. It was the Floribundas.

She crept silently to the doorway and paused again, listening. Her mother was talking now.

"Oh, fiddlesticks! There's no need to be turning on Olympia. She may be new to the chapter, but she's done nothing to make us doubt her loyalty to the cause. I think we should tell her. She's bound to find out anyway."

"Find out what, Frances?" Anna Marie's lofty voice purred sardonically. "I don't believe we've said what we're talking about. Have we?"

Jennie Ruth belched.

"Oh, let's stop pussyfooting," Virginia ordered. "We all know what we're talking about. We're just afraid to talk about it."

"Speak for yourself, dear," Delores piped up in her usual saccharine tone. "I believe that honesty purifies the soul. Why, even those with the darkest stains on their characters can benefit!"

"You!" Virginia bit back. "You wouldn't know honesty if it bit you on the bum. Paying cash under the table for—"

"Well, hello there," Randall greeted, making Leigh jump a foot. Her father had just emerged from the steps to the basement. He shut the door behind him with a clunk and smiled at her. The voices in the living room went quiet.

"Hi, Dad," Leigh returned. She was happy to see him, even if his timing was terrible. But it was clear that he would not be staying. He was wearing his coat and his car keys were in his hand. "Where are you off to?"

"Emergency surgery," he replied. "That old collie the Mackeys have always refused to spay has finally come down with a pyo, and it sounds like she can't wait." He threw a nod toward the living room and lowered his voice. "Glad you came by. Your mother could use some time alone with you."

Translation: I don't suppose you can get these whackadoodles out of my house before they drive my wife even more insane, please?

Leigh sent the appropriate unspoken message back.

I can try, but I'm no miracle worker.

Randall smiled at her as he walked out. "Thanks, Leigh."

No sooner did the back door close behind him than Frances's most annoying sing-song voice called to her from the living room. "Leigh, dear? Is that you? Would you like to come join us?"

No. No, I would not.

A vision floated through Leigh's head of her now twelve-year-old daughter, sitting behind a metal and plastic desk at her middle school, writing an essay on pony care or looking forward to getting a candy-cane gram from a secret admirer. Allison had no idea that at some point during the night, some deranged nutcase — quite possibly one of the deranged nutcases sitting in her grandmother's living room right now — had flung her scorched notebook out the window of a car in a cowardly attempt to intimidate the Harmon family into silence.

But Leigh knew it. And the more she thought about it, the angrier she got.

She stepped out into the living room. She made eye contact in turn with her mother, Virginia, Anna Marie, Delores, and Jennie Ruth. Then she sat down, crossed her legs, and smiled.

"Yes," she answered her mother smoothly. "Yes, I would like to join you."

Chapter 18

Back when Leigh's favorite soap operas were still on TV, she had an ongoing fantasy of being teleported into the middle of a tense romantic scene. She would be magically integrated into the cast so that the couple in question already knew her and were not surprised by her presence. Once there, she could fix *everything.* She would tell the guy straight out that the paternity test had been tampered with, and that the baby was his, not his brother's. And she would tell the woman that the guy never did have an affair with her supposed best friend — that it was all a plot dreamed up by her evil mother-in-law. Leigh could cut off two months' worth of plot angst at the knees and push those characters straight into their Happily Ever After.

It would be *so* gratifying.

Right now, sitting in her mother's living room in the midst of five-sevenths of the remaining Floribundas, she felt a giddy surge of power. An evil, giddy surge of power.

"So," she asked innocently. "What are you ladies up to today?"

The Floribundas exchanged some incredibly obvious guilty looks.

"They're helping me to pack up the decorations, of course," Frances answered, gesturing to the boxes and piles around them, which Leigh honestly hadn't noticed. "Yesterday we all agreed to rest up, although of course I did give the house a thorough cleaning. But today all the borrowed decorations have to come down so that we can return them to the Flying Maples as soon as possible."

"They were the ones who called 911 about the anthrax," Virginia said matter-of-factly.

"We know nothing of the kind," Frances argued. "That could have been anyone."

"It could have been. But it wasn't. It was them," Virginia insisted.

"Oh, will you stop with that?" Anna Marie snapped. She had stepped down to ordinary mascara this morning as opposed to false eyelashes, but her foundation was still so heavy it cracked at every wrinkle, and she wore the same ancient, flip-style wig. "If the Flying Maples really wanted the tour to be a failure, why would they loan us all these lovely decorations in the first place? If you ask me, those women saved our skin!"

Virginia, Delores, and Jennie Ruth all gasped in affronted horror.

"I daresay we could have managed," Delores proposed primly. "The house was received wonderfully well. Everyone has said so! There were only a handful of people still here when Lucille passed, and they have no idea how close they came to being poisoned themselves."

Frances dropped the macramé reindeer she was holding. Its bells tinkled as it slid off her lap and onto the floor. Frances hastily scooped it back up again, acting as if nothing had happened, but her face was visibly paler.

Leigh's own cheeks grew hot. "When I came in earlier," she said conversationally, picking up a piece of bubble wrap and enfolding a tacky gold candle trimmed with fake snow and plastic holly, "it sounded like you were trying to decide whether or not to tell Olympia that Lucille wanted to defraud her insurance company."

She kept her eyes up, even as she wrapped the candle. Noting the women's reactions was important.

Jennie Ruth's response was as expected, which meant the usual: her eyes were blank and her mouth hung open. From the rest of them Leigh expected various degrees of panic. And from one of them — she dared to hope — a flash of guilt.

She should have known better. The Floribundas never made anything easy.

Virginia's horse face practically shone with ghoulish delight. Leigh could see the same thrill in Delores's china-doll visage, but at least Delores attempted to hide it. And although Anna Marie's face didn't change much — perhaps due to excessive Botox treatments — her blue eyes sparkled with obvious interest.

Leigh saw no guilt anywhere.

"Oh, my," Virginia said with a rather girlish giggle. "Are we being frank, then? My word, Frances, I didn't know you had such loose lips!"

"Said the pot to the kettle!" Frances retorted. She threw her daughter one of her most severe disapproving looks, but it had the opposite effect than intended. Leigh was only too happy to see her mother get her mojo back.

"Well, does Olympia already know too, then?" Anna Marie asked, sounding annoyed. "Perhaps we're wasting our time with all this pussyfooting."

"No," Frances replied confidently. "Olympia has no idea of Lucille's… plans. I'm sure of that. But as I said before, she'd bound to find out soon. It's going to wind up being part of the investigation."

"Not necessarily," Anna Marie hypothesized. There were decorations all around her, but she wasn't doing a thing. Sitting in the wing chair in her flaxen wig, shiny gold-threaded woolen sweater, and bright red slacks, she looked like a blond Cleopatra again. "There wouldn't be an investigation at all if Little Bobby wasn't such a blooming idiot."

Murmurs and tut-tuts of agreement sounded from all around.

"I mean *honestly*," Anna Marie went on, "it's not that what Lucille suggested wasn't tempting, you have to admit. Lord knows Eugene and I could always use a little extra. But even if you weren't worried about sending your soul straight to hell, there's still the likes of Bobby to deal with. I wouldn't trust that imbecile to strangle a chicken!"

"Mortal sin!" Jennie Ruth bellowed.

Evidently, Leigh was not the only one who was surprised to hear her speak, because the other women all turned and looked at her for a moment. Nonplussed, Jennie Ruth immediately shrank back in her chair.

"Well, I'm Presbyterian myself," Virginia contributed, wrapping up a plastic snowman lamp, "but you do have to ask yourself, how wrong is it if the party in question *wants* to go?"

"One might consider it a kindness!" Delores chimed in, folding her hands angelically beneath her chin. "A service to help a dear friend's last wish come true, to provide for the financial security of her beloved child. And yet, if you *did* help her, the law would have every right to throw you in a cell with an ax murderer and take away your underwear."

The women all blanched.

Virginia cleared her throat. "Yes, well. Be that as it may, I still don't think it's such a horrible crime. Not that I want any part of it, mind you," she clarified, looking at Leigh. "I'm just saying nobody loses, really."

"The insurance company loses," Frances pointed out. "A swindle is a swindle, Virginia."

Virginia scoffed. "Insurance companies make plenty of money. You're not getting me to feel sorry for them. Why, they'll cover Harry's little blue pills without a peep, but when I want to try the latest female enhancement—"

"Camptown ladies sing this song, doo-da, doo-da!" Delores sang loudly, putting her fingers in her ears. She shot a look at Jennie Ruth, and the other woman immediately smashed her palms over her own ears.

"Oh, for heaven's sake," Frances said peevishly. "Do hush up about that, Virginia. We've all heard it before. This is a serious matter!"

Virginia hushed up, and Delores stopped singing. Cautiously both Delores and Jennie Ruth uncovered their ears.

Virginia quit was she was doing and studied at each of their faces in turn. "Indeed it is," she said in a whisper, her gray eyes twinkling mischievously. "Come on, ladies. 'Fess up. Somebody here helped Bobby. Who was it?"

Leigh held her breath. She watched the other women's faces carefully, but much to her annoyance, now they *all* looked guilty.

"Oh, for Pete's sake, Virginia," Anna Marie said with a laugh. "If one of us *did* do something illegal, we're certainly not going to admit it now! Why would we?"

"But I want to know!" Virginia replied, whining like a child. "I can't stand it! Shouldn't we stick together?"

"There is no *together!*" Frances said hotly. "Not in this!"

"Perhaps it was Sue," Delores suggested pleasantly. "She's always had a strong stomach."

Virginia shook her head. "Sue was laid up all weekend. Her stomach may be strong, but her bowels have got a virus something terrible. I went over this morning to see if she could come and help out, and as soon as I stepped through the door I could smell—"

"Virginia, dear," Frances interrupted. "We do not need the details of Sue's illness. She clearly had nothing to do with this."

"I was surprised Lucille even asked her," Anna Marie mused. "Sue never could stand Bobby. She was always telling Lucille she should cut him out of her will altogether and leave everything to the American Legion."

"Ladies, please," Frances interrupted. "I don't believe we should be discussing anything amongst ourselves that we do not also wish to share with the police."

"Wish to share?" Anna Marie repeated. "Don't talk nonsense, Frances. Why would we want to help the police? It's nothing to do with me."

Virginia also looked at Frances with alarm. "Of course not! If the police knew what Lucille was planning, they'd tell the insurance company. And then Bobby would get no money at all!"

Leigh's pulse rate picked up. Her mother was in a bind. If Frances admitted to having spilled the beans already, she'd be pilloried. But if she didn't admit it, someone might be motivated to prevent its happening in the future.

"Oh, I'm certain that none of *us* would say anything," Delores announced. "Certainly we wouldn't want to risk keeping our dear friend's dying wish from coming to fruition, would we? That would be so horribly self-serving! And none of us are in the slightest bit selfish, I'm sure."

Anna Marie scoffed. "Speak for yourself. You won't see me running to the police, but I'm not sticking my neck out just so somebody else can get a windfall, either. Particularly not some idiot like Bobby. Has anyone thought that maybe Lucille *did* just die of a heart attack or something?"

"Oh, dear, no!" Virginia cried, sounding scandalized. "That would be terrible! She would be devastated."

Delores shook her head vigorously. "Oh, no, her funeral plans are far too costly for that."

Leigh did a double take. "Funeral plans?"

Delores's pale eyes lit up with enthusiasm. "Such an event it will be! And *so* Lucille. Her casket will be carried to the cemetery by a horse and carriage."

"Black horses!" Jennie Ruth insisted.

"Black horses," Delores repeated happily. "Bagpipes will be played by men in black-watch tartan kilts. And the burying is to be done by hand, with shovels. Preferably in the rain."

Leigh would wish she hadn't asked, but the change in subject did seem to have gotten her mother out of the hot seat.

"That's never going to happen," Anna Marie said sourly. "How's Bobby going to pay for all that when there's no guarantee he'll get the insurance money right away, if at all? I kept asking Lucille, what's he supposed to do, keep her on ice?"

Virginia frowned. "Don't be such a party-pooper, Anna Marie. I'm sure Lucille made some sort of arrangement. She knew how much we were looking forward to her funeral."

Leigh felt a sudden, intense need to go outside and stand in the sunshine.

"Well, likely nobody's going to get any money if goody-goody Frances here decides to flap her lips to the fuzz," Anna Marie pointed out.

Whoops.

All eyes had turned back to Frances, and Leigh could tell from the russet tone rising in her mother's cheeks that righteousness was about to triumph over self-preservation.

"My mother didn't have to say a word," Leigh lied, thinking quickly. "I hate to burst your bubbles, but the police and the insurance company both are already onto Lucille."

Five sets of eyes moved instantly to Leigh.

"There's a thing in the industry called flagging," she rattled on, pulling words out of wherever in her anatomy she could reach them. "Lucille already collected once on an accidental death policy, and that puts her in a whole different category of suspicion when it comes to being involved in another one. They've been watching Lucille from the get-go, and working with the police to look for evidence of fraud. It's a good thing none of you are involved, because if Bobby tries to collect, he *is* going to get caught. The best thing for him to do would be to just let it drop."

None of the women moved. The room went completely silent. Leigh wished she could look at their faces, but she was too afraid to let them read hers. She had always been a lousy liar. She hoped that none of the Floribundas had ever been in the insurance business.

"How do you know all this?" Anna Marie asked suspiciously.

Leigh shrugged. "I know a lot of police stuff. But the insurance thing is common knowledge, really." Oh, she was *so* going to burn!

"Your family does seem terribly cozy with the police force around here," Virginia noted, her voice assuming a snide tone. "Your daughter seems interested in police work, as well. Such a curious little dear, she is!"

Stay cool.

"Allison?" Leigh said offhandedly, putting every ounce of willpower into her acting skills. "She did get a little overexcited on Saturday, asking all those silly questions. But you know how girls are at that age. One day it's one thing, the next day it's something else. I was afraid that Lucille's death had really upset her, but yesterday she didn't even mention it. All she cared about was her birthday party! And this morning she went off to school all obsessed over some fundraiser things the student council is putting on." She forced out a chuckle. "Can't keep that girl focused on anything more than five minutes these days."

Leigh avoided looking directly at her mother. She wasn't worried about Frances giving her away, even if every word she'd just spoken was a lie. Whether Frances approved or not, she was sharp enough to understand what Leigh was doing. But if Leigh were forced to face her mother's three-alarm scowl, her own involuntary cringe would give them both away.

"It could be anemia," Virginia diagnosed. "Particularly if the poor girl's monthlies are heavy. You should make her eat more red meat. She's not one of those vegetarians, is she?"

Leigh had no idea how the conversation had moved from insurance fraud to vegetarianism, but she was all for it. "Actually, she's been making noise lately about wanting to 'go veg.' But I'm not sure it's a good idea. What do you think?"

Virginia obliged by rattling off various organs that could suffer permanent damage from lack of protein, and Leigh's mind checked out. The other Floribundas, who showed an equal lack of interest in the topic, began busying themselves with the packing again. All except Anna Marie, who analyzed lint on her clothing and studied the weather through the side window.

"And what about you?"

Leigh realized after a few seconds of silence that Virginia was asking her a question.

"Do you find that eating yogurt stabilizes the pH in your lady parts?"

Mercifully, the doorbell rang. Leigh jumped to answer it, but before she could turn the knob Olympia was already entering.

"Hello, there!" the tall woman said merrily, peeking around the door. "Sorry I'm late. But I brought muffins!"

Leigh glanced back at the other Floribundas. Although they were smiling in greeting, their spines had stiffened. Leigh supposed it made sense that they wouldn't completely trust Olympia, since they had all known each other for decades while their newest president had only been around a few months.

Olympia stepped into the dining room and placed her tote bag on the table. Leigh watched as, ever so briefly, Olympia's gaze rested on Lucille's empty chair. A dark look — sadness? irritation? annoyance? grief? — flashed across her features before she forcibly averted her eyes. When she turned back to the Floribundas, she made an attempt at a warm smile.

"I know this has been difficult for everyone," she said as if making a rehearsed speech. "Clearly you were all very close to Lucille, and I'm sure her passing came as a shock. Not knowing her as well as all of you did, I haven't been affected quite as deeply, so I've taken it on myself to smooth over the situation."

The other Floribundas exchanged suspicious glances. "Smooth over?" Anna Marie asked. "Smooth over what, exactly?"

Olympia blinked at her. "Why, the PR debacle, of course!" she replied with surprise. "Lucille's death during the event has been an absolute nightmare of negative publicity for the Holiday House Tour. Or at least it could have been, if not handled properly!"

"Oh, right," Virginia said with disinterest. "I guess we didn't really think about that."

Olympia stared at them all blankly for another second. "Of course not. You're still grieving. That's why I handled it. I was on the phone with the Regional Coordinator and the committee chair all day yesterday, I've smoothed things over with both of the women who were punching tickets on the porch, and I've personally reached out to all the guests we had to excuse from the house early — at least all the ones I could locate. And I've deflected several potential issues with reporters."

She leaned onto the arm of the couch and smiled broadly, exposing her prominent front teeth. "So... you're welcome!" She threw her palms up at her sides and cocked her head endearingly.

The Floribundas did not seem endeared. Leigh found their reaction odd, until she realized that Olympia lied so often none of them had any way of knowing whether she'd actually done those things.

"That's wonderful, Olympia, thank you," Frances said, in the same voice she might use to praise a young grandchild for a stick-figure drawing. "You're right, of course. We've not been thinking of that sort of thing. But it is very important for the reputation of the chapter."

"Hear, hear!" Virginia agreed. "Were the ticket sales good?"

"Oh, they were marvelous!" Olympia crowed. "The best in the whole history of the tour!"

The women clearly wanted to believe that.

"Don't you all worry about a thing," Olympia continued. "I can continue to handle the regionals and the media. You take as much time as you need to recover. I'm an emotional rock. Always have been, you know. Things like this can cripple some people, but not me! Just rolls right off my back."

Jennie Ruth harrumphed.

"Seems to me you were flat *on* your back for a while there," Anna Marie said with a smirk.

Olympia's smile faded. "If you are referring to my… episode, I assure you that was a medical issue. I heard Leigh calling for me and I tried to move too quickly. It had nothing to do with emotions."

"Why, of course not, dear," Delores agreed. "I'm sure you didn't even catch a glimpse of Lucille's lifeless corpse before going down."

"I've seen lots of dead bodies," Virginia commented. "When I was in high school, I used to do housecleaning up at the old funeral home by the chocolate factory. But Harry, now, he's a sheep in wolf's clothing. Talk about passing out at the sight of blood — that man can't stand a paper cut. He was all out of joint about Lucille dying, wringing his hands over whether that booze he put in the punch could have pushed her over the edge. I told him that was hogswazzle. We all know Lucille drank gin like a fish!"

"Lucille always did enjoy a little nip before bed," Delores said fondly. "But how good of Harry to be concerned! After all, I do believe she'd cut back lately. And the sicker one gets, you know, the more harmful even small amounts of alcohol can be."

Virginia threw Delores a glare.

"My Melvin has nerves of steel, but then that's to be expected in a doctor," Olympia said proudly. "Nothing gets to him. He deals with life and death on a daily basis, you know."

"Oh, how exciting!" Delores cooed. "I wasn't aware that one could die of hemorrhoids."

"My husband is a colorectal surgeon," Olympia clarified icily. "He saves lives on an hourly basis. He has been awarded special honors by the Mayo Clinic and he personally pulled the bullet out of President Reagan after the assassination attempt!"

Leigh had been having enough trouble trying to read all the women's faces before; adding Olympia to the mix was giving her whiplash. The Floribunda president was hopelessly confounding. She had made little effort to conceal her irritation with her husband at the house tour, yet now she spoke of him as if he were a saint. And why was she praising his stoicism, of all things, when Melvin was one of the few people present who seemed genuinely saddened by Lucille's passing? Surely Olympia could think of something nice to say about the man that wasn't total hogwash!

"Well, I daresay my Harry hasn't lost any sleep over Lucille's going to a better place," Virginia said loudly, ignoring Olympia's outburst and steering the conversation back to her own husband. "He knew she was ready to go. But he is worried that he'll get in trouble, if not for the booze, then for the mistletoe." Virginia's voice lowered. "And I'm a little worried about that too, to tell the truth. He admitted to the police about hanging a sprig of the stuff up over the punch bowl. He didn't think a thing about it at the time, but Lord, it looks bad. What if some of it *did* drop off in Lucille's punch?"

Leigh shot a glance at her mother. Frances's complexion was ashen again.

Dammit!

"There's no way," Leigh said quickly. "Like Lydie said, only one berry fell, and we saw it immediately. You all drank the punch. It wasn't crystal clear because of the cider, but it wasn't so murky you couldn't see through it."

Delores spoke in her most comforting tone. "Of course! And how fortunate for all of us, since *hundreds* of people could have been poisoned to death otherwise. But truly, no one could blame that little girl if she accidentally ladled out one leaf or a twig, could they? My, no. And one could only expect that afterwards, the sweet child might be too frightened for herself to admit such a thing." The diabolically evil angel face smiled smugly.

"Excuse me," Frances blurted, putting aside whatever she was wrapping and hastening to her feet. She turned her back on the women, hid her face with her hands, and escaped up the stairs.

Leigh stared daggers. "No mistletoe was served in the punch," she said acidly. "My niece may be young, but she's not an idiot. Nor is she a coward." She got to her feet. Lenna did, in fact, have some issues where bravery was concerned, but the wagons had circled and Leigh's gun was drawn. She took two steps after her mother, then turned around. "You know, some people say things that are mean and upsetting on purpose, but instead of taking responsibility for the hurt they cause, they pretend they meant to say nice things." She glared straight at Delores. "Now *that's* being a coward."

She turned again and started up the stairs. No sounds followed her from the living room as she made her way to the master bedroom and shut the door behind her. Frances was sitting on her bed, staring forlornly at the wall. Leigh sat down next to her. "I punched Delores in the face," she reported. "You want me to beat up the rest of them?"

To her delight, Frances actually smiled. "No, dear," she replied. "That won't be necessary. I'm fine."

"No, you're not," Leigh said with a sigh. "Having Lucille pass away so unexpectedly, here in your house, was terrible for everyone. But there's obviously something else going on with you. You want to tell me about it?"

"Heavens, no," Frances said.

Leigh wasn't sure how to respond to that. "Okay," she said finally. "But you should get it off your chest somehow."

Frances shook her head. "I appreciate your concern. But talking won't help anything. It's… in the past. I just want this investigation to be over with." She stood up. "I don't know what came over me, really. I should go back downstairs."

Leigh felt the sting of failure as her mother stepped away.

"By the way, what was all that nonsense about Allison?" Frances asked, turning around.

Leigh decided to explain as little as she could. No way was she going to distress her mother further over the charred notebook. "Maura said that the less interested Allison seems to be in this whole thing, the less worried anyone scheming in insurance fraud might be about her note-taking."

Frances drew in a sharp breath. "None of the Floribundas would hurt a child!" she said adamantly.

Leigh would love to share her mother's confidence. "Virginia said something about our family being cozy with the police. How much do the Floribundas know about my relationship with Maura?"

Frances looked troubled again. "I mentioned to Virginia yesterday that the case had been handed over to the county detectives. I also mentioned that the detective we spoke with was your friend. I... I thought everyone would consider that comforting. Why? Does it matter?"

Leigh blew out a breath. "I suppose they would have found out anyway."

So, given Virginia's mouth, any or all of the Floribundas could have known by last night that Allison had a direct connection with the detective investigating the case. The question was, would knowing that fact make a guilty party more likely to threaten Allison... or less? Leigh's brain began to hurt.

"You needn't worry about the Floribundas," Frances insisted. "As I've said before, I've known these women for decades, and I can assure you that none of them is completely morally bankrupt. I know they've become a bit... rough around the edges over the years, but they do all still care deeply about the beautification of the community. And that is becoming an increasingly rare trait in younger women today."

Leigh prepared herself for another "no one under sixty considers it their civic duty to weed and seed the medians" lecture, but to her surprise, none came. Instead, Frances stepped over to the vanity and looked in the mirror. She picked up a tissue and dabbed at her eyes.

"I mean it when I say that I appreciate your concern," she said in a milder voice. "It's nice to know you care about your dear old mother. But you really shouldn't worry about me. I'll be fine."

Leigh watched as Frances reapplied her favorite orange lipstick. A mother's protectiveness for her children never stopped, did it? Reversing the flow must seem unnatural. Leigh felt a wave of sympathy. She also felt a long-standing twinge of guilt. "Listen, Mom. Now that Lucille is gone, there's something I need to apologize for. I lied to you."

Frances put down the tube of lipstick and turned around. She looked hurt. "Lied to me?"

Leigh nodded. "Lucille never liked me, you know. She always said I had a smart mouth and was too much of a tomboy. When Warren and I got married she did send us a toaster. But it was *her* toaster. The surface was greasy, the cord was frayed, and burnt crumbs were falling out of it. I don't even know if it worked. I was afraid to plug it in." She held her breath. "Long story short, Lucille was right. I never sent the damn thank-you note."

Frances grabbed a tissue to blot her lipstick, then inspected her work in the mirror. The reflection showed her newly orange mouth twitching with a grin.

"I know that, dear," she replied.

Chapter 19

Leigh slipped out of her parents' house the back way while Frances returned to her guests in the living room. Standing outside in the cool December sunshine, Leigh felt relieved to have escaped the lion's den. But with visions of Allison's charred notebook still flashing behind her eyes, she remained anxious. She fidgeted with her car keys as she remembered Maura's most recent instructions. *Let me handle it. Keep Allie away from the Floribundas. Act as if you've washed your hands of the whole business and have no interest in it.*

Leigh winced. She'd already screwed up the third one, hadn't she? But keeping Allison safe was all that mattered. She looked at her watch. She was supposed to be working at home today, getting a jumpstart on a new project. Forget that! Warren was supposed to be home around two — she would be nice and let him enjoy a few more hours of productivity before she collapsed in his arms in a heap of raw nerves. The two of them would have just enough time to rally and put on brave faces before Allison stepped off the bus after school and they locked her in her room forever. And in the meantime?

Inspiration dawned. In the meantime, she would find out once and for all what the heck was bothering her mother.

She strode across the yard to Lydie's back door and knocked. Her aunt appeared within seconds, wearing a shimmering fuchsia silk bathrobe and holding a steaming cup of tea. "Well, hello," Lydie greeted.

"Hello," Leigh returned with a grin. Her aunt had never been one to sleep late. She'd also never been a "fuchsia silk" kind of woman. "Nice robe."

Lydie grinned back. "Thanks. It's new."

Leigh didn't bother to ask how, why, or from whom she'd gotten it.

Lydie didn't bother to tell her. "Come in and have some tea with me. I just made a whole pot of herbal."

Leigh accepted the invitation and enjoyed the smooth, amber tea, which tasted of pumpkin-pie spice. Then she told her aunt straight out about finding Allison's burnt notebook on the lawn. "I couldn't bring myself to tell Mom about it," she explained. "She's determined to believe that none of the Floribundas is actually dangerous, even though she's not at all sure they wouldn't stoop to assisted suicide and insurance fraud! But you know how hyperprotective she is of the grandkids — catch her in the right moment, and she'll go apoplectic over a hangnail. And right now, with her nerves so completely strung out like this…" Leigh rubbed her face with her hands. "If she *did* get worried about Allison, I have no idea how she'd react. If she flipped out on the Floribundas, and one of them really *is* pathological, God only knows…"

"I see your point," Lydie said with concern. "Her nerves are most definitely strung out. That is true."

Leigh removed her hands from her face. "Potato salad," she said grimly. "Aunt Lydie… You've got to tell me! What the hell does potato salad have to do with any of this?"

Lydie sighed. "It's all in her mind, Leigh. But that doesn't make it any easier to get over."

Leigh waited.

"Your mother and I threw a party on our sixteenth birthday," Lydie began finally, sounding tired of the topic with her first sentence. "It was my idea. I was the one who pushed for it. I wanted to invite a bunch of our friends from school to have a cookout at the house. We didn't have much of a yard, but it was big enough to gather and play some music and dance on the patio, and we figured people could spill around to the front porch, too. Neither of us were dating yet, exactly, but there were boys that Frances and I had our eyes on, and we desperately wanted them to come. We were afraid your grandparents wouldn't allow it, but they did, as long as we kept the party outdoors and paid for all the food and made sure that everyone behaved themselves and that everything was cleaned up afterwards."

Leigh smiled to herself. Her Grandma and Grandpa Morton had been a little on the strict side. She could imagine that gaining permission for such a party would be a coup. Especially since the couple's wild-child older daughter Bess had already thoroughly besmirched her own reputation.

"So we got busy and sold some baked goods and did some

gardening for people and saved enough money to buy the food and decorations." Lydie's eyes began to sparkle as she talked. "It was August, but we had the maple tree strung up with Christmas lights and streamers and giant paper flowers, and we bought fancy invitations and mailed them. It was a magical time, no doubt about that. It was a treat just getting ready for it."

The lights in her eyes faded a little. "The day before the party, Frances came down with the sniffles. Nothing serious, just a summer cold. She was upset because her nose was all red and she wanted to look her prettiest for Gary Tarkinton, but otherwise she felt okay. So we finished off the cooking and the baking and such, and before we knew it, the party had started."

Leigh tried to picture Frances at sixteen, all dolled up and ready to flirt with some guy who wasn't Randall, but the image wouldn't come. Of course, she couldn't imagine her mother flirting with her father, either.

"Everything went beautifully for most of the day," Lydie explained. "The food was all very good, and everyone had a fun time. The weather was cloudy, and it sprinkled on and off, but that wasn't a problem until right near the end. Then it really began to rain, and that's when the trouble started."

"*Rain* ruined your party?" Leigh asked skeptically.

"Of course not. We were teenagers. And it wasn't a storm, just rain. Your grandpa already told us we weren't allowed to move the party into the house, though, so we had collected some umbrellas and tarps just in case. We held them over us like tents, which was kind of fun. Although some people just ran around and got wet anyway."

The last vestiges of pleasure on Lydie's face slipped away. "But that's when people started getting sick. The boy your mother liked, Gary, was the first one it hit. He threw up all over himself. And then it was like a plague of Egypt. Everyone was dizzy, and sick, and faint. Poor Gary was so bad we had to call his parents, and later they called a doctor. Everyone else went home, and some of their parents called doctors, too."

"That must have been horrible," Leigh commiserated. "Did everyone get sick?"

"No, although it seemed like it at the time," Lydie answered. "I suppose for most of them it was a touch of hypochondria. In truth, there were twenty-some-odd people at the party, and only four got really sick, with maybe half a dozen more complaining of some symptom or other. Frances and I didn't feel sick at all, but we both felt like we could have died, just the same. We had no idea what could have happened."

Leigh could imagine the nightmare. "The potato salad?" she asked.

Lydie nodded gravely. "The doctor who treated Gary came over to the house the next day and was asking all sorts of questions. He said it was food poisoning. When we told him what we'd served he said that most likely it was the potato salad, and Frances nearly dropped to her knees, because she'd made that all by herself. Your grandma argued about it — she told the doctor that all the ingredients were fresh, and that even though the bowl did sit out a while, it had been refrigerated all morning and it wasn't that hot a day. But when the doctor saw that Frances had a cold, he asked her if she'd been sneezing, and of course she had been. And he went on and on about how bacteria from your nose can get into the food and then pretty soon you're poisoning the whole neighborhood."

Lydie's dark eyes flashed fire. "He wasn't the least bit tactful with his words, either. And your mother was absolutely beside herself. She went straight to her room and cried for I don't know how long."

"That's awful," Leigh agreed, knowing she would feel just as bad. "Poor Mom."

"It got worse," Lydie continued. "Gary was quite ill. Much worse than the others. And naturally that horrible doctor reported his theory to Gary's family. So when Gary got back to school and Frances ran up to him all eager to make sure he was feeling better, the first thing he did was tag her with a nasty nickname."

Oh, no.

"Filthy Francie," Lydie recalled with bitterness. "Filthy, filthy Francie. Sneezing in the potato salad, poisoning half the school. He was hateful. Truly hateful. As if she'd done it to him on purpose! How either of us could ever have thought that boy had a shred of decency in him is beyond me. He made your mother's life a living hell for the rest of high school. That horrible nickname stuck. Her embarrassment became a running joke. People would look at her in horror every time she'd offer to share her lunch or split a soda. God forbid she should sneeze in class — all the boys would keel over and play dead!"

"That's so mean," Leigh murmured. She felt a twinge of nausea as she imagined her mother on her hands and knees in a hazmat suit, scrubbing the kitchen floor with industrial-grade cleansers. The whole OCD cleaning thing… holy hell, was that how it started?

"It was horribly mean, especially considering your mother was plenty traumatized by what happened even before that," Lydie replied. "It took her a very long time to get over it. It took years before she felt comfortable cooking for anyone outside the family. And she never has really enjoyed the responsibilities of being a hostess, as proud as she is of her spotless house. It's just plain sad. And now, *this*…" Lydie's face turned red. "Well, it makes me so mad I could spit, frankly."

Leigh knew the feeling. She was racking up more and more things to be angry about, and it was doing nothing for her Christmas spirit.

"So you can understand, now," Lydie finished, "why your mother has been acting so strangely. I know it seems over the top, but the mere suggestion that Lucille was poisoned to death *in her house* has unleashed so many bad memories that her conscience has practically come unhinged. I've talked till I'm blue in the face trying to make her see that the two events aren't connected. That it's not her fault whether Lucille was poisoned intentionally, accidentally, or not at all. But nothing I've said has made one iota of difference."

"Oh, my," Leigh mumbled. "That's not good. If she won't listen to you, she sure as heck won't listen to me. Even if she is talking to me more, now."

Lydie's eyebrows lifted curiously. "Talking to you more, now?"

Leigh nodded. "I guess because… well, because she's not talking to you as much. She's been calling me more."

"I didn't realize," Lydie said, looking thoughtful.

"So what else can we do?" Leigh asked. "How can we get through to her?"

Lydie shook her head. "I don't know, honey. Your father's tried too, of course, but she won't listen to him either. They didn't meet until years after all this happened, but as you can imagine, hearing the story didn't faze your father in the slightest — he shrugged and told her it didn't sound like any big deal to him, that it could have happened to anyone and that she shouldn't care what Gary said because he sounded like a jerk anyway." Lydie smiled a little. "I daresay that your father's cavalier attitude was a big part of what attracted her to him."

Leigh contemplated the thought. How interesting. "But he can't get through to her now?"

"It's tough to talk someone out of feeling guilty," Lydie replied. "Besides which, over the years your mother has realized that your father doesn't belabor that emotion under any circumstances. So I suppose she's discounted his opinion."

Leigh smiled. Feeling guilty, in her father's opinion, was a waste of energy. If you did something wrong, you made amends the best you could, and then you moved on.

Must be nice.

"There must be something we can do!" Leigh insisted.

Lydie said nothing for a moment. She took a long drag on her tea, then set down the mug. "I'm going to be honest with you, Leigh. I'm worried about your mother, and I've tried to do the best I can for her. But I'm tired."

Leigh looked up at her aunt with surprise. She couldn't remember the word "tired" ever having passed Lydie's lips before. Her aunt was like the Energizer bunny.

"I've given your mother plenty of time to come around where Mason is concerned," Lydie went on. "But the wedding is almost here. And she still hasn't accepted him."

Oh, Leigh thought sadly. *That* kind of tired.

"And quite frankly, I'm fed up," Lydie confirmed, a steely edge entering her voice. "There's no reason I should have to choose between my sister and my husband, but Frances is making me do it. She can pretend to accept him, but she's a lousy pretender. She still thinks I'm making a mistake, and we both know that's the bottom line. I'm tired of trying to change her mind and failing. She's wrong about Mason, but if she can't see that, I don't know what else can give. Mason has nothing to apologize to Frances for — any sins he ever committed were against me, and if I've forgiven him, what business is it of hers? Mason has done everything he can to make things right. He's been so patient with her! He bears no ill will. How much longer am I supposed to stand by and allow her to treat him like he's practically less than human?" Hurt warred with anger in

Lydie's eyes.

"No one could blame you for losing patience with her," Leigh said softly. "I wish there was something I could do."

Lydie rose abruptly and poured herself another cup of tea. "You're already doing it," she said more positively. "You've accepted Mason as a member of the family."

"He's always been a member of the family," Leigh stated. Then her tone turned teasing. "He's just staking out new territory now. Someone might want to inform Harry Delvecchio, though. Lenna said he was quite persistent in his attentions to you the other day. She said he even nabbed you on the lips under his traveling mistletoe."

Lydie grimaced. "Oh, that dreadful man! I can't believe he was pestering *me!*"

Leigh studied her aunt's incredulous expression with amusement. Had Lydie not looked in a mirror since Mason came back into her life?

"I mean, he was flirting with women your age, for heaven's sake!" Lydie continued, returning to her chair. Somewhere in the house a door opened, then closed with a thud. "So why was he spending so much effort hanging his foolish mistletoe over my head? Hanging around the kitchen acting like he was some fine—"

"Who's this?" Mason asked, walking into the kitchen carrying a bag of groceries and a cup of takeout coffee.

"Nobody," Lydie answered, burying her face in her mug.

Mason's eyes slid sideways to Leigh. *Like I believe that,* his gaze said with humor. He began to put away the groceries. "Are you talking about something that would upset me?" he asked Lydie casually.

"Yes," she answered without hesitation. "But I can handle such things on my own, Mason. I've been doing it for a very long time now and I can manage just fine, thank you."

Mason finished his unpacking and sat down. "You've been doing everything for yourself for a very long time," he replied. "All the more reason you should let me take a little of the load off your shoulders."

Lydie's dark eyes sparkled at him. "You can clean out the gutters."

Mason laughed. He leaned over and kissed her on the cheek.

"Anytime you want, Mrs. Dublin."

Leigh wished her mother could see the two of them like this. But naturally, whenever Frances was around, all three of them were wound up tight as drums.

"I've got to get dressed," Lydie announced, rising again. She threw a look at Leigh. "Entertaining men in my nightclothes! Really, how scandalous!"

Leigh grinned as Lydie departed. Her aunt's new outlook on life was such a joy to witness.

"So, what brings you over?" Mason asked Leigh. "Is your mother doing any better?"

He bears no ill will, Lydie had said. Clearly, it was true. Leigh brought Mason up to date on the situation, grateful for another sounding board. The threat to Allison continued to eat away at her stomach lining, and she wasn't sure how much longer she could last before ruining Warren's day.

Mason listened attentively, but when she was finished, he shook his head in disbelief. "I don't know, kid. I can't see any of those women going through with a scheme like that. The insurance fraud, I mean."

Leigh frowned. The way he said "those women" sounded suspiciously sexist. "Why not?"

He shook his head again. "Wrong profile. It's too high risk. None of those ladies are on the brink of financial ruin, are they? Are they really in a place where they're willing to risk jail time for a windfall? Besides which, they're not even looking at an instant payout. They'd have to wait years to be safe, and waiting years is a tough enough sell for people in my age bracket. Besides which, the scheme is a long shot at best, and even then it all depends on her son, who doesn't strike me as particularly dependable."

Leigh felt guilty for doubting Mason. Sad to say, the man did have some experience with criminal psychology.

"Now, if they're irrational, then anything's possible," he admitted. "I don't know the women. But Lydie seems to think they've still got all their marbles, even if they are odd."

Leigh wished she could be as sure of that. But in *her* experience with criminal psychology, people who appeared to have all their marbles could and did do some pretty horrifying things.

"It's the son I don't get," Mason mused, scratching his bristly chin as he leaned back in his chair. "The man clearly has no idea how to run a clean fraud operation."

Leigh couldn't help but smirk at the note of smug superiority in his voice. "Oh?"

Mason's eyes flickered over to hers. She tried to stop smirking, but she wasn't quick enough. He frowned. "You want my opinion or not?"

She stifled herself. "Yes. Please. Sorry."

He grumbled. "If the son arranged with a third party to give Lucille a fatal overdose of something, with the idea being that he would blame it on the assistant later, why the hell would he barge into your mother's house and accuse the assistant of incompetence just minutes after he found out about Lucille's death?"

Leigh thought about it. "To get everyone thinking in that direction, so he could ensure there was a proper autopsy with a toxicology report and everything?"

"Well of course that's what he'd *want* to happen, seeing as how he's guilty," Mason answered. "But if he was innocent, would anything about that make sense?"

Leigh saw his point. "If he was innocent, he would have assumed she died of natural causes."

"Of course," Mason continued. "But the story he's trying to sell the police is that even though he's innocent, his *very first* thought at hearing the news was 'oh, my God, the assistant killed her.' Well, that raises a pretty awkward question for him, doesn't it? Namely, why he and his mother would employ such an incompetent in the first place."

Mason scoffed. "What he should have done is sit tight for a day or two at least. Then he could have used any old excuse for why he's suddenly suspicious of the assistant. That she's acting weird. That he's noticed some of Lucille's pills were missing. You see?"

Leigh released a long, shuddering breath. "So you think Bobby is definitely acting guilty, but you don't think any of the Floribundas would agree to work with him? I don't get it, then. What *is* going on? Who's trying to scare Allison?"

Mason's weathered forehead creased. "It's possible Lydie doesn't know the Floribundas as well as she thinks she does. She doesn't know the newest one at all — she told me that. Either way, it's this Bobby I'd be worried about."

"But he couldn't have taken Allison's notebook," Leigh insisted. She was starting to feel shaky again. "He wasn't there. He had to be working with someone inside the house!"

Mason put a hand over hers. "I know it seems obvious that the two things are connected. But we really don't know that. Burning a child's notebook and throwing it out a car window is a coward's act. Someone that Allie took notes about could have gotten paranoid after the police got involved, even if they had nothing to do with Lucille's death. We still don't even know for sure that Lucille's death *wasn't* from natural causes."

Leigh sniffed. She couldn't afford to be so hopeful. "You just said Bobby acted guilty!"

"Oh, he is," Mason said confidently. "Guilty of trying to plan an insurance fraud. But that doesn't mean he succeeded."

Leigh stared. "You mean... Lucille could have died before they got a plan worked out?"

Mason shrugged. "Why not?"

"But then what would Bobby do?" Leigh speculated. "How would he handle it?"

Mason shrugged again. "How do you think?"

Chapter 20

Even sitting inside Lydie's kitchen, Leigh could hear screams and shrieks coming from her parents' house next door. She and Mason got to their feet and rushed outside.

Virginia was power-walking across the Koslows' front yard toward her car, her bony arms flying in all directions. "Evacuate! Evacuate!" she screamed.

Delores came next, moving almost as quickly, while behind her Jennie Ruth lagged a bit. Jennie Ruth was clearly doing her best to keep up, but her oversized body had evidently not been so taxed in a while. "Oh, do hurry!" Delores chirped while Jennie Ruth wheezed and panted.

"You are all being ridiculous!" Olympia scolded from the porch, her hands planted on her hips and her face angry. Frances stood beside Olympia, looking equally perturbed.

Leigh stopped running and tried to slow her frantically pounding heart. "It's all right," she said to Mason, grabbing at his sleeve to stop him, too. "It's just the really crazy ones."

Mason swore. "Are you sure?" He surveyed the scene, still on edge, but no doubt as skeptical as Leigh when it came to taking the hysteria of a Floribunda at face value.

He was not, however, breathing nearly as heavily as Leigh, which was irritating. The man was almost seventy! She *had* to start exercising. "Mom?" she called up to the porch. "Is everything all right?"

Frances looked down, saw Leigh and Mason standing together in the yard, and visibly stiffened. "Everything's perfectly under control," she replied curtly.

Mason laid a hand on Leigh's arm. "I'll take off," he said. "You let us know if there's anything we can do, though, all right?" He turned and walked back toward Lydie's house without waiting for an answer.

The hysterical Floribunda contingent had reached their cars and were now peeling away. God help any other motorists in the area.

"What on earth are they flipping out about?" Leigh demanded. She didn't mean to sound so cross, but her mother's attitude toward Mason was wearing on her. Lydie was right. Something had to give. Soon.

"They're afraid of the Flying Maples," Olympia answered, sounding exasperated.

"The new chapter is trying to murder us all, haven't you heard?" yelled the sarcastic voice of Anna Marie from inside the house. No doubt her majesty was still holding court on the couch.

"A woman named Carol Ann called," Frances explained. "She asked if it would be all right if she came by to pick up the bin."

Leigh tried not to roll her eyes. "Well, that explains everything."

"Virginia may call the police," Frances stated.

Olympia waved a dismissive hand. "They'll ignore her. Let's just get the bin ready to go, shall we?" She looked at Leigh. "Would you mind?"

Leigh helped Olympia carry the plastic container out through the door and down the porch steps. It was fairly heavy, but it had sturdy handles, and Olympia more than carried her weight. "You're strong," Leigh commented, not without a hint of jealousy.

"Rowing machine," Olympia replied proudly. Leigh tended to believe her until she added, "I was the first woman ever to land a spot on the men's crew at Princeton."

They had just set the bin down on the grass when a silver SUV pulled up and double-parked with its lights blinking. The driver, a merry-looking woman of around seventy with bleach blond hair, popped out immediately, as did the passenger, a woman of around the same age with gray hair in a short, spiky cut. They popped open the back of the vehicle and then smiled rather self-consciously as they came forward.

"Hello," the blonde greeted. "I'm Carol Ann. I'm so sorry to hear about your loss. But I understand your house looked beautiful and that everyone who came through thought it was marvelous. I hope the decorations made things easier for you."

The Floribundas on the porch seemed stunned for a moment. Even Anna Marie, who had risen for the occasion, seemed speechless when confronted with such utter and complete normalcy.

"They were a wonderful help," Frances said finally. "We

couldn't possibly have decorated the house properly without them. Thank you so much."

The Flying Maples smiled. "Oh, you're welcome. It was nothing," Carol Ann returned. "We'd already done the work, after all, and they were simply sitting there. I'm glad they were of use. But we do have to start returning them."

"Yes," the other woman chimed in. "Believe it or not, the owners of some of these gems still decorate with them every Christmas!"

"How precious," Olympia offered, finding her voice. "Thank you again. What do we... owe you?"

The Flying Maples laughed and picked up the bin. "Oh, for heaven's sake! Forget about it. You would have done the same for us, I'm sure."

Silence ensued.

"You need any help?" Leigh asked as the women moved toward the open back of their SUV.

"No, no, we've got it!" Carol Ann called back pleasantly. "Merry Christmas!"

"Merry Christmas," the Floribundas returned.

The Flying Maples loaded the bin inside, got back in their SUV, and drove away.

"Well," Anna Marie said snidely. "They were scary as hell, weren't they?"

Olympia and Frances exchanged a concerned glance, and Leigh tried to read their eyes. Had they really believed that the anthrax prank call had come from the Flying Maples? If so, they had to doubt themselves now. Despite the cloak-and-dagger nature of the bin's original drop-off, Carol Ann and friend had seemed innocent as the driven snow.

Leigh heard multiple car doors slamming.

"Yellowbellies!" Anna Marie called out as Virginia, Jennie Ruth, and Delores began to straggle back down the sidewalks. Evidently, they'd only been circling the block until the danger passed.

"You can never be too careful!" Virginia defended, making a show of watching down the road in the direction the SUV had departed. "We don't know why they were *really* here."

"Hello!" called an unexpected voice from the across the street. The women all looked up to see a middle-aged man with a large potbelly waving at them with an anxious smile on his face.

Bobby Busby. Leigh tensed. *What the —*

"I, uh…" he said in a friendly, but anxious voice. "I was driving by and saw that you ladies had something going on, so I thought I'd go ahead and stop in."

The Floribundas all stared at him in silence. If he wasn't anxious before, any normal person facing the sight of six stressed-out Floribundas now would be.

"I thought I'd see if you wanted me to dispose of any of the greenery I brought over," he offered, removing a grimy cap from his head and combing a hand through his thinning gray hair. "I mean, if you're throwing it out anyway, well, I can certainly make use of it at the store."

"You can have it," Frances said quickly.

Leigh wasn't surprised at the reply. Frances had never wanted to use real greenery in the first place. If the man was willing to come in and remove the boughs before they started gathering dust and dropping "those horrid needles," Frances would be all for it, any illegal shenanigans on his part be damned.

Leigh steeled herself. God knew she'd had enough of the Floribundas for one day, but if suspect number one was going back into her parents' house, then so was she.

Ten strangely quiet minutes later, Bobby was stuffing the last of his donations into a yard-size trash bag in the living room while every other pair of eyes watched him closely. More interesting was that Bobby had also been studying the Floribundas. As he had wandered about the house removing wreaths and untwining garlands, he had not-so-covertly fixated on each of their faces in turn. But he had said nothing to anyone.

"I think this is the last of it," Frances announced, handing him the sprig of mistletoe she had only just discovered hanging on the ceiling over the toilet in the half bath.

"You don't want to keep any of that?" Bobby asked. "It lasts a good long time if you dry it."

"I think not," Frances replied, her voice clipped.

Bobby shrugged, dropped the mistletoe in his bag, and tied it off.

"It's *poison!*" Jennie Ruth boomed.

Bobby's head jerked up to look at her. His eyes were wide for a moment, but just as quickly, he released a breath and relaxed. "Oh, no. You're thinking of the European kind. This is American mistletoe — Phoradendron. Worst you'd get from eating it is a belly ache."

"Are you *sure?*" Delores asked suspiciously. She stared hard at Bobby.

Bobby stared back at her. Nobody said anything else.

Leigh began to get seriously creeped out. What was wrong with this picture? "I'm sorry about your mother, Bobby," she heard herself say. She wasn't sure why she'd said it. It just seemed like the kind of thing that *should* be said, as opposed to all these nerve-wracking pregnant looks.

"Thanks," he said mechanically. He looked at each of the assembled faces again. "I guess you might be wanting to know... they got the 'preliminary' autopsy done. It says my mom died of cardiac arrest, which basically just means her heart stopped. But they still don't know why." He shouldered the bag and took a step towards the door, even as his gaze continued to move from face to face. "I asked for a full toxicology screening. They said they're going to do it. But it's going to take a couple weeks, probably."

"What about her funeral?" Delores practically shouted. Then, seeming to realize her volume was out of character, she moderated her tone back to cloying. "Dear Lucille did *so* have her heart set on that horse and carriage tripping along in the rain. I do hope that financial considerations won't force you to renege on making her fondest wish come true?"

Bobby studied the older woman with a frown on his face. Then he shrugged. "I don't know."

And with that pronouncement, he walked out the front door. As he moved through it, a low-hanging string of lights snagged on his cap and pulled it from his head. The cap landed on the floor near Olympia's feet, and Bobby didn't immediately reach for it, no doubt expecting she would do the normal, expected thing and hand it back to him, especially since his hands were full.

But Olympia was a Floribunda. So instead she cringed, let out an audible "ugh!" of disgust, and jumped back a foot. Leigh looked from the dirty cap on the floor to Olympia's expression of disgust, and felt a flash of insight as to why her mother and the Floribunda president got along as well as they did. Olympia was a germophobe.

Leigh stooped down and picked up the cap herself. It was indeed disgusting. The original navy blue color was simultaneously dirty, faded by the sun, and striped with the salty white bands of old sweat stains. She handed it back to Bobby and he replaced it on his head with a grateful nod. Beside her, Leigh could sense Olympia wincing with revulsion. As soon as Bobby was out the door, Olympia produced a miniature bottle of hand sanitizer, gave herself a squirt, and held it out to Leigh. "Here!" she ordered. "Quickly!"

Oh, yeah, Leigh confirmed. *Definitely a germophobe.* But she held out her hands and accepted the offering. The truth was, her fingers did feel greasy.

Olympia repocketed the sanitizer, watched through the front window as Bobby drove off, then turned around and threw her hands into the air. "And what was *that* all about?" she demanded.

The Floribundas went deadly quiet again.

If Leigh had any doubt that Olympia was the only member of the chapter who was *not* aware of Lucille and Bobby's insurance fraud plans, she put the idea out of her mind. The Floribundas were, to a one, intentionally hiding something from their newly minted president. And Leigh was not the only person who could see that.

"Well?" Olympia repeated impatiently. As Leigh watched, the look in her eyes changed gradually from mild annoyance to shocked hurt.

"What exactly is it you're asking, Olympia?" Frances said finally, breaking the tension.

"Nothing," Olympia answered shortly, frowning at them all. "Clearly, nothing. I have to go." She crossed to the coat rack and picked up her things.

"But… do you have a ride?" Frances asked.

"I'll call," Olympia snapped back. She opened the door for herself and stepped out.

"Some people tend toward the touchy side," Delores said lightly. "I understand they don't mean to be rude. But still, one does wonder…"

Leigh tried hard to block out the rest of Delores's sniping. "Why does she need a ride?" she whispered to her mother. Frances was standing close to the window, and as Leigh stepped to her side she could see Olympia heading down the street at a brisk walk.

"She doesn't drive," Frances whispered back. "She's passed out before. Something to do with keeping her medications balanced. I do hope she isn't too upset, but Maura asked that we not speak of Lucille's plans to anyone who didn't already know about them. And I'm sure that Olympia didn't know, because everyone insists they didn't mention it, even Virginia!" She sighed. "They still don't trust Olympia, and they don't want to ruin things for Bobby."

Leigh thought a moment. "Maybe Lucille trusted her."

Frances shook her head. "Lucille always thought there was something funny about Olympia. That she was hiding something. Lucille told me flat out that she didn't trust her."

"When was this?"

"A week ago!"

Leigh looked through the window again. Olympia was making a cell phone call as she walked. Her gawky, tall form turned the corner and disappeared from sight. Leigh bid another farewell to her mother and headed back outside herself. She still had nowhere in particular to go, but she was unable to take one more nanosecond of the Floribundas. Perhaps in the time she had left to kill she would drive to the clinic and watch her father work. There was nothing like watching the expression of a few anal glands to reground one's psyche.

Leigh had only just crossed the street when a car rolled up beside her and slowed down. She looked over with a start, at first believing the car to have no driver. Then she realized that the balding head barely sticking up above the wheel was that of Melvin Pepper.

"Hello, Ms. Harmon," the doctor said politely. "I'm sorry if I alarmed you. I was just looking for my wife."

Leigh tried to calm her breathing. She was jumpy as a cat. "Olympia just turned the corner, walking that way," she explained, pointing.

Melvin seemed confused. "Just now? She was at your mother's house, then?"

Now Leigh was confused. "Didn't she call you for a ride?" Come to think of it, Melvin had arrived way too fast for that, unless he'd been sitting down the street waiting.

He seemed embarrassed. "Why, no. I've been looking for her. She hasn't been answering my calls, and I was getting worried. But I thought she might be here, helping to clean up or something."

Leigh studied the doctor's face. He was clearly anxious. Today, everyone alive was anxious! "She was there, but she left," Leigh explained again. Then her mouth kept going. "Why exactly are you worried about her?"

Melvin did not seem to take offense at the nosy question. "It's just that she's not been quite herself lately. I suppose it's because of losing Lucille so suddenly like that. The two of them were rather close, I gather."

The last part was news to Leigh. "They were? Oh, I'm sorry. I didn't realize."

Melvin looked thoughtful. "I didn't either. I knew they spoke on the phone and visited, but Olympia's been so very upset..." He stared out the window another moment before breaking his reverie. "I'm sorry," he said, putting the car back into gear. "I really must catch up with her. Thank you so much, Ms. Harmon."

"You're welcome."

Leigh stepped toward her car again, but kept watching as Melvin's sedan cruised around the corner and out of sight. Olympia and Lucille? Close? Frances insisted that Olympia didn't know about the fraud plans, that Lucille hadn't trusted her. But could Frances really be sure of that? What if Lucille had lied to her?

For that matter, how well did Frances really know any of the Floribundas? She was so certain that none of them would hurt a child...

Leigh stopped moving. She pulled her phone out of her bag and dialed her husband's number. "Warren?" she pleaded the second he picked up. "Can you come home early? I need to talk to you about Allison."

His pause lasted only a second. "Sure. I'll be right there."

Chapter 21

Leigh leaned into her husband's side as they stood on their front porch in the cold, looking out at the sky. It was a beautiful, clear night, and although their quota of visible stars wasn't so great in the suburbs, the ones they could see were all twinkling brightly.

"Allison took it pretty well, I thought," she said, digging her hands in her pockets and hugging her coat to her.

Warren tightened his long arm around her shoulders. "Yes, she did," he answered. "She's old enough now to understand the 'why' that comes with the 'don't.' It also doesn't hurt to have Mo being the one giving her the bad news."

"You mean delivering the punishment," Leigh said with a sad smile. "For Allison, this is basically house arrest. You know she'd be back over at her Grandma's house if she could, sniffing around and asking more questions. She can't help herself."

Leigh shivered, and Warren rubbed her arm briskly. It had turned sharply colder, but they were used to talking outside in the evenings. It was the only way they could be completely sure they wouldn't be overheard, since Allison moved like a cat and appeared to have bionic ears. "Her heart didn't seem to be in the tree-trimming," Leigh added. "Did you notice?"

The Harmons put up most of their Christmas decorations right after Thanksgiving, but they had always waited until after the twins' birthday to put up the tree. Today they'd gone all out with the traditional celebration, which included picking out a live tree, carting it home, and then decorating it with all their handmade treasures. The popcorn-string tradition had been abruptly discontinued after Chewie's first Christmas, but otherwise the ritual remained essentially unchanged over the years.

"Oh, I think she had fun," Warren assured. "I think she was just anxious to get back to her computer."

Leigh lifted her head and looked at him. "Her computer? Tonight? Why?"

"So she could dig into her birthday presents, of course," he said with surprise.

Leigh relaxed a little. "Oh, you mean the genealogy database." For a moment she'd been worried. But she really should try to stay calm. Maura had come over earlier, met with them both, and examined the charred notebook. As soon as school let out she had spoken with Allison herself, explaining what had happened and then recommending that the girl have no contact with anyone from the Holiday House Tour or go anywhere without a parent until further notice. She had deftly sidestepped all of Allison's attempts to ferret out additional information, and she'd somehow managed to do it without making Allie feel like a kid. All of which was wonderful. On the downside, however, she'd also given Leigh no useful information and had told her only — in so many words — to be quiet and stay the hell out of it. Maura had also brought the unwelcome but not surprising news that she would soon officially be removed from the case.

"I don't think it's the genealogy database Allison was anxious to get into," Warren replied.

Leigh stiffened again. She didn't like something in his tone. "Well, what else did we get her?"

Warren stared down at her with his trademark "oh no, not this again" expression. "We discussed this already. At length."

"Well, I can't remember," Leigh said with annoyance. Curse her over-forty mom brain!

"One was a membership in a genealogy service that gives her access to public birth and death records and military and immigration records and things like that," he answered.

"Yeah?" Leigh prepared herself.

"The other was a people finder service that will let her perform background checks."

Holy crap.

"She especially wanted that one," Warren reminded. "And you said it wouldn't be a bad idea to know if any adults in her orbit had criminal records or were listed as sex offenders."

Leigh blew out a breath. She did have vague memories along those lines. "But I didn't think she would use it to get more involved in a police investigation she shouldn't be involved with in the first place!"

"I don't know why not."

Leigh glared up at her husband, but he merely smiled and put his other arm around her. "It's all public information," he assured. "The service just makes finding it easier. No one will know she's looking at it, and we're not letting her out of our sight. It'll be all right. She's a smart girl."

"Why do you think I'm so worried?" Leigh said with a moan. She closed her eyes and buried her head in his shoulder. "Allison should be making crafts and crushing on pop stars and baking sweets and hanging out with other twelve-year-old girls, not sitting in front of a computer researching backgrounds on a bunch of a geriatric delinquents! Face it, Harmon. Our daughter is weird."

Warren laughed out loud. "Leigh, you're weird. I'm weird. It's a miracle of genetics we had one normal kid."

She smiled into his shoulder. "Good point."

Her fingers had been curling and uncurling around a tiny ball of paper in one of her otherwise empty coat pockets, and its presence began to bug her. She pulled it out. The sight of it ripped the smile from her face immediately.

"Look at this," she said with disdain, handing it to Warren. "If I'd never seen this stupid thing, I probably wouldn't be half as freaked out right now."

Warren let go of her, unwrapped the small slip of paper, and moved it into the dim glow cast out the window by their Christmas tree. "The blaxe you brew for your adversary often burns you more than him?" he read.

"That's the one. Cheery, isn't it?"

"I'm guessing it's supposed to say 'blaze,'" he surmised.

Leigh considered. The x was right next to the z on a keyboard. It made sense.

"'Brew' isn't the right word, either," he continued. "I've heard a proverb like this before. I think it's supposed to say 'the fire you kindle' or something like that. You make a fire for your enemy, but it burns you instead. Get it?"

Leigh frowned. She grabbed the piece of paper and stuffed it back in her pocket. She liked having a smart husband, but only when he didn't show her up. "The point is," she explained, "it got me all freaked out about poisoning. I had it on my mind even before Lucille died. If I hadn't, I'd be able to believe now that she died of natural causes. Because despite all the craziness, that really does make the most sense."

Warren studied her face in the dim light. "But you think she was poisoned?"

Leigh shook her head. "I don't really *think* anything. I just don't feel good about it. I had a premonition that something bad was going to happen, and it did, and now I feel like the danger is still out there. And I can't reason myself out of feeling this way."

Warren wrapped his arms around her again. They said nothing else, but simply stood in the cold silence for a while, watching the December stars.

"Mom? Dad?"

The tiny voice sliced its way into Leigh's groggy consciousness. "Mom!"

Leigh opened her eyes. She was in bed, it was still dark outside, and the ceiling light was on. Allison was sitting on the edge of the mattress, dressed and ready for school. Warren was just waking up as well. "What time is it?" he asked. "Is something wrong?"

"No," Allison said quickly, but calmly. "It's a few minutes before your alarm's supposed to go off. I woke you up early because I want to talk to you. And we won't have enough time otherwise."

Leigh jolted to full alertness. "What is it?"

"It's a couple things," Allison began, talking more slowly than usual. Leigh got the feeling her daughter was trying hard not to get her parents any more upset than necessary, given the circumstances.

It wasn't working.

"First off, I don't know if you saw it before you went to bed or not, since your phones are in the kitchen, but Aunt Mo sent us all a text late last night."

"No," Leigh said, sitting up straight. "What did it say?"

"Bridget's gone AWOL," Allison reported calmly. "You know, Lucille's assistant? It doesn't mean anything to us necessarily, but Aunt Mo wants us to call right away if any of us see her or hear from her. And stay away from her, of course."

"Of course," Leigh echoed soberly. Bridget? Disappeared? The idea wasn't too surprising, since the woman seemed afraid of her own shadow. But was she running because she felt guilty, or because she was afraid of something or someone else? Could it be both?

Leigh felt a sudden pang of terror. Had Bridget *run,* of her own free will, at all?

"Why would Bridget take off?" Warren asked.

"That's another reason I wanted to talk to you," Allison explained. "I found out some interesting things about her."

Leigh tried to calm her pounding heart. Bridget was fine. Why must her brain always leap to the worst possible conclusions? "What's that, Allie?" she asked, failing to hide the squeak in her voice.

"Well, Bridget grew up in Beaver County, and she never had any kids of her own. She didn't get married until she was in her late thirties. Her husband was older and had grown kids and she moved in with him and his parents. I think she was taking care of them. Not long after they died, Bridget's husband divorced her."

"Nice," Leigh grumbled.

"He was the one who filed, yeah," Allison agreed. "Anyway, after that she started working as an assistant for elderly people. But she ran into trouble about a year ago. The man she was taking care of died, and his daughters sued her for negligence."

Leigh leaned forward. So Bobby hadn't been making that up. "Seriously? How did you find this out?"

Allison smiled a little. "It's all in the public record, Mom."

A vision of Bridget's fidgety nervousness floated before Leigh's eyes. It was replaced with the memory of the assistant's response after Lucille was proclaimed dead, when Bridget had begun to blubber from her chair, *this cannot be happening again!*

"The case was dismissed," Allison continued, "I'm guessing for lack of evidence, but the documents I saw didn't get into a whole lot of detail. It was a civil case, not criminal, but it was a mess. I don't know how she could have afforded a lawyer. And you'd think it would make it really hard for her to get another job."

Leigh mulled the thought. "Yes," she said soberly. "You'd think it would."

"But Lucille and Bobby Busby hired her," Allison stated.

Yes. They did. Leigh needed coffee. She smelled coffee. She had to be imagining it, though, because Warren wasn't out of bed yet.

"Here, Mom," Allison said cheerfully, handing her the steaming mug that was sitting on her bedside table. "Yours is over there, Dad."

Leigh and Warren exchanged an incredulous glance. "Okay, Allison," Warren asked with a laugh as he reached for his. "What is it you really want?"

"Nothing!" she insisted, raising her palms in a gesture of innocence. "I just wanted to wake your brains up." She paused a second. "And make sure you didn't get mad at me."

Leigh sipped a hot dose of sweet caffeine. *Ah, nectar.* Thank God for coffee machines even a twelve-year-old could operate. "We're not mad, honey," she assured. "Thank you for the coffee."

"There's something else," Allison continued, the tightness in her tone extinguishing any joy from the moment. "Something I really don't know what to make of."

Leigh took a large gulp of coffee. She steeled herself for the worst again.

"I keep feeling like I should tell Aunt Mo," Allison said, "but then I think that's stupid, because the police must already know. It's just that she can't tell us about it, which is annoying. It's a whole lot more fun talking to her about this kind of stuff when she's *not* working the case. I mean, you think you're having a discussion with her, but then you realize you're not, because she's not really telling you anything from her side, you know?"

Leigh chuckled. "Welcome to my world, kid."

"Anyway, the thing is, Olympia and Melvin Pepper don't exist."

Leigh sputtered as a drop of coffee detoured down her windpipe. "Excuse me?" she coughed. "What do you mean, 'don't exist?'"

Allison waited until her mother could breathe again. "I mean that I can't find them on any database I should be able to find them on. The people we know exist, obviously, but those can't be their real names."

Leigh felt a chill. "Fake names?" she murmured.

"Why would they be using aliases?" Warren asked. "This is the president of the chapter? And her husband?"

Allison nodded. "Strange, isn't it? Olympia's a pathological liar, Dad, so it's hard to know what she's making up. She doesn't seem to do it to be mean or anything. She just... does it. So maybe she makes up names she likes, too. Maybe she thought calling her husband 'Dr. Pepper' would be funny. Who knows?"

Warren threw Leigh a hard look, and she knew what he was thinking. In the political and financial realms in which he worked, people didn't go around changing their surnames just for kicks. If you took on another identity, you generally had a damn good reason.

"I tried to look them up another way, since they both have kind of unusual first names, but I didn't get anywhere," Allison complained. "You wouldn't believe how many MDs are named Melvin!"

"Proctologists?" Leigh muttered, still trying to think of a single good reason why the couple should need to go incognito.

Allison's lips screwed up with annoyance. "Well, *that* would have helped. I didn't know what kind of doctor he was."

"Well, if this woman lies about everything, how do you know he's a doctor at all?" Warren asked.

Leigh remembered watching Melvin as he attended to Lucille. "I don't *know*, but I really think he is," she answered. "At least, he was. My mother said he was a proctologist and that Olympia was a tax attorney, and that they'd both recently retired. Of course... Olympia could have told her anything. But I have noticed that the more boring it sounds, the more likely it is to be true."

"Well, that's really weird, then," Allison said, slumping her thin shoulders.

"What's weird?" Warren asked.

"I heard Lucille and Bridget talking," Allison explained. "Olympia's been telling everybody that they sold their house in Rochester and that they're renting a condo while they shop for another house here. But Bridget has seen both Olympia and Melvin down where she lives, in Perry North, going in and out of one of the scummiest apartment buildings in the neighborhood. Lucille thought they were living there because the truth was they were dead broke."

Leigh took another swig of coffee, but her chill persisted. *On the brink of financial ruin.* Those were the words that Mason had used. Words to describe someone desperate enough to commit insurance fraud.

Leigh's alarm clock went off with a deafening screech. She and Warren both jumped, splashing warm coffee all over the blanket, and for a moment Allison looked like an actual twelve-year-old as she exploded into a fit of giggles.

"Sorry about that," she twittered. "Guess I should have reminded you to turn it off."

"It's okay," Leigh replied, swinging her feet out of the damp bedcovers.

Allison's tone turned serious again. "Anyway, I was wondering if you thought we should warn Grandma about Olympia. Aunt Mo didn't tell *her* to stay away from either of the Peppers, so maybe they do have a good reason for not using their real names. Maybe they're in the witness protection program or something."

Right. If Melvin's safety depended on Olympia keeping her mouth shut, God help him.

"I'll call Maura and ask her," Leigh promised. "But you're right, if she thought Olympia was a danger to Grandma in any way, she would have warned her already."

"Maybe I can find out more before the bus comes," Allison murmured to herself as she walked out the door. "A *proctologist* named Melvin…"

Leigh closed the door behind her daughter and threw her husband a determined look. "That girl is going to school and coming straight back home and she's not getting out of our sight otherwise until this mess is over with."

"Agreed," Warren said heavily.

"Who knows what else she's going to find out as soon as she gets back on that computer?" Leigh lamented. "Maybe it should mysteriously disappear while she's at school."

Warren's eyebrows lifted. His face showed an expression halfway between sheepish and terrified.

"What?" Leigh demanded.

"Her birthday presents," he replied. "They have phone apps."

Chapter 22

Leigh paced back and forth in her living room as Chewie napped fitfully by the couch, eyeing her with a sleepy but wary look. The corgi had paced with her for a good part of the day, but his short little legs were tired, and his efforts hadn't profited him much. Still, he seemed reluctant to close both eyes, lest he miss the moment if Leigh happened to suddenly veer off into the kitchen and the vicinity of his treat bin. Finally, after seeming to despair of her ever sitting down again, he heaved himself up, walked to the kitchen doorway, and sprawled his chunky body across the opening like a trip wire.

Then he closed both eyes.

Leigh smiled at him and then turned to look out the window again. She had tried to work. She had managed to scribble down a dozen pages' worth of ideas on a print ad campaign for an incredibly boring line of industrial dehumidifiers. Some of her ideas were even decent. But Maura still had not called her back, and Leigh was ready to jump out of her skin. Warren was holed up in the basement den, also working from home today, and also uptight. Maura had replied to Leigh's early-morning voicemail with a brief text saying that the Harmons should keep Allison home after school and not worry about Frances, and that Maura would call at some point. But those assurances weren't good enough.

Leigh still, desperately, needed to *do* something. But what?

Her eyes moved to the portable landline phone currently sitting on the coffee table. It had been quiet all day, which was odd. Why hadn't her mother called? Frances had taken to calling at least once a day, and often twice, ever since Lydie had begun spending so much time with Mason. Leigh hastened to the phone and dialed her parents' number.

Frances did not pick up until the fourth ring.

"Mom?" Leigh asked, her tone panicked. "Are you okay? Is everything all right over there?"

A beat of silence passed. "Why yes, of course, dear. Why

shouldn't it be? Is everything all right with you? And my grandchildren?"

As Frances's own voice rose from perfectly calm to increasingly frightened, Leigh wanted to kick herself. "We're all good," she said quickly. "The kids are at school. I just hadn't heard from you in a while, that's all."

"Oh," Frances replied, sounding confused. Then she sounded amused. "Did you miss the sound of my voice, then?"

There was really no good way to answer that question.

"I'm waiting on a call from Maura," Leigh said instead, changing the subject. "And I'm getting impatient. I was hoping she'd have an update for us, but she's supposed to hand over the case sometime today, I think."

"Yes, that does always seem to happen," Frances agreed. Now she sounded distracted. "Listen, dear, I'd love to chat with you, but I'm a bit busy at the moment getting everything ready for the meeting."

"The meeting?" Leigh repeated. "What meeting?"

"Why, the Floribunda chapter meeting, of course."

Leigh couldn't believe her ears. "Mom, you can't— I mean, you just met with the Floribundas yesterday!"

"Oh, don't be ridiculous," Frances asserted. "We were just cleaning up a bit, then. This is a *chapter meeting*, dear. We have business to conduct."

"But," Leigh protested, wishing she could lock up her mother right along with Allison. "Can't you postpone, under the circumstances?"

"Why on earth should we do that?" Frances retorted. "The Floribundas *always* meet the first Tuesday of the month! And I *always* host the December meeting. Why, it's tradition!"

Leigh closed her eyes and breathed deeply.

"Besides," Frances continued, "we have important new business to conduct! Lucille was an officer, and we must hold a vote to replace her. You can't expect us to continue operations without a duly elected sergeant-at-arms! Who would shut Virginia up? We'd never get a *thing* done!"

Leigh gave up. "Is Olympia going to be there?"

"She *is* the president. She will be running the meeting. She even has some new business of her own. As secretary, I've just added it to the agenda."

"What new business?"

"Our meetings are closed to the general public," Frances stated. "Unless you'd like to apply for a prospective membership?"

Leigh stifled a primal scream. "No, Mom. Just be careful, okay? Do whatever Maura said to do."

"I shall, dear. And the same goes for you."

Leigh agreed and hung up. Her mother obviously remained convinced that none of the Floribundas themselves were a danger to herself or to Allison. Leigh was not so sure. But her hands were tied. Maura had insisted that she would handle the reporting of appropriate case information to Frances herself, warning Leigh that any rumors reaching the Floribundas by way of Leigh would necessarily cast more suspicion on Allison. Maura had also assured her that, aside from the same risk by association that all the Floribundas faced, Frances had no particular reason to fear for her own safety.

But Leigh couldn't stop worrying. She began to pace again.

What was Olympia up to, after all? Melvin's worries about his wife's emotional state yesterday afternoon had hardly been comforting. He seemed to think that Olympia was close to Lucille, but Leigh had seen no evidence of that. True, Olympia had fainted when she'd caught sight of the old woman's head lolling. But such a sight could be horrifying even for a stranger. Then again, the whole fainting episode could have been an act.

No matter what was going on with Olympia, Bobby Busby's actions still made no sense. The night Lucille died, he'd acted guilty as hell. But why had he come over to the Koslows' house yesterday? What could he possibly have been fishing for? If one of the Floribundas *was* his accomplice, the smart thing to do would be to stay as far away from her as possible. And if his accomplice *wasn't* one of the Floribundas, why was he there at all? Why would he and Lucille hire a personal assistant who'd been sued for the death of a previous employer in the first place?

Leigh collapsed on the couch in a heap. The conjecture was driving her crazy. If it weren't for the blasted notebook being thrown on her lawn, she might believe that Lucille had died of a heart attack with no "help" whatsoever. And why not? Bridget could still have panicked and skipped town, fearing she'd be blamed. Bobby could have been caught off-guard, thinking his accomplice had gone trigger-happy.

Yes, Leigh could believe that Lucille had died naturally. *Except* for the notebook. And of course, there was still the baffling business of the "snowing anthrax" prank call, which had accomplished nothing except to panic everyone by sending the police to the house before Lucille had even died!

Leigh sat up again. Yes… that *was* odd.

A coincidence?

Surely not.

Her cell phone made a siren sound, and Leigh scrambled up like a mad woman. Chewie awoke from his slumber and pawed at the air like an upside-down turtle before getting his stubby legs underneath his plump belly again. Leigh dove for her cell, which she had left plugged up on the kitchen counter.

"Maura? What's up?"

"Chillax, Koslow," the detective said smoothly. "I'm just reporting in, as promised."

Leigh breathed a little easier. She looked at the time. The middle school should be letting out now. Soon, she could gather her little family together and bolt the doors.

Warren appeared at the top of the steps, and Leigh put Maura on speakerphone. "Did you know the Floribundas have another meeting at my mother's house today?" Leigh asked the detective.

"She mentioned that, yes."

"And you're okay with that?"

"The police department isn't in the habit of forbidding friends of the deceased from seeing each other, even in the case of a suspicious death," Maura answered calmly. "Although I have advised your mother privately to avoid both Bobby Busby and Bridget, if that makes you feel better."

"It does," Leigh admitted.

"Is there anything else you can tell us?" Warren asked.

"There is one thing," Maura answered. "I intend to visit your mother later this afternoon and tell her this myself, but if you see her before then, that's okay, too. Because of the anthrax call and the fact that Ms. Busby ate and drank refreshments also served to the general public, the medical examiner ran some tests to rule out the more obvious causes of food poisoning or contagion. I'm sure your mother will be happy to know that there was no evidence of either."

Leigh was very happy to hear that. "Good to know."

"However," Maura went on, "there were some other abnormalities in the bloodwork that led the ME to order a full toxicology screening."

Leigh's heart fell again. "Meaning?"

Maura blew out a breath. "Meaning, in general terms, that such a ruling usually tips the scales away from a natural death and toward something like a medication overdose."

Now Leigh felt sick.

"Which could have been entirely accidental," Maura finished. "All that can be said at this point is that further toxicology testing is needed. And those results are going to take a while, I'm afraid."

Leigh looked up at her husband. Even Fiji didn't sound safe enough anymore. "You up for some winter camping in the Yukon?"

Warren smiled nervously. "Do they make heated tents?"

"Calm down, kids," Maura soothed. "Everything's going to be all right. Just keep Allison with you today. I've got to go — another case breaking. Ciao."

The policewoman hung up abruptly, and Leigh and Warren shared an uneasy look. "Allison isn't a threat to anybody. At least not anymore," Leigh told herself and him, again. "I acted like I never even found the notebook in the yard, which is perfectly plausible — I might not have. And I told all the Floribundas that Allison couldn't care less, and they *should* have believed me. Unless Mom already told them about her peculiar... hobby. Oh, I don't know *what* those women are thinking!" Leigh dropped her forehead on the counter.

Warren put a hand on her shoulder and gave it a squeeze. "We're just being cautious, remember? Whoever threw her notebook on our lawn was sending a message that Allison should stop butting her nose into the matter, and as far as anyone else could possibly know, she's heeding that warning. End of story."

"I hope you're —" Leigh jumped as her phone sounded again, this time with the happy jingling sound that indicated a text from Allison. She picked it up and read the screen.

> Don't freak out or anything, but Bridget just showed up outside the school.

Leigh freaked out. She fired back a series of questions as fast as her index finger could type, and Allison responded with frustrating slowness.

> NO she was not threatening me. She just waved from a distance. I think she wanted to talk to me but I motioned that I couldn't and I got on the bus. End of story.

And then again, two seconds later.

> Calm down, Mom. I'll text Aunt Mo myself.

Leigh tried to slow her breathing.

"Allie's safe on the bus," Warren assured, reading over her shoulder. "She'll be home in minutes."

Bridget. Bridget who had gone AWOL as of last night, avoiding the police. Why the hell would she show up at Allison's school? What could she possibly want?

What had Allison seen?

Theories zipped painfully through Leigh's frayed neurons. Why did Bobby Busby even need a Floribunda when he had Bridget the incompetent personal assistant right there by his mother's side? Bridget could stage an "accidental" overdose, even take the heat for it, and Bobby would still collect his money. He could even sue her for negligence, collect from *her* insurance too, and then someday down the road, the both of them would be better off! Bridget could declare personal bankruptcy, start working fast food, bide her time... what did she have to lose, really?

Her freedom, of course. But only if she got caught! And she'd be less likely to get caught if the accident happened in a public place, with plenty of people about, perhaps even with a bit of chaos going on or even during a full-out panic which would distract everyone's attention *and* make Bridget's "honest" mistake more understandable...

What had Allison seen during the anthrax scare?

"We've got to call Maura," Leigh shouted, jumping up.

"I already did," Warren replied, hanging up his phone. "I had to leave a message. She's on that other case."

Leigh's phone jingled with another text from Allison.

Do NOT freak out, Mom. But I think Bridget is following the bus.

Chapter 23

Leigh was in the basement garage with her hand on the car door before Warren's words got through to her. "Unless you have the bus route memorized, there's no point!" he pleaded, shoving her coat at her. She had grabbed her keys and her purse, but that was all.

"Besides," Warren continued to reason, even though he looked every bit as flustered as she felt. "You don't know where they were when she texted. The bus could be here any second. The smart thing to do is just to go out and wait!"

Leigh thought about it. Then she released the door handle, shrugged on her coat, and headed outside. They raced up the drive together and out to the edge of the highway. "I don't see it," she panted.

"No," Warren agreed, looking both directions. "Not yet." He glanced at his phone. "Still nothing from Mo. I'll call the locals. They may think I'm crazy, but I don't care."

Leigh did not care either. She breathed heavily of the frigid air and continued to stare in the direction from which the bus normally came. When had it gotten so *cold?* There were no gloves in her coat pockets; her hands already felt like blocks of ice. She reached for the phone she had stashed in her pants pocket and was barely able to turn the screen on. There was another text from Allison.

> You're not panicking, are you? I really think she just wants to talk to me.

Leigh did not care what Bridget wanted. She sent a reply.

> Just stay on the bus until you see us! We're waiting for you outside.

Allison's response made clear that she took after her grandfather Randall.

SIGH. Please, Mom. No drama.

A couple hundred years later, Leigh's heart lurched as she heard the familiar hoot, squeak, and hiss of bus brakes in the distance. She looked to see the blunt yellow nose of the Bluebird school bus pulling onto the main highway from the next crossroad. "They're here!"

Warren stepped up to her side. He had finished his phone call, although she had no idea what he'd said. They watched in nervous silence as the bus rattled its way up the highway and closed the distance between them, making one more infuriatingly slow stop on the way. "Is there a car following it?" Leigh asked, squinting.

"I can't see," Warren replied. "But there almost certainly will be, whether it's Bridget or not."

At long last, the bus neared them and began to slow. "Would jumping on board and throwing her over my shoulder qualify as drama?" Leigh quipped, scanning the windows.

"Stay right here," Warren warned.

The bus stopped. The folding door bent open with a groan and their tall, red-headed son hopped out, grinning at them. "Gee, you guys must have really missed me today," he joked.

Leigh started to answer, but Allison stepped out right behind him, her small face red with embarrassment.

"What's up?" Ethan asked.

The bus door slammed shut and the engine revved. "Where's Lenna?" Leigh asked as soon as her voice could be heard over the din.

"She has cheerleading, remember?" Allison said with exasperation. "You're supposed to pick her up later because Aunt Cara is giving her presentation today?"

Oh, right.

Leigh's eyes were focused on her daughter, making sure she looked whole and well, but Allison's gaze was fixed on something else. "There," she said suddenly, pointing down the road. "I think that's her car."

Leigh and Warren stiffened like soldiers drawn to attention. Indeed, a very old rat-trap of a car which had been one in a line of several caught behind the bus had begun to pull off the road. They watched, stunned, as the woman behind the wheel waved at them with a gloved hand, then turned off into the private drive beside them and parked on the gravel shoulder.

"What is she thinking?" Warren murmured.

"I told you she just wanted to talk to me!" Allison pleaded. "I got to know her on Saturday. She's okay."

The child's words had no effect on her parents' defenses. As the frumpy, gray-haired woman in the tattered wool coat got slowly out of her car and walked toward them, Leigh grabbed her daughter by the shoulders and loomed over her from behind. Warren stood beside and a little in front of the two of them, squaring his shoulders and pulling himself to his full, impressive height. Neither of them had a weapon, of course, and Warren had about as much experience fist-fighting as Leigh did racing stock cars, but Bridget had no way of knowing that. He looked imposing, and Leigh knew that he, like she, would fight as dirty as necessary with no guilt whatsoever if this harmless looking, diminutive, middle-aged witch laid so much as one chipped fingernail on their daughter.

Ethan, who had never received an answer to his earlier question and clearly had no clue what was going on, took in the situation with a quiet glance and then came to stand on the other side of his mother and sister. He squared his own thin shoulders, crossed his arms over his chest, and stood up to his full height. Then he glared at Bridget with a studied frown in perfect imitation of his father.

Leigh so wanted to hug the boy. But it really wouldn't be appropriate right then.

"Um," Bridget said uncertainly, stopping about ten feet away from the family. "Hi. I'm sorry. I didn't mean to scare anybody."

"Too late," Leigh replied. She thought about informing Bridget that the police were on the way, which *could* be true. But it would only allow the fugitive a head start in escaping them, and truthfully, the personal assistant looked more pathetic than menacing at the moment. "What do you want?"

Bridget's expression had turned timid as a fawn. Her hands and voice shook a little. "I just wanted to talk to Allison," she bleated.

Leigh was completely, thoroughly unmoved. "So talk!" she ordered.

Bridget's eyes turned teary. "I... I told you I didn't mean to scare her. I just didn't know how to get in touch with her again." She looked at Allison and managed a pitiful smile. "I didn't know your last name, Allison. I just knew you were somebody's granddaughter. I was so… flustered. But we talked about your school, and I remembered that. So that's where I went. I'm sorry."

Her voice cracked, and Allison piped up confidently. "I wasn't scared."

Leigh resisted the urge to tell her daughter to go to her room. "Get to the point, Bridget," she barked.

The personal assistant nodded agreeably. She took in a deep, shuddering breath. "I just wanted to tell Allison that it's really important that she tell the police absolutely everything she saw happen with Miss Lucille on Saturday." More tears began to fall. "I'm in such horrible, horrible trouble, and I didn't do anything wrong!"

Bridget lowered her head and began to sob, and Leigh and Warren exchanged a pensive look.

"Allison has already given a detailed statement to the police," Warren explained. "It's on the record. If you're here to try and convince her to change something, you can forget it."

"No!" Bridget protested, her voice suddenly adamant. "No, I want her to tell the truth!" She looked directly at Allison. "You saw *everything*. I know you did. If you could only remember it, it would help me prove I didn't do anything wrong. Please!"

"What exactly is it you think she saw?" Leigh asked.

Bridget shook her head, sending her frizzy gray locks into further disarray. "There's nothing in particular! It's just… everything. They think I *gave* her something. I know they do. But I didn't! Miss Lucille had her lunchtime pills with her taco and she wasn't due for any more until bedtime. They keep asking me what I did right before she fell asleep… what I gave her to eat and drink. And I told them, but they don't believe me!"

"I remember everything she ate and drank," Allison announced.

"Tell me!" Bridget begged. "Oh, please. Tell me what you remember!"

"Why do you need to know?" Leigh argued.

Bridget flailed her arms. "Don't you see? I'm so afraid! I can't let… I can't go… Last night I slept in my car!" She broke down and started crying again.

Allison twisted in Leigh's arms and turned around to face her parents. "There's no reason I can't tell her what I already told the police," she reasoned. "I think it will make her feel better, and then she won't think she has to keep running. Wouldn't that be better for everybody?"

Leigh still wanted to send both her children inside the house and lock the doors behind them. But she could think of no credible argument. She and her husband exchanged another look.

"All right, Allison," Warren answered for them. But he kept his own hand on the girl's shoulder as she turned toward Bridget again.

"What I remember," Allison began, speaking confidently, "is that by evening we were all getting tired and hungry, even though we had that late lunch. Lucille had been complaining about being hungry for hours, but it was right around seven, when the crowds started dwindling, that she told you to go steal some cookies for her. I remember she said 'and don't get caught!' because she didn't want anyone to know she was breaking the oath."

"That's right," Bridget agreed, nodding enthusiastically. "And did she ask me for punch, too?"

"No," Allison replied. "Just cookies. She specifically wanted one of Jennie Ruth's strawberry date cookies and some of Delores's little ones from the cookie press. But not the ones with the shiny metallic sugar balls, because those always got stuck in her dentures."

Bridget smiled broadly. "Yes! Yes, oh, you do have a good memory!"

Leigh studied the woman. If Bridget *didn't* want Allison to tell the absolute truth, she was an amazing actress.

"You left the room, and Lucille passed some gas really loud," Allison continued. "Then she looked at me and said, 'control yourself, child!'"

Ethan laughed out loud as Allison imitated the old woman's scolding tone. If Leigh wasn't so uptight she would have chuckled herself; both her kids were good mimics.

"Oh, she did that to everyone," Bridget said with an agitated wave of her hand. "I've even heard her blame her doctor. What next?"

"That's all she said to me. She pretty much ignored me," Allison went on. "When you got back, you were holding a cup of punch and a napkin full of cookies. You put the napkin on the table and she yelled at you to hide it in her lap, and you did."

Bridget continued smiling broadly, nodding encouragement. "You told the police all this?"

"Of course," Allison replied. "I thought at first that you brought the punch for her, but instead you drank it really quick."

"I was afraid she'd take it!" Bridget declared. "And I was thirsty, myself. I couldn't carry two cups and the cookies, too."

"You could have drunk yours in the kitchen and then asked for another one for her," Leigh pointed out.

The personal assistant blinked several times. "I guess so. I didn't think of that."

Despite her best intentions to remain cynical, Leigh believed her. She thought back to Bridget's appearance in the kitchen that night. The personal assistant had come in and gotten served — and sneaked out the cookies — just before Leigh noticed the mistletoe berry floating in the bowl. The mistletoe was already on the ceiling then, so Bridget's cup must have been served after Harry spiked the punch. "Did you taste alcohol in the cider?" she asked.

Bridget immediately looked contrite. "The police asked me that, too! And yes, I guess I did. But I didn't really think about it. It just tasted good to me."

"Did it occur to you that Lucille shouldn't have alcohol?" Leigh accused.

Bridget started looking teary again. "I didn't give her any!" she insisted. "I drank the whole cup! But… no, not really. The doctors always told her she shouldn't drink, but she did anyway. She always had a little gin before bed, and her son knew about it and he told me to let her do what she wanted, that it hadn't killed her yet. That's what he said, 'It hasn't killed her yet!'"

Bridget turned back to Allison. "Go on, please!" she begged.

"Well, you drank the punch, and Lucille started eating her cookies," Allison reported. "She said the strawberry one was 'subpar' and that Jennie Ruth was 'getting senile.' But it looked to me like she ate the whole thing. Then she started in on the smaller ones. She yelled at you because one of them had some sprinkles on it she didn't like. You asked her if you could have that one and she said no."

Always the charmer, Leigh thought uncharitably. Someday, she really did hope to be enlightened as to one positive quality of the late Lucille Busby.

"That was when you came in, Mom," Allison said, looking up at Leigh. "You asked me about Lucille sneaking cookies. Olympia walked in, too, and said something about how well everything was going. Then Lucille started coughing. Bridget reached for the glass of water that was on the floor, but she knocked it over."

"Why *was* the glass on the floor?" Leigh interrupted, remembering her mother's fear that punch had spilled on the carpet.

"Lucille wouldn't let me leave it on the table!" Bridget defended. "Everything was set just so with the decorations and all, and she couldn't hold it in her lap. What else was I supposed to do with it?"

"Anyway," Allison went on determinedly, "Lucille was still coughing. Bridget, you went out to get water, and Grandma came in."

Bridget nodded enthusiastically. "When I got back, all four of you were there with her, and she had a cup of punch in her hand. But *I* didn't give it to her! Did I?"

"No," Allison answered. "Olympia did."

Bridget's eyes bugged. "Olympia? I didn't know if it was her or Frances. I wasn't paying any attention before — I mean, to who had a drink with them. And then I had to leave again to get a towel. You told the police all that?"

"Of course," Allison confirmed.

Bridget's chest heaved with a sigh. "Oh! Oh, that's wonderful. I... I didn't know."

"Why do you think it matters so much?" Allison asked pointedly.

Bridget wiped her reddened eyes with a hand. "Because I've been thinking about it. How... I mean *when* she might have... you know." Bridget turned to Leigh with a guilty look. "I kind of lied to you that night," she said miserably. "Miss Lucille does nod off in her chair sometimes, but I was really surprised that she fell asleep then. She was so worked up from all the excitement, I expected her to just get crankier and crankier. But by the time I finished sopping up the water from the carpet, she was all mellowed out, and just a couple minutes later, she was out like a light."

Bridget's eyes got teary again. "I was surprised, but God forgive me, I was just so *glad!* When I went to throw away the napkin and the empty cups it occurred to me that maybe she got a little alcohol in her punch, too, and that's what made her sleepy. I didn't worry about it because that's why she drank the gin at home, to help her sleep. Anyway, she seemed peaceful, and she wasn't yelling at me anymore, and I never thought—" The assistant's voice broke down again.

Leigh looked at her husband, who lifted one eyebrow back at her. The woman was pretty damned convincing.

"Lucille drank the entire cup of punch that Olympia gave her," Allison said to her parents. "I wonder if she noticed alcohol in it. She did say, 'I like that one. Fruity.'"

Bridget raised her head. "She said what? 'Fruity?'"

Allison nodded.

Bridget looked from Leigh to Warren. "That's funny. I'd say it had a bitter tang, if anything. It was cognac. Right?"

Leigh nodded. "But… we don't know if Olympia got her punch before or after the bowl was spiked. There might not have been any alcohol in her serving."

"Lenna might remember if she served Olympia before or after Harry came in and hung up the mistletoe," Allison piped up. "Or Grandma Lydie might know."

"But if there wasn't any alcohol in it, why did Lucille fall asleep?" Bridget insisted. "She didn't say she felt bad." Her hands flew to her mouth and her voice turned frantic again. "Unless it really was poisoned!"

Olympia. Leigh's pulse began to pound in her ears. "Allie," she whispered too quietly for Bridget to hear, "what did you write about Olympia in that notebook? The one that was stolen?"

Allison turned to face her mother. "Nothing about what happened with Lucille. Just medical stuff that Virginia told me."

The pounding pulse continued. "What kind of medical stuff?"

Allison motioned for Leigh to bend down a little. Leigh did so, and her daughter whispered in her ear. "She has this condition called Conn's syndrome. It's where her adrenal glands don't work right. I don't really understand it, even after Grandpa explained it to me. But it causes high blood pressure and problems with electrolytes, and if you don't treat it, you can die of a stroke. Olympia is on medication, but Virginia said it's tough to dose correctly because she has some other health problems too. So her blood pressure can go low or high. It's made her pass out a couple times, which is why she doesn't drive anymore."

Leigh straightened up. She needed to let some of the blood flow out of her head, otherwise she couldn't hear over the pounding in her ears. After a few seconds, she bent back down again. "You wrote all that down?" she asked.

"Of course," Allison whispered. "It means that Olympia had a lot of medication on hand. Probably stuff that could have been bad for Lucille. Because Lucille had congestive heart failure, and early kidney failure, too. There are all kinds of drug interactions and—"

"I get the picture," Leigh said faintly, straightening again. She reminded herself that every bit of this information was already in the police department's hands. She reminded herself that she had always considered every Floribunda a suspect. But those reminders didn't help.

Frances liked Olympia. Frances trusted Olympia. Frances was with Olympia *right now.*

Leigh recalled with sudden, icy clarity the eloquent speech she had made to the Floribundas about how Allison wasn't interested in the case anymore. They had all been gathered in her mother's living room at the time.

All of them *except* Olympia.

"Leigh?" she heard Warren say. "What are you thinking?"

They spoke on the phone and visited, Melvin had said of Olympia and Lucille. *The two of them were rather close, I gather.*

Leigh could stand it no longer.

"If you'll excuse us, Bridget," she said firmly. "There's somewhere we have to go."

Chapter 24

"I can't believe you made me leave cheerleading early just to go to my Grandma's house!" Lenna whined. "It was *so* embarrassing!"

"Sorry," Leigh said insincerely. Warren was driving their van as fast as he safely could, but the extra time it had taken to pick Lenna up at the middle school had fried what few nerves Leigh had left. They had only been fifteen minutes early to pick Lenna up, which was certainly better than abandoning her at the school. At least Mathias wasn't Leigh's responsibility; he had basketball until dinnertime on Tuesdays and his dad picked him up then. Her plan was to drop off all three kids at her Aunt Lydie's house, then go babysit her mother until the Floribundas left. Then she and Frances were going to have a very long, very honest, and no doubt very upsetting conversation. Preferably with Warren there. The world's most perfect son-in-law might have no independent knowledge of the situation, but if he vouched for Leigh's opinion, Frances would give it twice the weight.

Leigh checked her voice mail on her cell phone and used an app to check her landline at home. There was still no response from Maura. Leigh had left a second message informing the detective that they had talked to Bridget and were now headed to the Koslows' house. The local police had been called off, but Leigh was perfectly prepared to place another call now if anything at the Koslow home appeared... well... out of control.

But that wasn't going to happen.

Allison's small voice piped up from the back seat. "Mom, I think Bridget's following us again."

Are you kidding me? Leigh swung around. Sure enough, the ratty old car was right behind their bumper. "She's not even trying to hide herself!" she said to Warren.

"Well, that's a good sign," he answered. "She probably just wants to know what's going on. You bundled us all in the car so fast... she seemed to have more she wanted to say. Or ask."

"Well, I can't help that," Leigh replied. "I'm not leaving my mother alone with Olympia."

"The two of them are very unlikely to be alone, you know," Warren assured. "It is an official meeting."

"I know," Leigh answered, feeling no better as dark visions played in her head of the Floribundas standing in a circle holding candles and wearing long red robes with thorns sticking out of their heads. "Hurry."

"Mom," Allison piped up again. "I haven't told you what else I found out about the Peppers."

"Do I want to know?" Leigh asked weakly.

"Well, I don't know if it's important, but it is kind of interesting," Allison answered. "Those databases are *so* cool, Dad! You wouldn't believe what I could find out, just over lunch!"

Leigh threw her husband a sideways glare. He smiled back sheepishly.

"Melvin's last name is Dumke," Allison began, consulting her pocket notebook. "He's spent most of his life in and around New York City. Olympia is his first and only wife. But get this: he didn't even meet her until after he moved to Rochester ten years ago!"

"Really?" Leigh said with surprise. "How long have they been married?"

"Not even seven years," Allison answered. "Isn't that wild? And he's her third husband. She's been married to a chiropractor and a radiologist. Widowed both times."

Leigh's heart dropped into her shoes. "Warren—"

"I know. I'm getting there as fast as I can," he insisted.

"They were both a lot older than her," Allison added. "So I'm not sure you should read too much into that. But I do think I know why she and Melvin changed their names."

Leigh sucked in a breath and prepared herself. They were only a block away now. "Yes?"

"Malpractice," Allison said grimly. "Melvin got sued. A bunch of times, all of them last year. I'm guessing that's why he retired. And why they sold their house. And why they moved to a low-rent apartment in another state where nobody knew them."

Warren let out a whistle. "Well, that makes sense."

"You found all that out with your birthday presents?" Ethan asked incredulously, pausing a moment in the app he was playing, which had been making exploding sounds the whole drive.

"Yep," Allison answered proudly.

"Sweet," Ethan replied. He returned to his game.

Lenna, who was in the third row of the van, was busy texting and paid no attention to any of them.

"Oh," Allison spoke up. "And Mom, Olympia's not a tax attorney, either. She's an accountant."

Leigh had no business being surprised by that.

"We're here," Warren announced, shifting the van into park. "As close as I can get, anyway. The Floribundas take up a lot of parking spaces."

Leigh hopped out and hurried the kids along. It was amazing how slowly middle schoolers got out of a car. In elementary school, the kids would be halfway across a parking lot before she could get her seatbelt undone. Now they stared at their phones like zombies and practically had to be pried out.

"Could you take them to Aunt Lydie's?" Leigh asked Warren when they finally began walking toward the houses. "I'll have to go to my mom's alone. She already told me their meetings are 'closed.'"

"So what are you going to do?" Warren asked.

"Sneak into the kitchen and wait it out," Leigh replied. "I can't let Olympia get her alone."

"You're not going to eavesdrop on the meeting, though, are you, Mom?" Allison asked innocently. "Because eavesdropping is rude and dishonest."

Leigh looked down to find her daughter directly behind her elbow, as expected. Her voice was convincing enough, but the girl's dark eyes couldn't hide a sassy glimmer of sarcasm.

"Of course," Allison went on, using her most mature tone, "eavesdropping *can* be an okay thing to do, if you're trying to protect somebody who might be in danger. Isn't that right, Mom?"

"I didn't—" Leigh gnashed her teeth. She could see her parents' house up ahead. "Your dad will explain it." She broke into a jog, then called back over her shoulder. "I'll text you!"

She did not let her gaze dwell on the look her husband was giving her. She whipped her head back around and focused on the mission before her. She had no intention of confronting Olympia Pepp—. Well, Olympia whatever-her-name-was. Leigh's only goal was to get the woman out of her mother's house, and then clue

Frances in on what had probably happened so that they could all stay away from the pathological liar in the future.

Leigh drew close to the houses, then skirted around to avoid being seen through her parents' living room windows. She crept up to the back door, found it unlocked, and quietly made her way into the kitchen. No way would her father be home — she wasn't worried about that. Nor were the Floribundas likely to congregate in the kitchen, as most women did. Frances's crowd liked to keep it formal, convening in the living room for the business meeting and eating — if food were involved — in the dining room on china plates.

At this moment, the women were in the living room. Leigh could hear their voices as soon as she entered. She crept over and leaned into the corner by the kitchen doorway.

"Anna Marie has done what she thought best, Virginia, dear," Delores was saying in her fake sweet voice. "Even if it might put us all behind bars, I'm sure that's not her concern."

"Oh, stuff it, Delores!" Anna Marie spat back. "I don't want to be president again! Do you? She was going to find out anyway."

"Oh dear, oh dear," Virginia was moaning. "I do believe she's in shock."

"Olympia?" Frances crooned. "Are you all right?"

Leigh couldn't help herself. She eased her way around the doorframe until she could just peer into the living room with one eye. She couldn't see much, but the sliver of the room she could see is where Olympia was standing, looking pale and totally adrift. Frances stood next to her.

"We wanted to tell you earlier, but really, it was better for you if you didn't know," Frances explained. "Once the investigation started, we were strongly advised not to talk about it at all."

"Everyone knew?" Olympia asked finally, her voice shaky. "Lucille asked every one of you to… to kill her?"

"Kill is such a crass-sounding word," Anna Marie retorted. "Assisted suicide sounds much better."

"The answer is no," Frances said forcefully. "Lucille did not ask me."

Olympia turned and studied her. "Oh," she said simply.

Frances's cheeks reddened. She looked affronted. "The point is," she continued, assuming a lofty tone, "your contention that you cannot continue to serve as our president because we do not trust you is incorrect. Anna Marie has proven that we do. We have told you one of our deepest and darkest secrets."

"There's more?" Olympia croaked.

"No," Anna Marie answered sharply. "Now, are you going to stay on as president or not?"

Olympia looked conflicted. She also looked horrified.

Leigh's head swam with confusion. If she didn't know her own mother, she would be calling 911 right now, ready to have all six of these women — plus the one who was home sick in bed — arrested for conspiracy. Conspiracy to commit *what* she still wasn't sure, but they sure as hell sounded guilty of something.

"I… Well, I…" Olympia stammered. "I still can't believe it. Are you saying that Lucille's son is in on this? And that someone really did… I mean… one of *you…*"

"Well, *I* don't know that," Virginia said defensively. "Do you, Olympia? Who does?"

Leigh couldn't see Virginia, but she got the idea that the woman's piercing eyes were floating around the room with an accusing look, because the women she could see were all taking a sudden, intense interest in either the floor or the ceiling.

"Mortal sin!" Jennie Ruth boomed out.

Maybe not a conspiracy, Leigh thought with relief. These women couldn't possibly work together well enough to join forces for evil.

A loud, angry rapping sounded on the front door.

"Good heavens!" Frances said with a start. "Who on earth could that—"

Virginia jumped to the window. "It's Bridget!"

Crap! Once Leigh had ruled out the woman as a threat to the children, she had forgotten her entirely.

"Bridget?" Frances questioned, even as she turned the knob. She had barely opened the door when Lucille's heretofore unassertive personal assistant burst through the opening and into the room.

"Where is she?" Bridget demanded, looking around frantically until her eyes alighted on Olympia, who had been standing behind her. "*You!*" she screeched. "*You* did it! You poisoned Miss Lucille!"

The Floribundas let out a collective gasp, and Olympia collapsed against the arm of the wing chair. "You… you're insane," she said weakly. She looked toward the door, but Bridget immediately backed up and blocked it. The Floribundas rose to their feet. Olympia pulled out her phone. She looked around at them all, her eyes wide and wild. "You're all insane!" She looked down at her phone and texted something.

"Do calm down!" Frances ordered gruffly. "And sit down! This meeting is still called to order!"

"Anna Marie is sergeant-at-arms!" Virginia groused.

"Clamp it, Virginia!" Anna Marie ordered. "Everybody *sit down!*"

The other women all groused and moved back a bit, but only Anna Marie actually sat down. The rest continued to hold their ranks in a menacing semi-circle around Olympia.

"I don't know what she's talking about!" Olympia declared. "I swear! I didn't know about any of this!"

"It was your punch!" Bridget continued, her whole body shaking. "Bobby blames me, everybody blames me. The police are trying to arrest me, to put me in jail, to ruin my life! But I didn't give her anything she shouldn't have had and I didn't do anything wrong!"

Leigh's feet fidgeted beneath her. She wasn't in the kitchen anymore. She couldn't remember quite how that had happened, but she was now standing at the edge of the living room. Of course Bridget would know about the upcoming Floribunda meeting — and she would expect Olympia to be there. Did Bridget hope to trick Olympia into a confession in front of everyone? Or was she just flipping out from pure emotion?

"You lie like a rug," Virginia accused Olympia. "How do we know you're not lying now?"

"I'm not!" Olympia insisted, rising to her full height. "It's true that I do… exaggerate sometimes. But it's just a little game I play!" She looked around at all their faces in appeal. "It's how I got this chapter on the Holiday House Tour, isn't it? And you were fine with my methods when I was helping you!"

"She does have a point, ladies!" Frances agreed.

"Murderer!" Jennie Ruth bellowed.

Olympia sank down on the chair arm again.

"Now, let's be reasonable," Virginia argued. "Even if Olympia did help Lucille along, we all know it was a kindness. Why, it was practically a fiduciary duty, if you think about her family!" She stopped and glared at Jennie Ruth. "So stop with the moralizing, you old fuddy duddy!"

"Virginia!" Anna Marie said hotly. "We are *not* alone!"

Virginia glanced up at Bridget. "Aw, hell," she said dismissively. "She's bound to know."

"Know what?" Bridget shrieked. "What's going on, here?" She looked past the women and over at Leigh. "You know about this, too?"

All eyes turned to Leigh.

Frances jumped. "Where did *you* come from?"

Leigh's cheeks flamed with heat. She'd long since forgotten the incognito thing.

She was saved from answering by Olympia, who rose again and made a move for the door. "Don't you dare!" Bridget demanded, blocking her again. "Not until you admit what you did! Tell them it was you and not me!"

"I don't know what you're talking about!" Olympia fired back.

"What was in the punch?" Bridget pressed. "I know it was the punch that killed her. It was the only thing I didn't give her myself! She was fine all day, awake and alert. Then she drank that one cup of punch and she nodded right off. Within *minutes* her eyes were closed. And she never woke up!"

Leigh watched in horror as Frances made a strangled sound. Her hands flew to her throat. "The punch?" she rasped. "My punch?"

"No, Mom!" Leigh cried. "Not your punch! If anything was in it, it was added later!"

"You added it!" Bridget accused, sticking a pudgy finger in Olympia's face. "What did you put in there?"

"I don't have to listen to this!" Olympia fired back, shoving Bridget's hand aside. "Get out of my way!"

"Let her go!" Leigh yelled to Bridget, who was attempting to block the door again. "The police will catch up to her!"

But Bridget wasn't listening. A catfight of a shoving match ensued at the door, with both women using their bulk to try and oust the other from the vicinity of the doorknob. Olympia was taller and had longer arms, but Bridget was plumper and nimbler, and the two banged around in a well-matched tussle while Leigh and Frances stood back in dismay and the rest of the Floribundas egged on the conflict with assorted screams, screeches, hoots, and whistles.

Olympia seemed about to get the upper hand when the front door burst open and both women tumbled into a heap on the floor.

"What the blazes is going on in here?" Mason demanded, stepping into the doorway with Warren close on his heels.

The room went quiet. Olympia and Bridget both adjusted their rumpled clothing and scrambled to a more dignified sitting position.

Frances cleared her throat. "Point of Order."

Olympia struggled to her feet and smoothed her hair. "Yes?"

"I move to adjourn."

Chapter 25

Olympia glared at Bridget from the relative safety of Mason's side. "I am leaving now," she announced with a theatrical tone. "I have come into your storied chapter, I have been willing to serve, and if I do say so myself, I have done an excellent job of it. And if this is the way I am to be repaid, I will tender my resignation via written correspondence." She turned to the door with her nose in the air, and both Mason and Warren made way to let her leave.

Leigh's shoulders sagged with relief. But her reprieve was short-lived.

"No, Olympia," Frances insisted, stepping forward. "Don't go. And don't resign. I, for one, do *not* believe that you poisoned Lucille Busby. I just don't believe it!"

Oh, Mom, Leigh thought miserably. *Don't say that.*

"Who else agrees with me?" Frances said confidently, looking around the room.

The other Floribundas looked back at her. Then they all looked everywhere except at her. Lips pursed and backs straightened. No one said a word.

"I see," Olympia said blandly. "Well. That's that, then." She stepped between the men and out onto the porch.

Leigh released the pent-up breath she was holding. But again, the feeling of relief didn't last. As Mason and Warren followed Olympia out the door, Leigh looked past them and could see that the children and Lydie had gathered outside on the lawn. *Fabulous.* She headed toward the door herself.

"Olympia did too do it!" Bridget insisted to Frances. "The only question is why!"

"Why?" Virginia repeated with a laugh. "That's not a question at all!"

"Of course it is!" Bridget cried. "Miss Lucille didn't have much money, but all she had and even anything she might get from insurance is going straight to Bobby! She was a hateful old thing, but that's no reason to kill her. And Olympia barely knew her! What could she possibly get out of it?"

Leigh stopped walking. Something was wrong.

Anna Marie sighed loudly. "Go home, Bridget," she said dismissively. "There are things you don't need to know. Okay?"

Bridget balled her fists and let out a shriek of frustration. Then she brushed past Leigh and stormed out the door.

"Wait!" Leigh called, following her onto the porch. Olympia was standing on the sidewalk now, facing away. She appeared to be waiting for her ride home. "What did you say?" Leigh asked. But Bridget kept walking. The personal assistant was down the steps and into the yard, not far from where Lydie and the children stood, when Leigh took a chance and grabbed her arm. "Please, Bridget, stop a minute!"

"What do you want?" she cried.

"How well did Olympia and Lucille know each other?" Leigh asked.

Bridget looked at her as though the question were stupid. She shrugged. "They saw each other at these meetings."

Leigh had a niggling worry that she was missing something. "I was under the impression that Olympia had been meeting with Lucille secretly," she confessed. "Maybe talking on the phone. And that the others didn't necessarily know about it."

Bridget's lips screwed up into a puzzled frown. "Well, that's news to me. I don't see how. I was with the woman practically every second."

"I see," Leigh murmured, not seeing at all. If Olympia had plotted with Lucille, how had they managed it? Had it all been done through Bobby? If so, why was *he* so confused?

"I'm telling you," Bridget said again, with conviction. "Whatever killed Lucille was in the punch. The punch that Olympia gave her. And I'm done running. I'm going to tell the police everything I know *right now!*"

"There was nothing poisonous in the punch!" Lydie protested hotly.

Bridget and Leigh swung around. Lydie and the children were standing within steps of them. The Floribundas were all either on the porch or spilling out into the yard, even Anna Marie. Mason and Warren had positioned themselves between Bridget and the still-waiting Olympia.

"Maybe not when you served it," Bridget argued. "At least nothing but a little harmless cognac! But there was something else in it after *she* got hold of it and gave it to Miss Lucille!" Bridget pointed at Olympia. Olympia lifted her chin again and turned her back.

Leigh heard an animalistic sound, rather like a whimper. Frances was clutching her throat again. She sank down to sit on the porch steps.

"Oh, good Lord, Frances!" Lydie objected again. "There was *nothing wrong* with the punch we served!"

"We never even served punch to Olympia!" an unexpected soprano voice piped up.

All eyes focused on Lenna. "Remember, Grandma?" the girl said to Lydie. "She tasted it at lunch and said she liked it, but once the tour started she wouldn't drink a thing."

A shadow passed over Lydie's face. "That's true," she confirmed. "Olympia never did take any punch. I remember offering it."

"She told me she didn't want to drink any liquids because too many people would be using the bathrooms," Lenna reported. "She said it was better to wait until they were properly cleaned or we all got home."

Leigh looked over her shoulder at Olympia. The chapter president was facing Lydie now. She was watching them all, but her eyes seemed vacant, suddenly. Unseeing.

A twinge of fear crawled up Leigh's spine.

"Well, she must have stolen some punch when you weren't looking, then!" Bridget insisted. "Because she certainly had a cup!"

Olympia remained standing stiffly for a moment, still staring. At the sound of an approaching car, she turned her head down the street, then bolted like a startled cat. She jumped straight up in the air, hit the ground running, and raced through the yard and back up onto the porch. She appeared to be aiming for the door, but, seeing her path blocked by numerous Floribundas, she stopped and spun around frantically, seemingly looking for someplace else to go. Finally she squatted down right where she was — hiding herself behind the brick porch railing.

"Wages of sin!" Jennie Ruth bellowed, pointing at her.

Everyone else simply stared, befuddled.

"Mom," Allison spoke up. "I saw Olympia, like, ten minutes

before Lucille started coughing, and she wasn't carrying a cup of punch then. If Lenna and Grandma say Olympia didn't get that cup herself, then she must have asked someone else to get it for her."

"Her husband!" Lenna exclaimed. "He got a cup the same time Bridget did. He must have given her his!"

Allison nodded. "And that cup would have been laced with alcohol, which could have put Lucille to sleep. But... Olympia only offered it to Lucille because she started to cough!"

Light flooded Leigh's clouded brain. God bless her daughter's memory! "Of course!" she agreed. She turned to Bridget. "Olympia didn't intentionally poison Lucille! Don't you see? She would have had to carry a tainted cup around for who knows how long, not taking a single sip of it herself, just waiting for a chance to offer it to Lucille! How much sense does that make? Especially when you always kept a glass of water on hand? Did Olympia ever offer Lucille a drink before that? Did she ever offer her anything?"

Bridget's air of confidence faded. "No."

"But the water glass *conveniently* spilled just before then, didn't it?" Virginia insisted.

"I spilled it," Bridget admitted glumly. "It was full before."

Everyone went quiet again.

"Well, hell's fire," Virginia muttered. "If Olympia didn't put poison in the cup, then what happened to Lucille? Did she really just kick the bucket? Surely that little bit of cognac couldn't have done it!"

Frances moaned louder. From the porch behind the railing came a gasp, then a muffled whimper.

There were some other abnormalities in the bloodwork that led the ME to order a full toxicology screening... Maura's voice floated through Leigh's brain like a heavy, noxious cloud. *A medication overdose...*

"Hello, there!" a deep voice called out. Melvin had to stretch his neck to stick his head out the window of his car, which he had just double-parked in front of the house. "I'm here for Olympia... She seemed very anxious to leave in her text. Is she inside? Is everything all right?"

A sudden coldness burned in the pit of Leigh's stomach. Kind, gentle Melvin. He had been so upset at Lucille's death. Genuinely shocked. Genuinely horrified.

Of course he was.

He'd intended to murder someone else.

"No," Leigh answered quickly, no less than three times louder than necessary. "She isn't here."

Melvin looked at her with confusion, raising one thick, bushy eyebrow. "Well, where is she then?"

Good question. Curse her lousy lying ability!

"She couldn't wait," said a small voice from the vicinity of Leigh's elbow. "She saw there was a rideshare, like, a block away. So she just took that."

Melvin appeared slightly disgruntled. "Well. That was fast."

"Yeah," Allison said brightly, smiling. For once, the girl was intentionally acting like a twelve-year-old. "I showed her how to use the app. It's pretty neat."

Leigh's heart pounded in her chest. Melvin Dumke the proctologist looked so impossibly normal. So thoroughly, fantastically, boringly mundane. *Olympia had a lot of medication on hand,* Allison had reported. *Probably stuff that could have been bad for Lucille.* A doctor would know just what to do with that medication, wouldn't he? Just what would, and wouldn't, be good for a woman with Conn's syndrome.

It was tough to dose correctly.

Leigh turned her head slowly up toward the porch. She had no idea what the Floribundas were thinking. They could rat her and Allison out at any second, and she would be at a loss to explain herself. She doubted seriously that Melvin carried any weapon, and both Warren and Mason were standing a few yards away, pretending *not* to be watching the man with every muscle tensed. Still, Leigh's teeth practically rattled in their sockets. If Lucille hadn't had that coughing fit… If Olympia had drunk her own cup of punch… Would she have passed out first? Then died of… what? A heart attack?

Leigh's gaze passed over the front of the house. The Floribundas had moved. They were all standing on the porch now, clumped up in a close, odd formation like they were expecting someone to take their picture, but hadn't gotten their order worked out yet. They were staring down at the people in the yard with chins and eyebrows raised, their arms folded mutinously across their chests.

They looked scary as hell.

Melvin followed Leigh's gaze. He twitched a bit. "Well," he said awkwardly, averting his eyes. "I suppose Olympia went on home, then?"

"I suppose," Leigh answered mildly. "She didn't say."

Her thoughts, as she gazed back at the good doctor, were anything but mild. Yes, if Olympia had drunk her own punch, she might have passed out. She had passed out anyway, just from the shock of seeing Lucille. *Someone* had been acting then, hadn't they? But the person acting had been Melvin, when he pretended to be surprised to find his wife on the floor. What really surprised him was finding out that she was perfectly fine.

Melvin had expected Olympia to have a fatal attack, hadn't he? And he expected that no one would question it. Because her condition predisposed her to that risk. There would be no reason for a toxicology screening at her autopsy. Not if he didn't request one. Not if there was every reason to believe that her stroke or heart attack was brought on by natural causes, like the stress of the occasion, or —

It's snowing anthrax over there!

Leigh's breath shuddered in her chest. Of course. Who better to push Olympia's buttons? To stoke her worst fears and phobias to a fever pitch? The timing had been perfect. Olympia would have collapsed in the middle of the chaos, and no wonder. After all, she was a known hysteric when it came to contagious disease!

"Are you all right, Ms. Harmon?" Melvin asked with concern. "You look a little peaked."

He looked so sincere. So humdrum. So harmless.

He was counting on that, wasn't he?

"I'm fine," Leigh answered. "Just a little cold." Indeed she was cold. Every part of her body was freezing. But she had no business complaining. The Floribundas were all far older than she was, and every one of them had rushed outside without a coat.

She shot another look at the porch. The women hadn't moved. To a one, they glared at Melvin as if daring him to breathe.

"I... uh... guess I'll be getting along then," he said uncertainly.

"Have a good day," Leigh lied. "I hope you catch up with Olympia."

He smiled back at her, displaying yellowed teeth with a hint of black at the gums. How the heck had a germophobe like Olympia handled being married to a proctologist, anyway? "I'm sure I will," he said heavily.

"Merry Christmas," Leigh lied again.

He exchanged polite waves with the others in the yard, then drove away.

"Oh, my God," Bridget said in shaky voice. "I've got to get out of here. I want to talk to the police!" She pranced about skittishly, looking down the street and wringing her hands. "Oh... my car's parked two blocks away! What if he comes back?"

"We'll walk you back to your car, Bridget," Warren offered, gesturing to Ethan. Then he stepped up and gave both Leigh and Allison a quick hug around the shoulders. "Tell everyone not to worry. I texted Mo. She'll be here soon."

Up on the porch, Virginia and Anna Marie were pulling Olympia to her feet. "Come on, now, dear," Delores chirped, reaching up to pat Olympia's pale cheeks. "It's not that bad. Why, my second husband used to threaten to kill me all the time!"

"All the time!" Jennie Ruth confirmed, nodding emphatically.

"That sneaky little mole!" Virginia ranted, stamping her foot. "The nerve of him! And to try such a thing at an official Floribunda function!"

"He thought he was so clever!" Anna Marie said snidely. She had thrown one of Olympia's arms around her own shoulders and was supporting her sagging frame. "Well, I guessed what he was up to!"

"Oh, sure you did!" Virginia scoffed. "Maybe thirty seconds ago, right along with the rest of us!"

"But why?" Lenna called out with suitable melodrama as she clung to her grandfather's side. "Why would her husband want to kill her?"

The Floribundas exchanged odd glances. Leigh wondered if they were shocked by the insensitivity of the question. Then she realized that was stupid. "Yeah!" Virginia clamored, looking at Olympia. "Why *would* the old fart want to do you in, anyway?"

"Did you get him to marry you without a prenup?" Anna Marie asked excitedly.

"I would *never* accept a prenup!" Delores said fiercely. Then her tone thickened to syrup. "I would simply explain that my wifely favors are to be shared only within the confines of *eternal* wedded bliss."

"Pants on fire!" Jennie Ruth snickered.

"I'm so cold," Olympia said dully.

"Well, of course you are!" Virginia replied. "Let's get her inside, women, and we'll warm her right up! Don't you worry about a thing now, Olympia. We all know what happened. The police are going to catch up with that slimy little scumbucket, and when we all start talking they'll be sure to lock him up and throw away the key!"

Olympia hobbled toward the house, supported by Anna Marie on one side and Virginia on the other. "Really? You'll do that for me?"

"Why of course!" Delores cooed. "You're a Floribunda, aren't you?"

"But... you thought I was a murderess!" Olympia protested meekly.

"Murderesses aren't all bad," Virginia said lightly. "Besides, we were defending another Floribunda, then. But Melvin is nothing to us. We protect our own."

"And that's you, lady," Anna Marie said, beginning to breathe heavily as she moved Olympia through the doorway. "You're one of us, now!"

"For-ev-er, Flor-i-bun-das!" Jennie Ruth sang. She brought up the rear of the procession, waited a moment for Frances to join them, gave up with a shrug, then pulled the door closed.

Frances, whose face had only slighter more color than Olympia's, had sunk down on the steps again. Her eyes stared out at nothing. Leigh and Lydie exchanged a defeated glance. Allison looked up at her mother with confusion, just as Lenna threw an equally baffled glance at her grandfather. "What's wrong with Grandma Frances?" she asked.

Leigh shivered. The sky was darkening to a thick, smoky gray. Frances had no coat on.

Mason took a step toward her. "It wasn't your fault, Francie," he said.

Frances startled as if she'd been struck. "What did you say?"

"I said it wasn't your fault," he repeated. "That someone tried to commit a crime in your house. With your bowl of punch. It's still nothing to do with you."

Frances made no response. She went back to staring straight

through him.

"Go on back in the house," he suggested, his voice mild. "You'll freeze to death out here."

"No, thank you," Frances said listlessly.

"Mason's right," Lydie agreed. "It's too cold to sit out here. If you won't go in your house, then come on over to ours."

"I don't think so," Frances said robotically. "But thank you."

Lydie's face clouded. Leigh could feel that same, angry heat radiating off her body again. "Girls," Lydie said, her voice mild again, albeit strained, "please go back on over to my house. I'd like you to put some hot water on. We'll all have hot chocolate in a bit."

"Okay, Grandma," Lenna agreed, releasing her grandpa and grabbing Allison's coat by the sleeve as she passed. "She said you, too!" she nagged her cousin. "I don't want to go alone, and it's cold out here. Come on!"

Reluctantly, Allison moved off.

"All right, Frances," Lydie spouted the second the girls had closed the front door behind them. "Now, you listen to me. I've had enough! I'm sorry about everything that's happened, but I am *not* going to let you keep treating the man I love like he is a piece of gum on the bottom of your shoe!"

"Lydie," Mason implored, "Don't—"

"You be quiet!" Lydie fired back.

"What?" Frances replied, looking at her twin with genuine surprise. "But I— I've been perfectly polite!"

"Well, 'perfectly polite' isn't good enough anymore!"

"Lydie," Mason said firmly, taking his fiance's hand. "Please, now isn't the time for this. Look at her, will you? She's not even *here*. She's back in the nineteen sixties."

Frances's head whipped up toward Mason. "I'm sure I don't know what you're talking about," she said haughtily, sounding more like herself.

Mason smiled a bit. "Oh, I'm sure you do. It wasn't such a big secret back when we were young, remember?"

Frances's face drained of color again. She threw a panicked glance at Leigh.

"Yes, Mom," Leigh admitted softly. "I know about your sixteenth birthday party. What I know is that it was the kind of mistake that could happen to anybody. You've only made it into something huge in your mind. And what happened then has nothing to do with what just happened here."

Frances looked like she wanted to crawl underneath the porch and die. "Doesn't it?" she moaned. "A woman was murdered because she drank punch that was served in my house!"

"*You* didn't poison that punch," Mason stated flatly. "And frankly, I've always had my doubts about that damned potato salad, too!"

Frances's eyes shifted. She looked fully back at Mason for the first time all night. "What are you talking about?"

"Food poisoning!" he answered. "I've had it myself. Seen it more than once. And it never happens like Lydie's described it at your party — with everybody getting sick all at once like that. That story never did make sense to me."

"A doctor said so," Frances replied. "He said I sneezed and it poisoned them."

"Yeah, well," Mason said skeptically. "The doctor wasn't there, was he? He was getting the story from other people. Didn't sound like he ran any tests or anything."

"For heaven's sake, Mason, what are you getting at?" Lydie asked. "The doctor said it was food poisoning. It all happened ages ago. What does it matter now?"

Mason huffed out a breath. "It might have happened ages ago, but if it didn't still matter to your sister, she wouldn't be so messed up in the head she can't tell her butt's sitting on frozen concrete."

As if taking some cosmic cue, the Christmas lights on the house suddenly switched on, bathing them all in a kaleidoscope of color. Evidently, Warren and the boys had used a timer.

"Gary threw up his s'more you know," Frances said feebly, oblivious. "I haven't been able to eat one of those things since. He threw up all over a bunch of people. And then one of them threw up, too."

"Frances, *stop*," Lydie said with frustration. "This isn't helping anything. Why can't you just forget about it?"

"Let her talk," Mason argued. "I never heard about the s'mores before. I thought they threw up the potato salad. That's one of the reasons the story didn't make sense! Food poisoning doesn't happen instantly. Some people get sick in a few hours, other people take half a day. It's spread out."

"Oh," Frances said thoughtfully, remembering. "Well, they ate the potato salad earlier in the afternoon, but nobody got sick right away. They got sick when it started to rain. The rain ruined everything."

"So one person threw up, then another?" Mason asked. "For all we know, the rest could have gotten sick to their stomachs just seeing the mess from the first guy!"

"Oh no, they were far too ill for it to be just that," Lydie insisted. "No one wanted the party to end. We were all having a good time. Even with the rain!"

"Wait," Mason interrupted. "How did you make s'mores in the rain? Didn't your bonfire go out?"

Lydie laughed. "Our father? Approve a bonfire? Are you kidding? We used a charcoal grill, same as with the hot dogs."

Mason's brow furrowed. "On your back patio?"

Lydie shrugged. "I don't remember where we had it. It was a little portable thing."

"Describe the scene to me," Mason insisted, turning to Frances. "Tell me what it looked like. When the very first person got sick."

"Mason!" Lydie objected. "I really don't see—"

"Please," he begged, his blue-green eyes beseeching as he looked into his fiance's face. Always the charmer, Mason's earnestness made him look boyishly attractive as he stood in the glow of the Christmas lights, and Leigh doubted her aunt could stand up to such pressure. In fact, she could not. Lydie cracked a smile.

Mason smiled back at her, then turned to Frances. "Tell me," he repeated.

"They were making s'mores," Frances began. "Gary was irritating me, because he was flirting with Patsy. I had asked him if he wanted a s'more, and I brought all the supplies out, and then he offered to make one for *her*." Frances's lips drew into a thin, tight line.

Leigh perked an eyebrow. Mason was right. Her mother's mind really was stuck in the sixties.

"It was raining," Frances continued.

"Where was the grill?" Mason asked.

Frances thought a moment. "It was out in the yard. The patio was the dance floor. It had been sprinkling on and off all day, but when it started to rain hard, I got an umbrella. We had gathered a bunch of rain gear and everyone grabbed something and made the best of it."

"Gary got sick then?" Mason asked.

"No," Frances answered. "Only after they made the s'mores."

"You mean you stood there with umbrellas roasting marshmallows?" Mason asked. "Come on, now. Think hard. Try to picture it."

Frances's brow furrowed.

"Gary didn't have an umbrella," Lydie interjected. "Don't you remember? He and Patsy and that crowd, they were the ones that got the tarp. They threw it over their heads like a tent."

"They did what?" Mason demanded.

"But I don't remember them making s'mores," Lydie continued. "All I remember is them being out in the yard, giggling and cutting up. And then Gary vomited and after that everyone started getting sick."

"Of course they were making s'mores!" Frances retorted. "But did they have a tarp? All I remember is trying to hold an umbrella for him."

"You got mad at him for flirting with Patsy!" Lydie insisted. "You stomped off somewhere, I think."

"Did I?"

"Oh, good Lord, above!" Mason said dramatically, slapping his knee. He grabbed Frances's hands and pulled her forcibly to her feet. "Francie!" he cried, smiling broadly. "Can't you see what happened? What really happened?"

Frances stared at him as if he'd gone mad.

"Those idiots threw a tarp over their heads and stood over a charcoal grill in the rain!" Mason explained. "They didn't have food poisoning! They poisoned themselves with carbon monoxide!"

Lydie drew in a sharp breath. "Of course. Why didn't we — but I didn't know. I never saw the grill. I guess I wasn't paying attention. Or if I was, I never thought — Well, not at that age, anyway..."

"Of course you didn't!" Mason said with a laugh. "You were only kids. Even adults don't always think how fast fumes can build up in a situation like that. If your parents didn't see what they were doing, and the kids threw the tarp off right after the first guy got sick, it wouldn't be obvious to anybody what had happened!"

"Oh, Mason," Lydie exclaimed. "You're right. You're absolutely right! They were dizzy and weak and nauseous, but only a few of them actually threw up. And they did all get sick at once! Why, I've heard before that the symptoms of carbon monoxide can be mistaken for food poisoning!"

"Exactly! So," Mason said happily, turning back to Frances. "To hell with that doctor from way back when. I'd bet my bottom dollar it wasn't your potato salad at all, Francie. What happened at the Holiday House Tour wasn't your fault, and what happened at your sweet sixteen party never was your fault either! What do you think of that?"

Frances's color had returned. In fact, her complexion was glowing. She said nothing in response to Mason's question, but, to Leigh's utter amazement, she fell forward like a ton of bricks — then threw her arms around Mason's neck and hugged him.

Leigh stopped breathing. A quick glance at Lydie showed that her aunt wasn't breathing either.

The embrace lasted exactly three seconds. Then Frances stiffened, pulled back, and whacked Mason solidly on the shoulder. "Do *not* call me Francie, you reckless imp of a scallywag!"

The silence that followed was deafening. Giant, fluffy chunks of snow began to fall from the sky. One fell directly on the top of Frances's head. Another hit Leigh in the nose.

A broad smile spread slowly across Mason's face. Then he laughed out loud. "Why, Francie! I do believe that's the nicest thing you've ever said to me!"

"Don't flatter yourself!" Frances fired back, turning to start up her steps. "I have better things to do with my time than stand out here in the cold arguing with the likes of you, Mason Dublin!"

The snow began to fall faster. It stuck in Frances's hair like dandruff and attached itself to Mason's half-grown beard.

"I have a houseful of guests to see to and a fellow Floribunda to pull back from the jaws of death!" Frances continued to shout. She turned at the door, looked back at Leigh and Lydie, and moderated her tone. "Thank you for your assistance. I can manage perfectly well from here."

She looked at Mason again. Her lips pursed and her dark eyes narrowed menacingly. But not even Frances could conceal the glint of pure glee behind them. "Don't you have second-rate knives to sell or something?" she asked caustically.

The snow continued to fall, spoiling her hairdo with an uneven layer of fuzz, even as her frown was marred by lips that twitched involuntarily... unbelievably... toward a grin.

Mason said nothing. He answered her with the twinkle in his eye.

Epilogue

"I made it!" Frances said proudly, slipping through the door Leigh held open for her and into the official "bride's room" of the quaint stone Methodist church they'd attended all their lives.

"With plenty of time to spare," Leigh assured. "No one else is even here, yet."

Frances smiled with approval at Allison's modest blue velveteen dress. "Oh, how lovely you look, my dear!"

Allison smiled back, even though the dress, which she thought made her look childish, was a sore point. Her cousin Lenna's equivalent emerald green was of a similar fabric and style, but the neckline was lower, making it look considerably more mature. Still, on this happy Christmas Eve afternoon, the girl was being an exceptionally good sport. Her Aunt Lydie loved the dress, and Allison was pretending to love it, too. "Thank you, Grandma," she said cheerfully. "You look pretty, too."

Frances practically preened. Her own dress was a very dark forest green, notably less fitted and stuffy than the sort she normally wore. Lydie had picked it out for her twin herself, and Frances, after pitching the expected fit about how inappropriate such a gown was for a woman "of a certain age," was clearly enamored of it. "You look nice too, dear," she said to Leigh, albeit with noticeably less enthusiasm. "You might just want to stand up a little straighter."

Leigh let the advice roll right off her comfortably slouched shoulders. She liked her own dress, which was a simple affair in royal purple. But she would like it a whole lot better if it wasn't styled so much like Cara's, making it impossible for anyone seeing them together not to make the obvious comparison between willowy perfection and middle-aged spread.

She planned to stand next to her mother.

"What happened at the will reading, Grandma?" Allison asked eagerly.

Frances's dark eyes danced. "Oh, my," she began. "You'll never guess! Well, the Floribundas got our benevolent fund donation, as we were expecting. And it wasn't very much, which we were also expecting. It was good of Bobby to invite us all — he didn't have to, you know. But Olympia was asked to come as our representative, and I think she appreciated our support. Anyway, Bobby's been in a rather generous mood these days!"

"I can't imagine why," Leigh teased. "With the accidental death policy having to pay out after all."

"Well, they couldn't prove anything against him, could they?" Frances said good-naturedly. "What he *might* have done if he'd found a willing accomplice was hardly relevant. Personally, I don't believe he would have gone through with it. It was always just talk. Speculation and hearsay!"

"I don't know, Mom," Leigh debated. "Maybe most of the women wouldn't have had the guts, but I still think Delores would have gone for it if she didn't have to hear Jennie Ruth yelling 'mortal sin!' for the rest of their lives."

Frances chuckled a bit, then sobered with a sigh. "You know… You may be right about that."

"But what happened at the will reading, Grandma?" Allison reminded.

"Oh!" Frances replied. "Well, the most exciting thing was that Bobby felt bad that Lucille had so little of her own money left to give the garden club fund. So he made a donation of his own, right then and there, for four times as much!"

"That was nice of him," Leigh commented.

"Well, he's loaded now. He can afford it. But the real shocker was who else was mentioned in Lucille's will. Besides Bobby and the fund."

Leigh and Allison waited.

"Bridget!" Frances exclaimed. "Do you believe it?"

"No," Leigh replied. "I don't. The same Bridget that Lucille constantly yelled at and called incompetent? Why on earth would she leave her money?"

Frances smirked. "All part of the plan, dear. You know Bobby and Lucille hired her specifically *because* of her spotty reputation. Lucille was so miserable she was ready to go anytime, but she wanted her death to look like negligence. The best way to do that was for it to actually *be* negligence. She rattled poor Bridget constantly, hoping the woman would make some terrible mistake.

A true accidental overdose would be the safest thing for Bobby, you see."

"*That's* why they put Bridget in the will!" Allison exclaimed. "To make it look even worse for her!"

Leigh shook her head with disgust. "That is diabolical on so many levels! Even if Bridget made an honest mistake, the bequest would give her a motive for murder, or at least a subconscious slip! They set the poor woman up coming and going!"

Leigh stared into the bright leaves of the poinsettia that sat next to the bride's vanity, and wondered again if she would ever uncover a positive attribute of the late Lucille Busby. It seemed unlikely, now that the woman was gone. But it was Christmas Eve, it was her Aunt Lydie's wedding day, and Leigh was feeling good.

She would give Lucille the benefit of the doubt.

"Their intentions were hardly laudable," Frances agreed. "But their actions had a good outcome, nevertheless. Bridget inherited a tidy little sum. I suppose Lucille figured that if the insurance scheme worked, Bobby wouldn't need that money anyway. Bridget was dumbstruck, as you might imagine. She practically floated out of the lawyer's office."

Allison giggled. "I can picture that!"

"How is Olympia?" Leigh asked. "Is she still staying with Virginia and Harry, or is she back in her own apartment?"

"Neither," Frances replied, straightening her hair in the mirror. "She had some, well, *issues* with Harry, so she only stayed with Virginia until she got the protective order against Melvin. Then she went back to her apartment. But she's never been one to enjoy living alone. So she's moved in with Delores and Jennie Ruth."

"Seriously?" Leigh asked with disbelief.

"Oh, yes," Frances replied. "They have plenty of space. And I do believe it's helped Olympia with her... difficulty."

"You mean the lying?" Allison asked.

Frances nodded.

"How?" Leigh asked.

"Well," Frances answered, "from what I understand, every time Olympia tells a fib, Jennie Ruth shouts, 'pants on fire!'"

Leigh and Allison both laughed out loud.

Frances laughed with them. Then her expression sobered. "She seems much happier now. Apparently, near the end with Melvin, things were pretty bad. She pretended everything was fine in public, and so did he, but he was a better actor. It drove her mad that he pretended to be so solicitous in front of us, when in private they barely spoke to each other."

Leigh lowered her eyes in embarrassment. Watching the couple at the house tour, she had never imagined that their hostility went both ways. She had been as bamboozled by Melvin as anyone, thinking it was Olympia's aggression that was off base.

"He did have reason to be angry," Frances admitted. "Olympia did bankrupt the man, after all. She told him she knew how to handle his malpractice insurance, and he had no reason to doubt her, not at that point. She was a certified public accountant, and she'd been a doctor's wife twice before." Frances sighed. "But she exaggerates her accomplishments, and she can be a real goose sometimes, and she just didn't realize that monkeying with his policy was going to leave him vulnerable like that. And after the first case, well — word gets out that you're 'bare' and settling claims and people come out of the woodwork, you know? Particularly in New York. Poor Melvin didn't have to do anything wrong to be ruined."

Leigh didn't suppose Melvin was the type to make stupid mistakes. He had certainly planned out his inconvenient wife's demise well enough. He could have taken his chances, pushed her into a heart attack or stroke with her own prescribed medications, and hoped for the best. Instead, he had carefully set up a scenario that would minimize the risk of an autopsy — at least one with additional toxicology screening. He knew that the anthrax prank call, however ludicrous, would shoot up her blood pressure and provide cover for her collapse. And her concerned husband could be seen there, hovering, trying to save her. And when he failed, there would be no reason whatsoever to suspect foul play.

Leigh had to applaud the elegance of the scheme. The potassium supplement with which he'd laced Olympia's drink came in the form of a grape-flavored liquid, which she was unlikely to detect amidst the multiple sweet and sour tastes already mixed in the punch. Fluctuating potassium levels were par for the course with her illness, as were swings in blood pressure. There would be no telltale signs of poisoning to raise red flags on an ordinary autopsy. The excess potassium would simply cause her heart to stop. Even better, he himself could sip the doctored drink without concern, as could almost any healthy person. It was an apple specifically formulated for Snow White.

How could he know that it would also kill Lucille? Was Melvin banging his head on the bars of his cell right now, cursing the irony of the fact that Olympia had gifted her drink to the only other person in the house likely to be susceptible to it?

Leigh stole a glance at her phone. Melvin probably wasn't in a cell yet. But with luck, he would be soon. The final toxicology reports had only just come in, and they'd been needed to shore up the charges. Maura had promised to let Leigh know when the detective in charge of the case had served the official arrest warrant.

No, Melvin had no way of knowing that Olympia would offer her drink to someone else. No one had any way of knowing that Lucille and Olympia, though they suffered from different conditions, were taking one medication in common — a medication intended to keep potassium levels high. Melvin might have constructed an effective poison for Olympia, but for the aged and feeble Lucille, he'd created an electrolytic perfect storm.

"Of course, neither one of them had any business jumping into marriage so quickly in the first place," Frances was still opining. "Olympia insisted she loved him — that they fell in love on a cruise in the Bahamas and that neither of them wanted to wait. But I think she was lonely and just wanted to be somebody's wife again — preferably a doctor's wife. She's all about public perception, you know. As for Melvin, I wouldn't be surprised if she's the first woman who ever said yes to him. He's not terribly attractive, you know. And for all his good manners, he turned on her like a snake when she disappointed him."

Frances sighed again. "You know, Olympia believes now that he would have divorced her right then and there if they'd had a prenup. But he was so giddy in love at the beginning that they eloped without one. So instead of asking for a divorce, he went behind her back to tie up all the assets he had left. He convinced her they were flat broke, then made her move someplace where nobody knew them. Until he could... well, you know."

Leigh knew.

"I don't believe they ever *really* loved each other," Allison said knowledgeably.

Frances and Leigh both turned to look at her. "You don't think?" Leigh asked with a grin.

"Not just because he ended up trying to kill her!" Allison protested. "I mean, *duh!* But look at Aunt Lydie and Uncle Mason! They've loved each other for over forty years. The whole time they were divorced, they still loved each other. Even when they were fighting, they never remarried anyone else. And even if Aunt Lydie made a mistake that bad, Uncle Mason would forgive her. Just like Aunt Lydie forgave all his mistakes. Even if it did take her a while."

Frances favored her granddaughter with a smile. "It didn't take your Aunt Lydie so long to forgive, dear," she said quietly. "It was me who took too long." Her eyes went moist. "Lydie would have welcomed Mason back into her life much earlier if it hadn't been for me."

Leigh gulped. Her mother and Mason had been fighting like cats and dogs ever since he'd debunked the myth of the poisoned potato salad, which everyone now knew meant that they were getting along just fine. Frances and Lydie were both in the best of spirits, they were close again, and everyone was looking forward to the wedding. But Frances had never made an admission like that one.

"I didn't think he was a good person," Frances continued, her voice barely a whisper. "I didn't think he had a good heart. And I was so afraid." She collected herself, then smiled a little. "But when he made me start talking about what happened at the party way back then, I saw something in his eyes. Something I hadn't seen in so long, I... well, I didn't even remember it, honestly. But I looked, and there it was again, and all at once I just knew that he wanted to make me feel better. And that was all he wanted. Such a simple thing. And entirely unnecessary. I'd been horrible to him. He owed me nothing. He could have been doing it to score points with Lydie, but I knew he wasn't. He just... he just wanted to make me happy."

Her smile turned sheepish. "Not that wanting to please me is any requirement for a beau of Lydie's, mind you. But I realized he wouldn't have cared one fig about my feelings if he wasn't a good man. An honestly good man. With a pure heart."

"Oh he is, Grandma!" Allison said happily, giving her grandmother a hug. "And they're going to be so happy together!"

Frances swiped a tear from her cheek. "Yes, love. I believe they are."

Leigh's phone sounded with a siren tone. She looked briefly at the screen, then turned off the ringer for the duration. She would pass along Maura's update after the wedding.

We got him!

Melvin would be enjoying a jail cell this evening after all.

"We're here!" Cara announced, practically floating through the doorway, her mother's dress in hand. Lydie followed next, all smiles, but still wearing her jeans and sweatshirt. Lenna came next, followed by Leigh's Aunt Bess. Cara and Lenna looked like mother and daughter royalty in their gowns, as expected. But Leigh's darkly tanned Aunt Bess, who was wearing a simple deep blue, scoop-neck satin drape, looked almost scandalously conservative.

"Lydie's choice," Bess whispered in Leigh's ear. "But I'm not wearing any underwear."

"Come on, Mom," Cara urged, pulling the dress she carried out of its bag. "I can't wait to see you in this! We don't have that much time!"

"It won't take five minutes," Lydie said dismissively. "I just have to slip it over my head."

"But we still have to do your hair and makeup, Grandma!" Lenna insisted.

"Yes, Mom," Cara agreed. "We let you pick out all our dresses — you promised to let us give you the full treatment. Remember?"

Lydie looked at the other women, her cheeks rosy with color. She didn't have to move her lips to smile. Her whole face had been one giant smile for weeks now. "Yes, I do," she agreed. "Let's do it."

Exactly forty minutes later, Leigh joined her handsome husband and son at the front of the church's sanctuary. Darkness had just fallen, and the candles were lit. Brass candlesticks of all sizes sat in every windowsill and upon the altar, and a giant Christmas tree covered with twinkling white lights filled the corner. Colorful poinsettias spilled across the chancel and out into the aisles, while green garlands with fragrant pine cones capped the ends of the pews. In a few hours, hundreds of people would gather to celebrate the church's regular Christmas Eve service. But for now, the space's quiet beauty was Lydie and Mason's to enjoy.

"You look beautiful," Warren told Leigh, giving her a kiss on the cheek.

"So do you," she praised, meaning it. The wedding was a small gathering of close family only, with the male guests consisting of Leigh's father, her husband, her son, and Cara's husband and son. All the men looked dashing in their dark suits, even Leigh's normally sloppy-looking father. But it was Mason in his jet-black tuxedo who stole the show.

"You clean up nice," Leigh teased him, noting his clean-shaven face. The wily charmer looked more fetching than she'd ever seen him, no doubt because he was radiating such high spirits.

"Thanks, kid," he replied, looking anxiously at the back of the church. "Let's get this show on the road, shall we?"

Everyone else laughed.

"You've waited over forty years, Dad," Cara said, hugging him. "What's five more minutes?"

"Too long," he proclaimed.

"Go ahead and start the music!" a familiar voice yelled loudly from somewhere in the back of the church.

Everyone laughed all over again.

"Classy, Mom!" Cara chastised, signaling the pianist.

"That's my Lydie," Mason chuckled warmly, taking his place up front by the minister. "Enough with the stuffy nonsense. Let's get married!"

Chords of familiar holiday music filled the air, and the family gathered in an informal cluster near the altar, just as Lydie had requested. There was no wedding party, per se. Just a bride, a groom, and a cloud of family as witnesses. Lydie might not have opted for a ceremony even this formal, but as a little girl growing up in the church, she'd often dreamed of walking down this very aisle. Their hasty elopement had precluded that happening before, but this time, Mason insisted she should realize her dream.

Of course, over a lifetime fully lived, Lydie's dreams had changed a little. And when the music swelled to a crescendo and the bride appeared, she was not clinging to the arm of a patriarch, nor was she wearing a dress of white.

Lydie stood all by herself, proud and straight and strong, in a dress of the brightest, boldest, cheeriest Christmas red this side of the North Pole. Lydie's hair was dyed to its natural soft brown, and it curled gently around her face in a modern, chin-length do. Her dark eyes were those of a movie star, thanks to Cara's skill with more makeup than Lydie's face had ever seen before.

She began walking forward, confident and unhurried, and Leigh almost laughed to watch the men's jaws drop. The bride's red satin dress was corseted and cinched at the waist, hugging curves no one knew Lydie had. The bodice's sweetheart neckline was complemented by a smart, tight-fitting shrug jacket of softer chiffon, and the straight skirt was of cocktail length, showing off way more than anyone normally saw of Lydie's smooth, lean legs.

The bride didn't just look beautiful. She looked beautiful *and* sexy.

And Mason looked like a very, *very* happy man.

Lydie made her way to the front of the church, her face glowing with satisfaction at the expression on her future husband's face.

"Surprised?" she whispered, smiling at him.

"Not a bit," he grinned back.

Lydie leaned in to kiss him.

"Um, excuse me?" the minister said, laughing. "We haven't performed the ceremony yet. The kiss is supposed to be at the end, remember?"

"That's okay," Mason answered, leaning in. "We never have done things the regular way."

They kissed as the music continued to play. Leigh shot a glance at her mother and found Frances smiling. Everybody else was smiling, too, except Cara, who was spouting happy tears.

Leigh let out a sigh of satisfaction.

It was a very merry Christmas.

About the Author

USA TODAY bestselling author Edie Claire enjoys writing in a variety of genres including romantic fiction, mystery, women's fiction, ghostly YA romance, humor, and stage plays. She is a happily married mother of three who has worked as a veterinarian, a childbirth educator, and a medical/technical writer. When not writing she enjoys travel and wildlife-watching, and she dreams of becoming a snowbird.

Edie plans to add a new installment to the Leigh Koslow mystery series each year. If you'd like to be notified when new books are released, you can sign up for the *New Book Alert* on her website: **www.edieclaire.com.** You may also visit her Facebook page at **www.Facebook.com /EdieClaire**. Edie always enjoys hearing from readers via email: **edieclaire@juno.com.**

Books & Plays by Edie Claire

Leigh Koslow Mysteries
Never Buried
Never Sorry
Never Preach Past Noon
Never Kissed Goodnight
Never Tease a Siamese
Never Con a Corgi
Never Haunt a Historian
Never Thwart a Thespian
Never Steal a Cockatiel
Never Mess with Mistletoe
Never Murder a Birder

Romantic Fiction

Pacific Horizons
Alaskan Dawn
Leaving Lana'i
Maui Winds

Fated Loves
Long Time Coming
Meant To Be
Borrowed Time

Hawaiian Shadows
Wraith
Empath
Lokahi
The Warning

Women's Fiction
The Mud Sisters

Humor
Work, Blondes. Work!

Comedic Stage Plays
Scary Drama I
See You in Bells

Made in the USA
Columbia, SC
03 August 2018